NO PRECIOUS TRUTH

Also by Chris Nickson from Severn House

The Simon Westow mysteries

THE HANGING PSALM
THE HOCUS GIRL
TO THE DARK
THE BLOOD COVENANT
THE DEAD WILL RISE
THE SCREAM OF SINS
THEM WITHOUT PAIN

The Inspector Tom Harper mysteries

GODS OF GOLD
TWO BRONZE PENNIES
SKIN LIKE SILVER
THE IRON WATER
ON COPPER STREET
THE TIN GOD
THE LEADEN HEART
THE MOLTEN CITY
BRASS LIVES
A DARK STEEL DEATH
RUSTED SOULS

The Richard Nottingham mysteries

COLD CRUEL WINTER
THE CONSTANT LOVERS
COME THE FEAR
AT THE DYING OF THE YEAR
FAIR AND TENDER LADIES
FREE FROM ALL DANGER

NO PRECIOUS TRUTH

Chris Nickson

SEVERN HOUSE

First world edition published in Great Britain and the USA in 2025
by Severn House, an imprint of Canongate Books Ltd,
14 High Street, Edinburgh EH1 1TE.

severnhouse.com

Copyright © Chris Nickson, 2025

Cover and jacket design by Piers Tilbury

All rights reserved including the right of reproduction in whole or in part in any form. The right of Chris Nickson to be identified as the author of this work has been asserted in accordance with the Copyright, Designs & Patents Act 1988.

British Library Cataloguing-in-Publication Data
A CIP catalogue record for this title is available from the British Library.

ISBN-13: 978-1-4483-1445-4 (cased)
ISBN-13: 978-1-4483-1611-3 (e-book)

This is a work of fiction. Names, characters, places and incidents are either the product of the author's imagination or are used fictitiously. Except where actual historical events and characters are being described for the storyline of this novel, all situations in this publication are fictitious and any resemblance to actual persons, living or dead, business establishments, events or locales is purely coincidental.

All Severn House titles are printed on acid-free paper.

Typeset by Palimpsest Book Production Ltd., Falkirk,
Stirlingshire, Scotland.
Printed and bound in Great Britain by TJ Books,
Padstow, Cornwall.

Praise for Chris Nickson

"A riveting read"
Booklist on *The Scream of Sins*

"Brimming with Nickson's trademark period details, memorable characters . . . but also filled with frightening twists, bloody violence, suspense, and danger"
Booklist on *Them Without Pain*

"Well-drawn characters, plentiful historical details, and a real feeling for Leeds in all its gritty glory"
Kirkus Reviews on *Them Without Pain*

"A dark and complex mystery"
Kirkus Reviews Starred Review of *The Scream of Sins*

"This gritty and surprise-filled mystery will enthrall both newcomers and series fans"
Publishers Weekly Starred Review of *The Dead Will Rise*

"Nickson's richly authentic descriptions of life in . . . Britain combine with a grisly plot and characters who jump off the page"
Booklist on *The Dead Will Rise*

"An action-packed mystery that provides interesting historical details about despicable crimes"
Kirkus Reviews on *The Dead Will Rise*

About the author

Chris Nickson is the author of eleven Tom Harper mysteries, seven highly acclaimed novels in the Richard Nottingham series and seven Simon Westow books. *No Precious Truth* is the first novel in the brand new Cathy Marsden thriller series set during World War II. Born and raised in Leeds, he moved back there more than a decade ago.

www.chrisnickson.co.uk

For Ann and Gerard Pollock, around the corner from Cathy

ONE

Leeds, 18 February, 1941

Cathy Marsden glanced up, startled to see it was dark. It seemed no time since dusk had started to gather as she entered the rooming house deep in Hunslet. But she'd only had one thing on her mind as she darted through the streets: hurrying back to the office to pass on what she'd discovered.

Across Leeds bridge, then up Briggate, the canvas gas mask case bumping against her hip. Under the old railway arch, with its dirty, torn poster of Mr Churchill, and the newspaper seller shouting for people to read about the Allies defeating the Italians in Libya. A relief to have some good news, she thought, but her battle wasn't in Africa. It was here in Leeds. She pushed herself to go faster, face set, feet pounding against the pavement.

Cathy willed people out of her way, making a hurried apology as she brushed past an old couple who dawdled along the street. Almost six o'clock, according to the clock above Dyson's jewellers. No time to waste. After a frustrating week of following hints that had taken them absolutely nowhere, she finally had a solid lead on the man they'd been seeking.

She waited as the traffic passed on Boar Lane, impatient to be moving. Less than a minute and she'd be there. She was breathing fast, heart thumping in her chest.

The scream came and she jerked her head round.

The little girl had strayed into the road. Three or four years old, wearing a brown coat with a pixie hood, grubby socks bunched around her ankles, clutching her teddy bear against her body, and paralysed with terror as the tram came towards her.

Cathy heard the screech of metal as the driver jammed on the brake. Sparks flew up from the tracks. Not a hope of stopping in time.

Six years as a policewoman had taught her well. Calmly, Cathy stepped out, clutched the girl's arm and dragged her back to the kerb as the tram rumbled past.

A fleshy, raw-faced woman was crying, caught in shock, squatting down and holding the child, shouting at her then pulling her close and hugging her.

Cathy spotted the bear in the gutter, picked it up and tucked it under the girl's arm.

'You don't want to lose him, do you?'

With a solemn stare, the girl shook her head.

'I—' the woman began, but Cathy saw a gap in the traffic, waving as she darted across the street and hurried away.

Only a moment, instantly forgotten. She had bigger things on her mind.

The building stood fifty yards up Briggate. It was completely anonymous, no sign, just a solid brick front and a thick metal door. She slipped inside just as the first cold drops of February rain began to fall, showed her pass to the guard, and took the stairs at a run.

All this had been planned as the grand new Marks and Spencer store where the Rialto cinema had once stood. Almost ready to open when war was declared and the Ministry of Works requisitioned the place. Counters and clothing racks were hauled away, replaced with row after row of desks. Only the signs on the walls offered a reminder of what it had almost become: *Ladies' Clothing. Childrenswear. First Floor, Menswear.*

Cathy stopped at the door with Special Investigation Branch printed in small dark letters on a board, taking a breath before she turned the handle. Derek Smith and Terry Davis looked up as she entered.

She beamed. 'I've found out where Rob Dobson has been hiding himself.'

'What? Where?' Derek said. He pushed a pair of glasses up his nose.

'How? We've been hunting all over—' Davis began, but she cut him off.

'He's calling himself Roger Leeson now. Less than an hour ago he was tucked away in that dosshouse down from Braime's on Hunslet Road. No doubt it's him. I've checked.' She exhaled and grinned. 'Is the boss around?'

'Right here,' came a voice behind her. She turned to see him leaning against the door jamb. Sergeant Adam Faulkner, military police, in command of the Leeds squad of the SIB, a cigarette dangling between his fingers. 'How did you manage to winkle him out?'

'A tip from a woman I know.'

He nodded his approval. 'Good job. Smithy, Terry, you go and round him up. Shake everything he knows out of his brain. Maybe we can finally break this damned thing and arrest Connor.'

A flurry of movement as they pulled on gabardine mackintoshes and hats and slipped out. Faulkner sat down at his desk.

From the corner of her eye, Cathy caught sight of someone else entering the room. Her eyes widened in disbelief. He wasn't anyone she'd ever expected to see in this place. She folded her arms and glared at him.

'What the hell are you doing here?'

TWO

Daniel Marsden was five years older than her, the clever boy who won the scholarship to grammar school. The one who passed everything without seeming to do a stroke of work while she studied deep into the night, struggling with her lessons and failing half her exams.

He was the boy people noticed. They remembered him, asked after him, always full of praise, with Cathy a poor second. When Dan landed a Civil Service job and moved down to London, she'd said nothing, but deep inside she'd been glad to see the back of him. After so many years she had the chance to move out of her brother's shadow. Even now, his Christmas visits each year felt like more than enough time together, watching everyone gather round him. She'd been quietly relieved when he'd said there was too much going on at the ministry last December to be able to come.

Now he was standing in the office where she worked.

He smiled. 'I like the way you've had your hair done. It suits you.'

Cathy felt herself bristle. At twenty-six, she'd spent four years as a woman police constable, then two more as a sergeant, before her secondment to SIB and a move into plain clothes. She'd had to fight for respect every step of the way. It had been the same when she started here. She'd needed to work hard to make the squad accept her. To understand that a woman could do this job. Cathy wasn't going to let her brother dismiss all that with a flippant comment. Just the sight of him here, where she'd built a place for herself, made the excitement and pride at finding Dobson wither away.

'I'm so very glad you approve.'

Dan shifted his glance away.

'He's been sent,' Faulkner told her. 'We're working with him.'

She turned, fire in her eyes. Like the other men in SIB, Adam Faulkner had been a police detective before the war. He'd been in London, a member of the Flying Squad. They were famous, the best Scotland Yard had; everybody in the country had heard of them. He'd joined the army, eager to defend his country, only to find himself shuffled into the military police. Recruited for the Special Investigation Branch when it was formed the year before, last July he'd been posted to Leeds to set up this new squad. A sergeant, like her, but his was an army rank. A good, fair boss.

'Sent?' Cathy asked. 'What do you mean, sent?'

Faulkner closed his eyes for a second. 'Your brother is with the Security Service,' he said.

She was silent for a moment, eyes moving back to study her brother's face. Dan? He was bright but . . . It had to be some kind of practical joke. He was a civil servant; that was what he'd always said. This? Never in a million years. It couldn't be. The Security Service? That meant MI5, secret agents, not a place a boy who'd been raised in a Leeds slum could end up.

'You didn't know?'

'Not a clue.' She shook her head. Her mind was reeling. Dan? How could it be true? She tried to scrape an ounce of sense from what she'd just heard. It just didn't seem possible. 'He always just told us he worked for the government.'

Faulkner gave a short bark of a laugh. 'I suppose that's true enough. These days he's with something called the Twenty Committee.'

'Twenty?' Cathy turned on her brother. 'Twenty what?'

'Twenty. XX in Roman numerals,' Dan replied. 'Double cross. Espionage.'

So bloody clever-clever, she thought. Like a bunch of overgrown schoolboys, making a game of everything.

'He's here to deal with a problem,' Faulkner continued. 'A very urgent one, and we're under orders to help him however we can. Very strict orders. That's on top of all our other work, of course,' he added, and she caught the resentment in his voice.

'This is more important,' Dan said.

'I'm not denying it,' he agreed. 'Tomorrow morning, as soon as everyone's here, he's going to give us all the details.' He checked his wristwatch. 'Why don't you two get off? It sounds like you have quite a bit of catching up to do.' He looked at

Cathy. 'I'll let you know what they sweat out of Dobson. That really was some very good work.'

The rain was still falling, a press of people all around them on the pavement. Full blackout, but after a year and a half it felt like second nature. No lamps or bright shop displays, windows all covered with tape. Sandbags around the doors. Not a light anywhere, only black and white stripes painted on the kerbs and lamp posts to guide them. She tucked her arm through his, raised her umbrella and led him through the streets.

Dan was carrying a leather suitcase, and stopped every couple of minutes to adjust his grip. Her eyes flickered towards him, still trying to take in what she'd heard.

Along Kirkgate, then waiting until she sensed a gap in the traffic to hurry across Vicar Lane.

A tram was sitting at the York Road stop. With a sigh she slid into a seat, her brother beside her.

'Do they know you're coming? Ma didn't say anything this morning.'

'I didn't even know myself until late last night,' he said. 'Had to make four changes on the way because of bomb damage on the lines. I only arrived a couple of hours ago.'

An urgent problem, she thought. A rushed journey. That had to mean something big. A flap. MI5, XX Committee. Her own brother . . . it spilled around, a jumble in her mind.

'They'll be thrilled to bits to have you home.'

'I don't know how much chance they'll have to see me,' he told her. 'It's work. I'll probably be gone all hours.'

Every seat was taken, and people stood, holding on to the straps. The familiar winter smells of damp wool and sour breath filled the tram. Nobody seemed to be paying them a scrap of attention. Still, best not to say too much where people could hear. No loose talk.

'Sounds like you've made a splash down in London. Is what the boss said true? About your job.'

He seemed to be weighing how much to tell her. Watching him, she could make out the lines around his eyes and mouth. The worry and the strain. Whatever he did these days was taking its toll.

'I started with them before the war,' he said finally. 'I've only been with this current lot since the beginning of the year, when they were formed. That's why I couldn't come up at Christmas; we were making all the preparations.' He chuckled. 'I'm the only northerner.'

'And the only one who isn't a posh boy?'

He looked straight ahead, and she saw she'd hit a nerve. 'I'm there because I'm good.'

He'd need to be, in company like that. 'How do you like it?'

The frown vanished as quickly as it appeared. 'It keeps me busy.' He opened his mouth as if to say something, then seemed to change his mind. 'What about you? Looks like you've done well for yourself, too. Your outfit has a very good reputation.'

'More than you ever expected from me?' she asked, and let the question hang like a challenge between them. Her tone hardened. 'I'm there because I'm good, too. Not to get the tea and do the filing, if that's what you were wondering. They tried to make me into a skivvy when I joined with the police. It soon stopped.'

He smiled. 'Sergeant Faulkner made it perfectly clear you pull your weight.'

'I do.' No need to be modest about that. She was a good copper and she'd taken to the SIB work like she'd been born for it. 'The boss is good. It was all very strange at first, but I like it.'

It had been far more than just strange; the move to SIB had upended her world. One day she'd been patrolling in town and checking on her constables, quite content in her dark blue uniform and proud of her three stripes. At the end of shift she'd been called in by her inspector and told she was being seconded to a unit she'd never heard of before.

'They're very new,' Inspector Harding told her. 'You'll only be there for a few weeks. You seem ideally suited for what they want.' She smiled. 'No uniform, either.'

'Yes, ma'am,' Cathy replied. The next morning she'd turned up at the Special Investigation Branch office in plain clothes to do . . . she didn't know what.

'The Branch was formed to go after big crimes that involve the army,' Adam Faulkner had explained. He was full of enthusiasm. A true believer. 'Most of the work we do is overseas. The

Middle East, places like that. But there are plenty of deserters here who've been trying to put together criminal empires. They're organized. You name it: lorry loads of goods nicked to order from NAAFI warehouses and railway depots; army quartermasters' clerks on the take who let them make off with supplies in exchange for a backhander; raids on government offices to steal coupons for petrol and food; rings working with doctors to forge exemption certificates from conscription. Some even make their own hooch and pass it off as proper booze. This isn't the local butcher fiddling the ration. It's rackets, lots of them, an industry, and some of them are making fortunes from it. SIB set up offices like this to see if we can stop some of the crime. Not a chance of halting it all.'

Cathy was an experienced copper. She believed she knew the city and its crime, that she'd seen it all. But she'd never heard a whisper of anything like this. Was she so naive?

'How much of it is there in Leeds?'

'More than you can imagine,' he told her. You know there are barracks up here. Sometimes I think half the people in the forces have rackets going. We get involved when deserters skip out on the army and start looking to crime to make real money. I'll tell you now, you won't have time to be bored.'

'What about the police? Isn't this what they do?'

'The force is stretched. Come on, you must have seen that for yourself. It's full of war reservists and special constables. We know, we were all in CID. Racked up plenty of service between us. The police and the military police are good, but they can only do so much. The men we're going up against are dangerous. They think making fortunes is more important than fighting the Jerries.' He nodded at the four other men in the room. Cathy had noticed them, quietly inspecting and assessing her. 'This isn't what any of us expected when we signed up to fight the Germans, but it's turned out . . . interesting.'

'It sounds as if you're doing something important,' she said.

'I think we are.' He gave her a broad, eager grin. 'The best bit is that these squads are still brand, spanking new. No one's quite certain of how far we can go, so we get to make it up as we go along.' The sergeant looked more thoughtful. 'The problem is, none of us come from around here. We've been floundering a bit. No local knowledge and we haven't had time to develop many real contacts. If we're really going to work effectively, we need someone who knows Leeds inside and out.'

This was a world away from anything she'd done. Policewomen dealt with women and girls. Lost children, not gangsters. Would she be able to cope with it? But . . .

'Well,' she told him, 'I'm born and bred here. I know it through and through.' Cathy watched his face. 'What I don't understand, though, is why you want a woman?' The question that had nagged at her since she'd been given her orders. Women on the force never had chances like this. There were no female detectives in Leeds City Police, and never would be, if most of the men at the top had their way. 'Why *me*?'

He laughed. 'You can blame my wife for that. She thought a woman's perspective might be useful. You look at things differently.'

'Sensible lass. Sounds like she has the right idea.'

'When I talked to our HQ, they agreed I could give it a shot. I asked around, and your inspector praised you to the heavens.' Cathy blinked in astonishment. Inspector Harding had always been very spare with her compliments. 'She thinks you're quick and resourceful. You've spent enough time as a copper to know how the system works.' A chuckle. 'And once you open your mouth, nobody will ever doubt where you're from.'

Cathy laughed too. She knew her accent was broad. Common as muck, someone had said once. Leeds through and through.

That had all happened last September, three days after the first air raid on the city. The three-week secondment had been extended once, then again and again. Five months later and she was still here, officially a police sergeant, but now with the Special Investigation Branch for the duration. She'd proved herself; most of them had come to accept her as part of the squad. Adam Faulkner had never been a problem. He'd treated her as an equal from the start, even taught her to drive the battered, rickety Humber they used. Three other members of the squad had been fine too, especially after she was able to dig up information that helped them crack a few cases. But she'd never won over Bob Hartley. He strode around with a permanent scowl, the type who wore his resentment like an overcoat. He ignored her, undermined her whenever the opportunity arrived. Nothing was going to change his mind.

Fine. She'd learned to live with it.

Once she understood the ropes and overcame her doubts, this had turned out to be the best job she'd had in her life. Everything she knew about Leeds, the people she'd met as a copper, it had all come in useful. And she'd learned more than she believed possible. The days raced by so fast that they blurred at the edges. Faulkner had been right; never a moment for boredom.

By the Shaftesbury cinema Cathy pulled the cord to alert the tram driver, and stepped down to the pavement. Dan was right behind her. The rain had passed, leaving a cold, clear sky. Moonlight reflected off the silver barrage balloons, platoons of them bobbing over Leeds. The city had been very lucky so far: only a few small hit-and-run raids since the one at the beginning of September that had catapulted the city into the conflict. Before that, all the danger and destruction had happened elsewhere. London, Liverpool, Hull. When they watched it play out on newsreels, read about it in the papers and heard the reports on the wireless, it didn't feel quite real.

Then it arrived. They heard the sirens, and the sound of the anti-aircraft guns and searchlights cutting across the sky made it all very real indeed. Under it all, the relentless deep drone of the German planes and the thick, terrifying explosions of bombs that seemed to go on forever had brought the war all the way to their doors.

Cathy had been on duty the next morning, still shaken to her core from the raid, scarcely a wink of sleep after the all-clear. In the daylight she'd seen the damage. Marsh Lane goods station a ruin, with locomotives and wagons upended like a toddler's tantrum. Houses destroyed. Lives and businesses shattered. So much rubble. And everywhere, clinging in the air, the stench of destruction. Cordite and burnt wood. Scorched papers blowing around.

Since then, the sirens had wailed regularly, and their howling had become part of the fabric of life. They'd learned a routine: dressing quickly, bustling down to the Anderson shelter in the back garden and trying to stay warm in the bitter nights. Waiting, waiting. Holding her breath and sending up prayers. Relief at the all-clear. Everyone knew Leeds was due another big raid soon, the only question was when. Each face she saw was scared. But they were helpless. This was what war was like on the home front.

Cathy walked a hundred yards along Harehills Lane and turned down the ginnel that led into the Gipton estate. She'd done it so often she felt she could manage it blindfolded.

'All this still seems strange to me,' Dan said. 'Like a maze.'

'Hardly surprising, is it? You'd scarpered to London before we moved here.' She and her parents had been rehoused from a damp, mouldy slum on Quarry Hill out to where the air was free of smoke and soot. Seven years ago, she realized. It felt so much longer, yet it also felt like yesterday.

They'd been one of the first families to arrive. The builders were still working on most of the estate when all their possessions were fumigated in the bug van and they were handed the keys. A brand-new house. Clean and dry. Fresh paint. An indoor toilet, no sharing. Hot water. A garden. Cathy had loved the place from the moment she walked through the front door.

Her mother thought they'd stepped into paradise. She'd walked around, touching everything, needing to make certain it wasn't a dream. Even now, with the huge estate complete, Cathy felt they were living on the edge of the countryside. Sometimes at night she'd hear owls hunting and the bark of dog foxes. Her little piece of heaven.

They crossed the street, and halfway down Brander Road she stopped with her hand on the front gate. Cathy looked at her brother. No expression on his face, mouth a thin line. Not an ounce of joy in his eyes.

'Welcome home,' she said.

'Is that you, Catherine?' her mother shouted from the kitchen. The same routine every day.

'No, Ma, it's Mr Churchill dropped by for a cuppa and your advice on the war.' She glanced at her brother. He was standing in the hall, looking uncertain. 'Come and see what I brought home with me.'

Mrs Marsden bustled through, wiping her hands on her pinafore. She stopped as soon as she saw her son, eyes wide.

'Henry,' she called over her shoulder. 'Come here. See who's turned up.' She looked Dan up and down. 'Oh my, luv. This is a real treat.'

Cathy slipped away up the stairs. Let them enjoy the reunion.

The meal was full of talk. Her mother peppered Dan with questions nineteen to the dozen, wanting to know everything about his work, his life. Was he courting? When was he likely to be conscripted? Was he looking after himself properly?

Her father listened, not adding much, but he wasn't one for words. He'd been gassed at Arras, early in the last war, the one that was supposed to end all wars. His lungs had been ruined, he'd turned into a shrunken husk of the big proud, beaming man in the wedding photograph on the mantelpiece. He lived on a pension from the government, not able to do much. He couldn't even walk more than a few hundred yards without becoming breathless and leaning on his stick. But the joy on his face at seeing his son said more than words.

Cathy washed the pots. A clean, shining sink, still spotless. Hot water from the immersion heater, a new range; the house really did have everything. Back in her room, she checked the blackout curtains before turning on the light. No fireplace up here; she could see her breath in the air. Pulling on her thick dressing gown against the cold, she sat and took the writing pad from her dressing table.

Dear Tom, she began, *the weather's been cold again. We've had a busy week.* After that the words seemed to dry up. Writing had never come easily, but this was a letter to her boyfriend, and she didn't know what to put on the page. She should have been able to pour her heart out to him. She was grateful when a tap on the door halted her thoughts.

'Come in.'

Dan, wearing a thick jumper, hands in his trouser pockets, shirt collar unbuttoned He looked around, taking in the old wardrobe, the map of the world she'd pinned to the wall and the dressing table with photographs tucked into the edges of the mirror before he spoke.

'I meant what I said about your hair, you know,' he said. 'A liberty cut, isn't it?'

She raised her eyebrows. 'Very good. Someone been teaching you, have they?' Her best friend Annie had done it a fortnight before, when she was home on leave from the WAAFs. He was right, though; it framed her face and made her feel glamorous.

He shrugged. 'I picked it up from chatter in the office. Dad looks fine.'

'Seeing you has bucked him up, that's all. He's already had more than his share of bad days this year.'

'And Ma . . .'

'Ma is Ma,' she told him. 'Looks after everything and worries, as usual. How many times has she asked for your ration book?'

That brought a smile. 'Three so far. It's in my case. I'll give it to her later.'

Family, an easy topic. She wondered why he'd come to talk.

'Adam Faulkner seems on top of things.'

'He's as sharp as they come,' Cathy told him.

'What about the others?'

'They're excellent.' No denying that, even if one of them wished she wasn't there. All quick, ready to act, able to think on their feet.

'This afternoon, before you noticed me, you started to talk about something. Big case?'

Cathy hesitated. He wasn't one of them, not a member of the squad. Still, he sounded interested and they were going to be working together. Maybe she should stop feeling she needed to compete with her brother.

'Someone stole an army petrol tanker. A full one. The man I found was the driver.'

He gave her a curious look. 'Why would SIB be interested in that? Isn't it one for the police?'

Interesting; he understood the lie of the land. 'Normally, yes. But there are rumours that a man named Jackie Connor is behind it. He's a local boy, got a finger in all sorts of pies. A deserter, ignored his call-up papers. That puts it in our territory. We've been after him for months, haven't managed to come close yet. He's a clever devil, greases the right palms. If we play our cards right, this one might make him come a cropper. It's commercial fuel, so they'll have to get rid of the red dye in it before they can sell it on.'

'That's not too difficult.'

'No,' she agreed, surprised that he'd know; she'd only learned that when they began to investigate the theft. Four methods: run the fuel through charcoal, aspirin, bread, or use the filters in gas masks. 'But a whole tanker is a lot of petrol. Smithy should be able to squeeze some truth out of the driver.'

'Smithy? Which is he? The one with the glasses?'

'That's him. He's one of the best interrogators I've seen.'

He appeared doubtful, but it was true. Derek Smith didn't look anything like a copper. He barely scraped past the height requirement, and hadn't an ounce of heft on his body. The quiet type, he seemed more like a clerk than anything. But he could listen, and he had the gift of asking the kinds of questions that sliced a person wide open. With a little luck he'd do it this time.

'If you're here for a bit, you'll probably find out what happens.'

His expression soured. 'I don't plan on being in Leeds that long. We need to take care of my problem very urgently. Rotten as it might be for you, you're stuck with me for as long as that takes.'

'It's serious, isn't it?'

He pressed his lips together and nodded. 'Deadly. I'll explain it all in the morning. This XX committee I'm with, we're even newer than your lot. It's run by an Oxford academic. So bright he scares me. I worked with him on a report about Dunkirk and he saw something in me. Recruited me for this.' He lowered his voice. 'Not a word to them downstairs, though.'

'Don't worry, I can keep my mouth shut.' Cathy frowned. 'Did they send you because the problem's in Leeds and you're from here?'

Dan pushed a hand through his hair. A few flecks of grey in there, she noticed. 'That's part of it. You know the way people think: I grew up here, so I must know the place like the back of my hand and still have all sorts of contacts. There's a lot more involved, though. You'll find out tomorrow.'

'If we fail—'

'We can't,' he said sharply, and she caught the fear under his words. 'Simple as that.'

Cathy felt a chill.

'Your agency,' she said. 'What are you, a spy?'

He laughed and shook his head again. 'Come on, can you really see me doing that? No, mostly I'm a desk jockey in the Security Service. It turned out I was pretty good at analysing things and using the results to predict what might happen. Before the war started, they needed people with those kinds of skills. I just sort of drifted into the rest.'

He made it sound plausible. But she had the sense there was more he hadn't said. Probably a lot more.

'The rest? What's that when it's at home?'

'Bit and pieces,' Dan replied. 'Honestly, I can't tell you. I've said too much already.'

He looked uncomfortable, even though he'd given nothing away. She decided to change the subject.

'Did you know I was with SIB before you arrived?'

'No. Dad never mentioned it in his letters. I thought you were still a bobby. It was Sergeant Faulkner who told me.'

'You can imagine what a shock it was for me to turn round and see you.' She hesitated. 'You've lost some of your accent.'

'I've worked on it. Protective colouration for life down there. Fitting in.'

'Does it help?' Cathy asked.

'A bit.'

She stared at him. 'Not proud of where you come from?'

He gave a wry grin as he opened the door to leave. 'Safer if I don't answer that.'

'We'd better hope there's not a raid tonight,' she said. 'The four of us will be like sardines in the shelter.'

His laugh was genuine. 'I live in London. I don't think any of us has had a full night's sleep since the Blitz began. I mostly take my chances at home. You open the blackout curtains in the morning and hope everything is still there. About the only good thing is the threat of invasion has passed.'

THREE

No raid, no sirens, nothing to disturb the night's sleep. Their breath bloomed as they strode up the hill to York Road. A dusting of frost on the grass. Cathy stepped over a lump of dog dirt on the pavement, dried to pure white.

She was dressed for the February cold with lisle stockings, a tweed skirt, thick jumper, and the good wool coat she'd bought at C&A to celebrate her promotion to sergeant. All made to last. Just as well; everyone knew that clothing would be on the ration very soon. A pair of silk stockings was already like gold dust.

Dan had been quiet and preoccupied all through breakfast. His eyes told the tale: whatever he'd been sent here to do must have rattled him.

The man walking beside her was a very different person from the one who'd rushed off to chase his dreams down to London and his Civil Service job. This one seemed careworn, weighed down by responsibility. He looked older than thirty-one.

He'd changed, but that was part of growing older. How many times had she shed her skin? She'd gone from schoolgirl to the council clerk who came to feel there was more in life than typing and filing. Applying to be a woman police constable, still with only a misty sense of who she might be. Then a promotion to sergeant, enjoying the responsibility. Now part of the Special Investigation Branch, overcoming her fears and becoming . . . she wasn't quite sure yet.

'I think you're just what we need,' Faulkner had said at the end of her very first day with the squad. 'You'll fit right in.'

'Thank you,' she said, still far from certain what she'd be doing. Part of her wondered if she could go back to the police.

Now . . . no regrets.

Without the war there'd have been no SIB, no opportunity for her. It had rushed up on them all, shattering that fragile sense of hope they'd had after Mr Chamberlain came back from Munich.

When the storm finally broke, everything normal vanished from her life. War altered it all.

It began with long days in uniform at the railway station in the day after war was declared, trying to control the children being evacuated to the country. Once they'd gone, she had the constant round of making sure everyone was following the new regulations. While the Germans were overrunning Europe, the world she'd taken for granted was breaking apart.

Churchill becoming Prime Minister put some heart into them all, at least until Dunkirk, with all the soldiers coming home. A few groups of them had been sent to Leeds, and she'd escorted some to their billets. One young man, no older than twenty, kept bursting into tears, unable to stop himself.

For the first time in her life, she felt truly terrified of what might happen.

The fighter pilots down south had beaten the Luftwaffe in the summer skies, and she felt Britain begin to hope. Without control of the skies, Hitler couldn't invade. Instead, he had his revenge. The Blitz. It was still raging on. London, all the port cities pummelled night after night. Coventry completely destroyed between dusk and dawn. Beyond any horror.

Cathy glanced at her brother as he gazed impassively out of the tram window at the tired buildings and bomb damage on York Road. He'd certainly have seen worse in London.

After he'd closed the door of her bedroom last night, she realized it was probably the first time the pair of them had ever really talked and shown themselves. Not much, cautious words, but it was a start.

Down by the Parish Church, One-Eyed Sam was selling his newspapers.

'Germans sink cargo ship,' he shouted. 'Read all about it.'

More bleak headlines as the Germans kept attacking the convoys. When would the tide begin to turn properly?

'I'd forgotten how black all the buildings are,' Dan said as they walked through town.

'It's always been that way,' Cathy told him. Every building was covered in generations of soot. 'You've been gone too long. Those are the rewards of industry.'

* * *

The air in the office was thick. Derek Smith and Bob Hartley were both smoking cigarettes, and Terry Davis had his pipe going. George Andrews sat back in his chair, gazing at the ceiling and rubbing a hand across his jaw.

'In case any of you don't already know, this is Dan Marsden,' Faulkner announced. 'He's Cathy's brother, but don't make too much of it. He's here from London. Our job is to help him however we can.' His voice hardened. 'Those are orders from the very top. We just happen to be in the right place at the right time.'

A nod, then Dan rose to his feet, clearing his throat.

'I work for something known as the XX committee. We were set up to try to turn the German spies who come here into double agents and have them working for us.'

'What happens to the ones who refuse?' George asked quietly.

'Prison or firing squad.' He spoke as if it was the most normal thing in the world. 'It's probably best if I start with a little background. Since Europe fell, we've had a stream of people coming over. Most are easy to catch. They *want* us to find them and help them. The German spies arrive that way, too; they try to pose as refugees and slip through. There are teams all along the coast that question everyone who lands. They weed out the likely spies and give them to us for a thorough interrogation. The ones we do turn are kept in safe houses. They're all separate, they don't know about each other. They send radio messages back to their bosses, passing on false information we feed them. We look after them well enough but keep them closely guarded. They each have handlers.' A worried silence. 'One of them has escaped, and the people at the top are certain he's on his way to Leeds. My job is to catch him.'

She felt as if her heart had stopped. Now she understood the strain on Dan's face. All the men were quiet, staring straight ahead, silent.

'Why would he come here?' Cathy asked finally.

'He claims he was sent over with orders to sabotage a couple of places here that are vital to the war effort: Kirkstall Forge, and the Avro factory in Yeadon that's making bombers.'

God Almighty, if he hit those . . . Faulkner raised his hand to halt the sudden flurry of questions.

'Soon enough. Let him finish.'

'The spy's name is Jan Minuit.' He held up a photograph of a man with dark, wavy hair and deep-set eyes. Not a film star, but definitely the type women would notice. 'He's Dutch. Five feet eleven, thirty-six years old, built like a rugby prop forward. I have plenty of copies for you to pass out to people. His English is fluent, only a slight trace of an accent. He's a trained engineer, worked in Warwick for a couple of years in 1934 and '35, so he's familiar with English life. The type who'd fit in easily enough, and his background means he'd know his way around a steel mill and an aircraft plant.'

'If he's Dutch—' Smithy began.

'Then why's he working for the Nazis? He claimed the Abwehr threatened to kill his family if he didn't. He seemed perfectly content to be caught, eager to cooperate. I sat in on a couple of the interrogation sessions. He was very convincing, clever enough to fool us.'

'How did he get away?' Faulkner asked. He'd been scribbling in his notebook.

'We don't know.' Dan muttered his reply, staring down at the desk. 'We're looking into that. It won't happen again.'

'Doesn't have to, does it?' Terry said. 'Once is enough. When did he go?'

'Early evening on Sunday. Look,' he said earnestly, 'one thing you need to understand is that this XX programme is just weeks old. Before us, the system was a hodgepodge. We caught the agents the Jerries sent, but we had no proper system for using them. We're still finding our feet and beginning to sense the possibilities of all this. Double agents really could change the course of the war. That's not an exaggeration. Minuit was one of the first we turned. If he manages to sabotage either of these places, it's going to be a huge coup for the Germans, and the government will probably close us down. Much worse than that, it's going to really hurt the country.' He stopped, swallowing hard as he looked at them. 'We *have* to catch him. It's as simple as that. That's where you come in.'

'Why not use the police?' Bob Hartley asked. 'There's enough of them to hunt for him and guard these places.'

'As soon as they get involved, word will leak out,' Dan replied.

'People will talk. A German spy on the loose. Can you imagine the panic? That would be a victory for the Jerries.' He shook his head. 'This isn't my decision. It comes from much higher up. It has to be absolutely hush-hush. Absolutely.'

A riot of thoughts rushed through Cathy's mind. Dan was right, they couldn't afford to fail. God, she wouldn't want the responsibility he was carrying. Catch this man or . . . Her brother lived in a world she couldn't begin to comprehend. Espionage, subterfuge, double agents, false information. Chasing spies. A war of lies.

Now she'd been pulled into it, too. A far cry from the vague, groundless panic about Fifth Columnists that had been flying around at the start of the war. This was real. Stopping Jan Minuit was vital.

Her mouth was dry. She reached for the mug on her desk and took a swig of cold tea as the wave of questions began again.

'What steps have your people taken?'

'We've informed those in charge at the Forge and the Avro factory. They'll be increasing security and issuing warnings about people trying to penetrate the area or befriend staff.'

'Do you know what name Minuit might be using?'

'When we picked him up, he had false papers as James Martinson. They were surprisingly poor forgeries. We took them, of course. He had nothing when he vanished. No identification, only the clothes he was wearing. Not even a shilling in change.'

Cathy knew that wasn't a big problem; it was easy enough to come by a new identity card and ration book on the black market – if you could afford to pay. The first thing he'd need would be money. Where would he get it?

'What about robberies close to where you were holding him?' Faulkner asked.

'We're still looking into it. But no report of stolen papers.'

'Does he have any contacts up here?' Smithy's turn.

'He never admitted to any. But it's possible he made one or two when he lived in England. He did tell us that he'd visited Leeds once on his way to a holiday in the Yorkshire Dales when he worked over here, but he claims he never went anywhere near Kirkstall Forge. The Avro factory didn't exist then.'

Terry Davis took the pipe from his mouth. 'How well guarded are these places?'

'Reasonably secure,' Dan answered after a little thought. 'The Forge has its own Home Guard force. But someone working alone, determined and clever . . .' He sighed. 'You see what I mean. The factory at Yeadon is a different matter. It's what's called a shadow factory. Camouflaged so it looks like part of the landscape to anyone in an aircraft. It's nationally important, so there are soldiers in charge of keeping it secure.'

Shadow factory. Her entire world had expanded since she became part of the squad. Now it was about to take another leap.

'What about his contacts from when he worked in England?'

'We're watching, but he hasn't approached any of them. My guess is that he won't. Too obvious. One curious thing about him is that he somehow developed a taste for cricket during the time he lived in Warwick. When he stopped here on his way to the Dales, it was to take in a day of Yorkshire playing Hampshire at Headingley.'

Not what she'd have expected. But people were full of surprises.

'Did he spend the night in Leeds?' George looked thoughtful.

Dan nodded. 'A guest house near the ground, he said. Minuit claims he doesn't remember exactly where, though. No street name, only that it might have been called Beaumont or something like that.'

Somewhere to begin, Cathy thought. Her eyes flickered towards Faulkner. He saw and gave a small nod.

'Do the Germans have anybody round here who might look after him?' Bob Hartley again. A loaded, dangerous question. He'd been doodling on a notepad and looked up to speak. Cathy could see the row of arrows rising up the side of his paper.

'As far as we know, they don't,' Dan replied after a long silence.

Hartley's voice was unforgiving. 'That's not really an answer. Just how far do you know?'

'We're eighty per cent sure.'

Not good enough and they all knew it. Anything less than complete certainty left too many doubts. She took a slow breath. Traitors walking around Leeds.

'Do you have any idea where the hell we can start with this?' George Andrews asked; she could hear the ripple of anger under the Liverpool accent. 'You want it all kept quiet. That's tying our hands. How are we supposed to find information? We need to talk to people.'

'You can still do that,' Dan said. 'Just don't mention the real reason. Your job is to go after deserters and criminals. Make out he's one of those.' He brought a sheaf of papers from the folder in front of him. 'These are transcripts of his interrogations, and some notes from the agent who was handling him. They'll fill in some of the details.'

'I read it yesterday,' Faulkner told them. 'Some very useful stuff in there. Take a good look through it all and let's see what ideas it sparks.' He glanced at Cathy, tilted his head and rose. She followed. He tapped Dan on the shoulder, and they took the stairs down to the canteen in the basement. The air was warm, damp with steam as the cooks prepared a hot dinner.

A pot of weak tea, listening to the clatter of pans all around them. Faulkner took out a packet of Players and lit one before he spoke.

'You two didn't look thrilled to see each other yesterday. I hope you've cleared the air. This is the most important job we've had, and I can't afford any family tiffs scuppering it.' He searched their faces. 'Is that understood?'

'Yes. We had a talk last night,' she said.

'There won't be a problem,' Dan answered.

'Good. We're going to need to move very quickly.' He chose his words with care. The canteen was bustling; too many people who might overhear. 'Dan, I'm going to pair you with George Andrews for today. He's been out to . . .' He caught himself before he spoke the names in public. 'To both those places you mentioned. He knows people there.' He passed over the keys to the Humber. 'Tell him to take you.'

'I just need to ring my office first. See if there's any more news.' He drained the cup and left. Faulkner watched him go.

'Well?' he asked her when they were alone.

She gave a small, wan smile. 'I think Dan and I will be fine.'

'Honestly?'

She nodded. 'Older and wiser. He's evasive on what he really does, and we're always going to disagree on some things, but we can do it without a flaming row.'

'Good. I really don't want to have to bounce you back to the police.'

She searched for a smile, the slightest trace of humour, but his face was deadly serious. It wasn't a threat. Just a simple statement of fact. He was right; this case was too big for petty squabbles.

'What do you think?'

She was trying to work that out. It seemed so daunting, hunting a spy. How could they do it?

And Dan. She wasn't sure what to make of him. The suit he was wearing was fine worsted, very well cut. Not from Burton's or Fifty-Shilling Tailor. That Melton overcoat hadn't come cheap, either. He was dressing like a high-flyer; he must be making good money down there. All that and the new accent . . . he'd remade himself. Shed that Leeds skin and happy to do so. He'd been so eager to leave, to find a life in London. Now he was back where he'd started, with everything riding on catching Minuit. A very dangerous game of snakes and ladders. Succeed and he was guaranteed a good future in the capital. Fail and—

'By the way, we brought in that man Dobson you found in the rooming house.' A very neat change of topic. 'Only took a few minutes before he admitted he was the driver of the petrol tanker.'

She smiled. 'What else did he have to say?'

'Not a lot. Smithy spent half the night questioning him, but he's not giving much away. Back for another try today.'

'I don't suppose he let slip who's behind it all?'

Faulkner leaned closer and whispered: 'No. But he gave a couple of hints before he could stop himself.'

'Oh?' She leaned forward.

'Enough for us to be pretty certain it's Jackie Connor. What we suspected. That lead made a difference.'

'Let's hope it goes somewhere.' A quick shrug. 'How's your family holding up with the bombing?' For months, London had been pounded night after night. It was in the newsreels and the papers.

She knew he was married to a woman called June and they

lived just a few streets away from his parents. A place called Carshalton, somewhere south of the city.

'They've been lucky so far. Still plenty of raids, not much damage where they are, touch wood.' He stubbed out the cigarette. 'Before we go, there's a couple more things.'

She frowned, baffled. 'What?'

'I was in Whitelocks having a drink last night and a man was mentioning he'd seen a woman who pulled a little girl out of the way of a tram. Had a description of her, too. Hair in a liberty cut. You know the reporters from the *Post* drink in there. A couple of them pricked up their ears. A bit of good news and all that.'

'Oh.' She'd completely forgotten about it. Her mind had been too full of what she'd found, then Dan's appearance sent everything else scurrying away.

'I don't suppose you heard—'

'Not a dickie bird.' She cut him off. He'd guessed; that was one person too many.

'Still, you might want to wear a headsquare for a day or two until it all dies down. That style is quite distinctive.'

Cathy nodded. 'You said a couple of things.'

'You'll like the other one. Bob Hartley's applied for a transfer to SIB in Glasgow. A lot closer to his family in Carlisle, he says.'

She felt a glow of satisfaction. 'No women in the Glasgow office?'

'None. They're desperate to have someone up there, but I can't spare him until this operation's over.'

Another good reason to find this spy soon. Very soon.

FOUR

Cathy read through the transcripts of Minuit's interrogations, then his handler's notes. The man who'd questioned him knew exactly what he was doing, setting traps to trip the man up, peeling away the layers of his personality so thoroughly that now she could believe she almost knew *who* they were hunting. Minuit came across as a calm man who seemed straightforward rather than ruffled by all the questions. Someone who appeared relieved to be caught, eager to cooperate.

He'd been friendly with the agents looking after him, his handler said. He seemed to accept all the restrictions on his life without complaint. Adapted well, cooked simple meals. Sent his radio messages to the Germans exactly as he was instructed, read, listened to the wireless. Apparently content to do what he was told for the rest of the war.

And underneath it all, a very slick liar, she thought as she stepped down from the tram outside the Skyrack pub in Headingley. Someone who'd fooled the experts and bided his time until he had the chance to flee.

'Do you know this area?' Faulkner asked.

'I should do by now. Every time England played cricket here, we'd be patrolling round in uniform. It always brought the prostitutes out in force.'

'Cricket did?' he said in disbelief. Hard to believe with its staid reputation.

'Honestly. I must have taken dozens in for soliciting. Evidently cricket fans are randy as goats.' Cathy pointed along St Michael's Road. 'The ground's just the other side of those houses at the end.' As they walked, she cocked her head. 'Tell me something: do you think we're wasting our time doing this?'

'I hope not,' he answered. 'He might come back to an area where he stayed before. But at least we're doing *something*. We need to be out and looking. What's the option, wait for him to turn up?'

The first hotel owner didn't recognize the photograph of Minuit.

'We're full up with munitions workers these days,' she said. She was a hawk-faced woman, grey hair as coarse as wire, looking as if she'd forgotten how to smile. 'First it was soldiers after Dunkirk, and we've had all sorts billeted here since. I know it sounds horrible, but with no cricket, the war has been the saving of us in this business.'

'What have they done with the cricket ground?' Cathy asked.

'Using it for storing vehicles. Lorries go in and out of there all the time.'

'That man we showed you,' Faulkner told her. 'He's a deserter and a criminal. If he shows up, ring us immediately.' He wrote down the office telephone number and put it in her hand. 'It's important.'

As they were leaving, Cathy turned. 'Do you know a hotel called Beaumont?'

'Course I do. That'll be Gwen Carpenter and her husband. Turn right at the corner and you can't miss it, pet. There's a sign at the front.' She made a sour face. 'Not much of a place, mind.'

They worked their way along the street, the bitter wind whipping up around them. Small hotels, houses converted for bed and breakfast and now busy with war workers. Minuit hadn't been to any of them. They left the office phone number and heard the promise to ring if he appeared.

Finally they reached Beaumont. It needed a coat of paint on the front door, but was clean inside, the woodwork glowing and smelling of beeswax and lavender.

'No,' Mrs Carpenter said when she studied the photograph. 'I've a decent memory for faces and I'd swear I've never seen him in my life.' A faint smile. 'I'd remember a good-looking chap like that.'

She was a small, neat woman with intelligent eyes, wrapped tight in a flowery yellow pinafore.

'We believe he stayed here in—'

'1935.' Faulkner supplied the year.

'That explains it. We didn't buy until the year after. My husband loves the cricket and we thought this would make a good retirement income.' She gave a small, rueful smile. 'Now there's no cricket for him and I'm rushed off me feet.' A brief smile. 'Sorry, luv.'

So much for that, Cathy thought as they trudged on to the next place. By noon she was tired of hearing herself ask the same questions. Her feet ached and she was hungry. Only one place to go in Headingley.

She led him to North Lane and a pair of stone houses that stood a few yards back from the road. No mistaking the smell: fish and chips. Charlie Brett's. Not on the ration yet, with a restaurant where they could sit in the warmth and eat some hot food.

Small talk as they ate. Always aware that someone might be listening. Then out into the cold once again.

'Back to the fray,' Faulkner said. He pushed his trilby down on his head and pulled up the collar of his overcoat.

'He's not here, is he?' Cathy said. 'In Headingley, I mean.'

'Probably not,' he agreed. 'But it's only a bit over forty-eight hours since he scarpered. With no money and no identity card, he'll find it slow going. He's probably not even in Leeds yet. But like I said, we have to start somewhere. There's that chance he'll come back around here.'

'A chance,' she echoed.

'Think of this as seeding the ground in case he does.'

'Do you believe we can catch him?'

'We have to, don't we?' But all he had to offer was a bleak look. 'I wouldn't want to be in your brother's shoes. I reckon our . . . friend is going to be a slippery bastard.'

The first time one of the squad swore in front of her, he'd blushed and apologized. Cathy replied with language to make a sailor blush and suddenly everything was easier. No need for any of them to walk on eggshells around her.

Three o'clock and still no luck. The day began to drag and the wind blew paper along the pavements and gutters. The tram rattled its way into town.

They'd begun to walk down the Headrow when Cathy stopped.

'You go ahead to the office. I've just thought of someone who might be able to help.'

'Oh?' He gave her a curious look.

'Another long shot. I'll be along in a few minutes.'

She strode away, down Albion Street, turning along Boar Lane to the railway station. On the way, she took the letter from her handbag and dropped it into a letterbox. She'd finished it last night, after Dan had gone. Writing to Tom, re-reading the letters he sent her, always distracted her from the darkness that kept growing around them.

They'd been a couple for the best part of a year. It had started on a Saturday night at the Majestic. A good band playing. He asked her to dance. They'd spent the next half hour moving around to the music, then talking until she missed the last tram and he walked her all the way home to Gipton.

After that, they began to see each other once a fortnight. Casual to start; soon it was every week. She had Sunday tea with his family; he came over to Brander Road to meet her parents as things grew more serious. Without thinking, they moved from going out to courting. She enjoyed his voice, his company, his gentle confidence about life and faith in the future.

At least she knew he was safe, stationed in Nottinghamshire with the Ordnance Corps, teaching mechanics how to keep the army's heavy vehicles running. He was due another leave in a month or so, a chance to be with him once more. Something to keep her going.

The railway station was like a cauldron as she walked in, the smoke and stink of the locomotives everywhere. All around, a sea of uniforms, voices rising and falling, a scrum of bodies around the NAAFI canteen.

Somewhere on a far platform, a train whistle shrieked as the engine gathered steam and a guard bellowed for the final passengers.

Cathy squeezed her way through the crowd to the Women's Voluntary Service desk. Janet Benson was sitting in her crisp uniform with the silver *Centre Organizer* badge, sipping a mug of tea while she enjoyed a short moment of calm in the storm.

She'd been a godsend when the soldiers stumbled off the trains after Dunkirk. Somehow she'd known the right things to say to coax a grin from a bone-weary soldier, the places to send them. A plump woman with a kindly face and the gift of instantly making everyone feel at ease. Very efficient, and like an encyclopaedia when it came to finding aid in Leeds.

'Hello, Mrs Benson.'

The woman squinted, trying to place Cathy. A few moments and she eased into a smile.

'Sergeant Marsden, isn't it? I almost didn't know you out of uniform. Off-duty today?'

'No such luck,' she laughed. 'No rest for the wicked.' A few words of explanation and she brought out Minuit's picture. 'Ring any bells?'

The woman had a particularly keen eye for faces. Once she saw someone, she'd remember them. A photographic memory was the way someone had described it. More like uncanny, Cathy thought. But useful. Minuit might come on the train. He might ask the WVS for help. Mrs Benson might see him.

Might.

It was no less likely than trying the guest houses near the cricket ground. Faulkner was right; they didn't have anything else. Not yet, anyway.

'No,' she replied slowly, taking her time with the photo. 'I'm positive I've never talked to him. A deserter, you said?'

'An important one. A criminal. Dangerous.'

She pushed her lips together. 'All I can do is keep a lookout for him. Is he likely to be in uniform?'

She considered the idea for a second. 'I doubt it.'

'I can watch for him. But I'm not here all the time.'

'If you can tell the others . . .' Cathy scribbled down the office telephone number on the back of the picture. 'Keep it. Ring us if you spot him. Please. It's important.'

'Of course.'

Cathy shouldered her way through the travellers. Not too difficult; she'd never been tiny, and those years on the force had given her plenty of muscle.

Out in the cold air, she breathed deeply. Janet Benson was alert. That was something. But it was all haystacks and needles. How the hell were they going to find one man in Leeds?

Dan and George were talking to Faulkner when she entered, and all of them turned to look at her. Cathy shook her head.

'What happened out at the targets?'

Andrews rolled his eyes. 'Your brother had us start off with a very cold walk along the canal.'

'I remembered we used to ride our bikes for miles along that towpath when I was a kid,' Dan said. 'It runs by the Forge. I wanted to check if anyone could work their way in through there.'

'Can they?' Faulkner asked.

'If they were determined, maybe.' He glanced at George. 'What do you think?'

'It would take a fair bit of work, but there are woods all around and the place could use sturdier fences. It was a good idea,' he admitted grudgingly. 'The head of their Home Guard unit wasn't too happy when we showed him.'

'Anything to suggest Minuit's been sniffing around the place?' Faulkner asked.

'No,' Dan said, 'but they said they'll beef up patrols around the perimeters, add more fencing and tell the people on the gate to make sure they examine all the lorries that arrive. Plenty comes in and out by train, too, so they'll be watching the tracks. We've got the River Aire running through the place, as well. It's like a colander. The real problem is that it's been around for centuries. Long before they needed to worry about sabotage.' He frowned. 'I talked to my bosses. There'll be an army squad out there tomorrow to take charge. That should help. Still, if Minuit's careful, he'll probably be able to find a way in somehow.'

Grim, Cathy thought. But if they knew the danger, they could try to stop it.

'What about Yeadon?' she asked.

'Completely different.' Dan's voice was brighter. 'It's new, about as secure as it's possible to be. He'd have a much harder job there.'

'But not impossible?' Faulkner was doodling on a pad.

'Nothing's impossible,' Dan began. 'Have you ever been out there? Banked walls covered with grass and the roof disguised so it looks like part of the landscape from the air. That's why they call it a shadow factory. One man *might* manage to get inside, but it wouldn't be easy. If he did, he could do some real damage. But they have a good perimeter and troops watching everything. He'd have a much tougher job than at the Forge.' He frowned, took a deep breath, then raised his head and looked around the faces. 'What scares me most is that he might be able to find some way to tell the Germans exactly where the factory is. If he manages that, the Luftwaffe could destroy it in a single night.'

She closed her eyes, scarcely daring to think about the consequences.

'Have your people turned up any trace of him yet?' Faulkner asked.

'Two possible sightings in London. Nothing confirmed. Evidently a couple of people have reported wallets stolen to the police—'

'Only two?' Faulkner asked in astonishment. 'The London pickpockets must have all joined up. Names?'

'We'll have them in the morning.'

'Then that's probably all we can do for today. By tomorrow he may have had time to find his way up here, so things could heat up a bit. Better be prepared.'

'Are the others still questioning the tanker driver?' Cathy said into the silence that followed.

'Smithy's been with him all day,' Faulkner told her. 'Bob's been following up on the things Dobson let slip last night. Let's see what comes of them. You two take yourselves off home.'

FIVE

'You said you sat in on Minuit's interrogation,' Cathy said as they turned down the ginnel from Harehills Lane and into the Gipton estate. 'Is that part of your this and that?'

'Some of it.'

Not really an answer at all.

'What about you being here?'

'I told you, hunting Minuit is part of my job. It makes perfect sense: I've met him, talked to him.' He gave a wry smile. 'That, and coming from Leeds, of course.'

'Fine,' she replied. 'But there's something I don't understand. If catching him is so vital, why did they just send you? Wouldn't a whole team have been better?'

'It would,' he agreed. 'I asked for it. But we simply don't have enough people. We're stretched beyond breaking point as it is. The brass thought it would be simpler to work with your outfit. You're already here and well established.'

She couldn't deny the sense of that.

'What did you make of him when he was questioned?'

'I spent most of the journey up here thinking about that. He was good. He struck me as genuine, very pleased to still be alive. He was my first, though, so I didn't have any way to measure.' Dan kept a thoughtful silence for a few seconds. 'He was fluent in English, friendly. Charming. You know, in a strange way I liked him.' Dan sounded embarrassed by the admission. 'He didn't just con me; he managed to fool a seasoned spycatcher.'

'Do you think he'd be able to convince others he might meet?'

'I'm certain of it.'

That was bad news, she thought as they walked down Brander Road. They needed some thread they could pull, a way to pursue him. But they needed it yesterday.

'SIB are military police. They carry guns.' His words interrupted her thoughts and in a strange way she felt grateful. Better than the doubts and questions swirling through her head. 'Do you?' he asked.

'The men all learned to use them in basic training.'

'Are you armed?'

Cathy laughed. 'Not a chance. I'm still Leeds City Police, I'm just there on secondment. I won't have anything to do with guns.' Faulkner had suggested once that she learn to shoot. She'd refused. 'Does that answer your question?'

'Yes.'

'What about you? Do you carry one?'

'I told you, I mostly work behind a desk.'

Mostly. Carefully spoken. 'There's far more to what you do than you've been letting on, isn't there?'

'Me? I get my orders and carry them out, the same as you. That's all.' His mouth twitched into a smile. 'You know, you not having a weapon makes me feel a bit safer if we have a bit of a ding-dong.'

She laughed again. He'd very deftly changed the subject and avoided her question. But Dan making fun of himself . . . times really had changed.

Her mother kept trying to prod the conversation into life as they ate. As soon as they'd finished, Dan put down his serviette and stood.

'That was very tasty, Ma. Sorry, excuse me, I need to write my report.'

'Our Daniel's become very serious.' Mrs Marsden scraped the plates into the swill bucket for the neighbourhood pig, washed them and passed to Cathy to dry. A pale, fleshy woman, she was only truly happy when she was worrying. She built up every tiny thing until it looked far worse than it was. 'He's peaky, too. Do you think he's poorly?'

'He's busy, Ma, he has a lot on his mind with work. We all do.'

'Are you sure?' she asked doubtfully.

'I'm positive. There's a war on.' Cathy's mouth twitched into a smile. 'You haven't forgotten, have you?'

She spent the evening in the living room, fire burning in the grate and a concert by the Henry Hall Orchestra on Forces radio. The melodies swam through her head – 'April in Paris', 'Here's

To The Next Time' – while she finished some small jobs she'd been putting off: mending a hem on one skirt, a seam just starting to come apart on a jacket, sewing a couple of buttons back on a blouse, darning the toe of a stocking. Exchanges of idle, pleasant chatter with her father while her mother put her head back and dozed in her chair. Comfortable, the same as hundreds of other nights they'd spent together.

The knock on the door took her by surprise. Almost ten o'clock. Very late for visitors. Cathy checked no light was showing, then turned the key in the lock. Nobody on the estate had a telephone; anyone wanting them had to come in person. Twice, Faulkner had turned up during the evening when they had urgent business. Her heart began to thump.

Had they found a lead on Minuit?

She peered into the night. It took a few seconds before she picked out a shape in the blackness and broke into a wide grin.

'You!' Annie Carter, her best friend from just around the corner, now in the Women's Auxiliary Air Force. A WAAF. 'Come in, they'd love to see you. I'll pop the kettle on.'

'I can't stop, honest. I've only got a forty-eight-hour pass and I haven't been home yet. Here.' She took Cathy's hand and guided it over the sleeve of her uniform. 'Feel that? Leading Aircraftwoman Carter to you now.'

'I . . .' She was stuck for words. From hairdresser to recruit and up to NCO, all in just over four months. A real achievement. They hugged. 'That's wonderful. I'm so proud of you.'

'Promotion came through last week. A bit like a lance-corporal. You'd better watch out, I'm catching up to you, Sergeant. I haven't even told me dad yet. He's going to be over the moon.' A torrent of words tumbled from her, the same as ever. 'God, can you believe it took me an hour to hitch a lift? In uniform, too. Even showed some leg. I have to dash. I stopped by to say I'll see you tomorrow night: we'll go dancing and have a proper catch-up. Just you and me.'

'I don't know if I can. Our Dan's here and we've got a big flap on at the moment.'

Annie was stationed at RAF Church Fenton, not far from Leeds. She knew the demands of war. She'd understand. It was all a long way from the nights when they'd go out dancing or their weekly trips to the Shaftesbury to see the new film without a care in the world.

'I'll stop by at seven and we can see then. You can tell me all about it.'

Another brief hug, then she hurried off into the darkness.

Upstairs, warmed by the quilt, Cathy began the new Georgette Heyer novel she'd borrowed from the circulating library at the post office. Another, gentler century, worlds away from Leeds and the turbulence of war. But she couldn't concentrate. Turning off the light, she lay in bed, wondering if the sirens would sound tonight. Warm clothes sat ready on a chair; slipping them on had become routine.

She closed her eyes and tried to sleep. But troubles and possibilities kept storming across her mind. None of them seemed good.

She was jolted awake. Three minutes past one as the siren began to wail. No panic; she had the routine down to a practised art. She dressed quickly, three layers, thick coat and socks, stout shoes. Pulled the eiderdown off the bed and wrapped it around her shoulders.

Cathy could hear her parents in their bedroom. Her father always needed a few minutes. She tapped on Dan's door.

'You'd better wear everything you have. It'll be perishing out here.'

'I'm just going to stay here.' He sounded groggy, not even half-awake. 'It's what I do at home.'

'No, you're not. You're going to get yourself down there. Ma will be at her wits' end if you don't. Stop faffing, get yourself out of bed and into the back garden.'

She was the first in the Anderson shelter, shivering in the damp chill as she lit the Primus stove and put a kettle on to boil. She helped her father down the stairs they'd cut in the earth and saw him settled and covered up as her mother fussed. Finally Dan appeared. She pulled the metal door closed and put a match to the wicks in the hurricane lamps.

Up and down the street, families would be doing the same thing. Everyone waiting, hoping. Praying.

Sometimes they played cards. Whist or three-card brag to pass the time. Tonight she sat, staring at nothing. Dan was quiet, eyes closed, as if he was sulking or trying to sleep. But all of them were alert for the distant note of engines and the crump of the ack-ack guns. Nothing at all. After an hour the all-clear sounded.

Leeds had escaped again. How long could that last?

Cathy examined her face in the mirror. It was a desperate sight, she decided; she looked years older than twenty-six. Haggard, dark shadows under her eyes from the broken night. A touch of foundation to try and hide them. Make-up wasn't on the ration yet, but it was already harder to find, and prices rose all the time.

A touch of lipstick, then she ran a brush through her hair. She looked again, pouted. It would have to do. Passable, as long as no one looked too closely. She tied a headsquare over her hair. Anonymous now.

'What about the tanker driver?' Faulkner asked Smithy. 'Squeezed anything more out of him?'

He shook his head and pushed his glasses up his nose. 'Just what we have. I've gone at him every way I know. Either he's being paid very well to keep his mouth shut or he's terrified. Even the idea of prison won't budge him.'

'Worth another go?'

He frowned. 'Honestly? I don't think so.'

'Bob, anything on those things we picked up from the tanker driver?'

'Not yet.'

Cathy saw the flash of frustration cross Faulkner's face.' He turned to Dan. 'Do you have the names from those stolen wallets?'

'Andrew Johnson and Carl Williams.'

'It's going to be a day of foot leather,' Faulkner told the squad. 'Doss houses, lodging houses. There are a few around the city centre. You know the routine. We all did it enough on the force. Go round them all. You have copies of Minuit's picture. Show it. Try them with those other names. Martinson, too, the one he was using when he was captured.'

'I'll talk to the people at St George's Crypt,' Cathy said. 'They know me.'

'Take your brother with you,' Faulkner said. 'I have something to do for an hour.' He glanced at his watch. 'Back here for half past eleven.'

They walked along the Headrow. Large water tanks stood on the islands in the middle of the road, painted in black and white checks to warn nighttime motorists. Past the blast wall protecting the entrance to Lewis's department store. Down Merry Boys hill, to the front of the town hall, then waiting by the stone lions. Cathy remembered the story she'd been told once: when the clock struck thirteen, they rose and turned round. A silly, innocent tale from an age when the world wasn't burning.

'What are we doing?' Dan asked. 'Why are we standing here?'

'You'll see soon enough.'

Right to the minute, Woman Police Constable Betty Rains rounded the corner. Exactly where she ought to be on her beat. A shout and the constable was standing in front of her, with a quick, interested glance at Dan.

'Morning, Sarge.' She was always eager, smiling, a woman who loved her job. 'I didn't recognize you at first with that headsquare. What can I do for you?'

Cathy brought the photograph of Minuit from her handbag.

'I want you to keep an eye out for him.'

Rains studied the face. 'He's a bit of a cracker, isn't he? What's he done?'

'Keep clear of him, Betty. A deserter and a criminal. Dangerous, so be careful. Keep that. Show it to the others.'

'What do you want us to do if we see him?'

'Let me know as soon as you can. Inspector Harding has the telephone number for SIB.'

'Yes, ma'am.' A crisp salute and she marched off past the art gallery.

'Do you have many women police in Leeds?' Dan asked as they moved away up Calverley Street.

'Not enough. Just six constables, me, with the inspector in charge. People tend to underestimate us, but we see a lot.'

'Going back to it after the fighting's done?'

'Probably,' Cathy answered after a moment. She'd couldn't think that far ahead. Not yet. 'What about you? Going to stick in this line of work?'

'Have to get through this first.' He had a tense snap to his voice. The lines were sharp at the corner of his eyes and mouth. This was consuming him. No surprise; too much depended on his success.

The door to the crypt under St George's Church was unlocked, sandbags stacked three deep all around. Their footsteps echoed off the flagstones and the thick walls as they walked down the stairs. Ahead, rows of beds, all tidily made and covered with coarse grey blankets. Netting over the few windows in case of a blast.

The place was famous throughout Leeds. It offered homeless men somewhere to sleep. Fed them, provided clothes if they needed them. Cathy had brought a few here when she was in uniform. A refuge for the desperate. If Minuit arrived in Leeds without money, he might come here for a place to sleep.

Mrs Burns sat behind the desk. This had been her kingdom for the last five years and she ruled it with a wise eye. A stringy woman, standing five feet nothing in her stocking feet, she looked like a strong breeze might blow her all the way to the coast. But woe betide anyone who crossed her. No time for nonsense or troublemakers, yet always with a few minutes to listen to the stories people carried in their hearts.

'I heard you'd been transferred, Sergeant,' she said, unwrapping a mint humbug. 'I wasn't expecting to see you in here again.'

'Work,' she said and took the photograph of Minuit from Dan. 'We're looking for him. He's an important deserter. A criminal. Has he been here in the last couple of nights? He might be calling himself James Martinson or maybe Andrew Johnson or Carl Williams.'

'No,' the woman replied with certainty. 'We've only had our regulars lately.' She gave a long sigh. 'Fewer of those, too. A couple more of them died during that bad cold snap last month.' She pushed the picture back across the desk. 'What do you want me to do if he shows his face?'

Cathy wrote down the squad's telephone number. 'Get in touch. Don't try and stop him yourself.' Her tone was firm enough to make the woman open her mouth in surprise. 'I mean that. Let us handle it.' Threepence into the donation box on the desk, then back out into the February air.

As soon as they walked into the office, Faulkner gathered up his coat. 'There's someone I want to see. You two might as well come along.'

'Will it help find him?' Dan asked.

'Not immediately. Maybe not at all.'

'Would you mind if I stayed here, then? I need to take care of some papers.'

'Where are we going?' she asked as he turned the key in the Humber. Nothing.

'Dammit,' he said. The problem had started a week before. No time to take it to a garage yet. They kept a screwdriver jammed between the seat and back on the driver's side to tighten one of the wires in the steering column. A moment of fiddling, and he tried again. The engine purred.

'Did you know there's an honorary Dutch consul in Leeds?'

'I did,' Cathy replied, relishing the astonishment on his face. 'His name's Henry Victor.'

'Have you met him?' He turned up Albion Street, along Woodhouse Lane and out past the university.

'Not him. I ended up chatting to his wife at some charity do. Inspector Harding was poorly so I substituted for her. Next highest female rank,' she explained when he gave her a quizzical glance. 'The family used to be called something like Willems, but his father changed it before the last war. Thought it sounded too German.'

'Do you think she'd remember you?'

'I doubt it. We only talked for a few minutes and I was in uniform.'

He nodded, thinking. 'See if you can have a word. Remind her.'

'All right. Why are we going to see them?'

'I know your brother reckons this spy will steer clear of Dutch people, but he could be wrong. Or someone might hear him speak and notice the accent.'

'Are we that desperate already?'

'More or less,' he admitted. 'I'm willing to try anything. There's a small Dutch community here. The Victors can pass the word.'

Cathy stared out of the car window as they took the turning for Adel. Big houses with long drives and green lawns. Everything clean and ordered. But it didn't make her want to live among the rich; a council house in Gipton was all she needed.

Henry Victor had thin grey hair and a jowly face with a drinker's red nose under playful, intelligent eyes. He shook their hands and listened politely before turning to his wife.

'Perhaps you could show Sergeant Marsden around,' he said with a gentle smile. 'She might enjoy the garden.'

'I believe we've been dismissed,' Mrs Victor apologized once they were alone. 'My husband . . .'

Cathy shook her head. 'It doesn't matter.'

'I have no idea what he means about the garden. There's nothing to see outside in February. Would you like a cup of tea instead?'

Sitting at the kitchen table, Cathy saw the woman watching her and chewing her bottom lip. 'You know, I'd swear you look familiar.'

A few sentences to jog her memory, a short laugh and five minutes of polite chatter about nothing.

'There's more to this than just searching for a deserter, isn't there?' Mrs Victor asked quietly. 'Even if he is a criminal.'

'We need to find him.' She said it firmly enough to discourage questions.

A pause before the woman nodded. 'There aren't too many Dutch here, but we know them all. I'll ask them to keep their eyes open.'

Cathy brought a copy of Minuit's photo from the folder and set it on the table. 'He's very broad, a touch under six foot.'

Mrs Victor raised her eyebrows and nodded approval. 'People would certainly notice someone like him. We'll make people aware.' She pushed her cup away, a signal they were done.

'Was she able to help?' Adam asked as they drove away.

'Not really,' Cathy replied. At the back of her mind, she could feel the clock ticking. 'Coming out here, even checking the hotels, it all feels like a waste of time. He's not a crook. We know he's clever.'

'We're doing whatever we can.' He paused. 'We're all out casting lines and hoping we get a bite on one of them.'

'We need more than hope.' It was all scattershot. They were floundering, there was no rhythm to the search yet.

'Maybe so.' He sighed. 'We're doing the things we know. The things coppers do. I'd love some good suggestions.'

'I wish I had a few.'

'Tell me, what do you make of your brother?' He said it lightly, trying to make it sound like a passing remark. But the question carried far more weight than that. Dan had climbed higher than he let on; that much was obvious, even if he wouldn't admit it. But now he looked as if he understood fear for the first time.

She took time to find the right words. 'He's like a man up on a tightrope. He's up there in the middle of a gale and trying to make it to the other side without falling off.'

A wasted day for everyone, she thought as the rest of the squad straggled back to the office, shaking their heads. Dan, though . . . she tried to read his expression.

'Have you come up with something?' she asked.

'I might have,' he replied. Suddenly they were all paying attention. 'MI5 has a man up here. I slipped out to see him this afternoon, and he's heard a rumour—'

'What kind of rumour?' Terry Davis jumped on the word.

'It could be nothing. From some . . . German sympathizers up here.' Cathy stared at him and he gazed back. 'Don't worry, we know exactly who they are. The only reason we don't haul them off is because they sometimes give us useful snippets of information. It's word that someone might be coming. Might even already be here.'

Her heart thudded.

'Nothing more concrete than that?'

Dan shook his head. 'He's keeping his ear to the ground. I need to keep our agent under wraps from everyone—'

'Of course. God forbid the right hand should know what the left hand's doing,' Hartley said, tossing his pen down on the desk.

'Leave it,' Faulkner said quietly. 'This is more than we've found so far.'

'He'll let me know as soon as he hears anything. Even a crumb.'

'We'll have to make do with that. You lot have worked hard. You look like you've all had enough of today.'

SIX

'What exactly do you do for these XX people?'
Dan had said a little about his work, but he'd stayed very spare on detail. Caution? Trying to make himself important? One thing was certain: there was more to his job than he'd revealed. She intended to keep prodding.

Dan looked up from the papers scattered around him on the bed. He was wearing his overcoat and fingerless gloves against the evening cold, frowning as he read.

'I already told you.' He smiled. 'This and that. But to Ma and Dad I'm a civil servant.'

'A lie.'

His response was a vague smile and a shrug. 'A small one. The world is full of them.'

Cathy was ready to push him. 'You're a bigger fish than you make out, aren't you? Sitting in on the interrogation of spies. Going to see a local MI5 agent. All the surprising things you seem to know. Being sent up here to hunt Minuit.'

His face gave nothing away. She heard the first hint of annoyance in his voice.

'I already told you: sending me made sense. I've met him, I've seen him move around and heard him talk. I can recognize him. It's part of my job.'

Perhaps. But . . . 'You didn't answer my question.'

He put down the papers and she saw the flash of anger cross his face. 'What do you want me to say? I told you I drifted into this. That's enough. Besides, if I denied it, would you believe me?'

'Maybe you could convince me.'

He shook his head. 'I'm not even going to try. There's no need.'

Someone had taught him how to slide around words.

'How dangerous is Minuit?'

He rubbed his chin. 'We were certain we had him pegged, but

we were wrong. He fooled an interrogator who's an expert at taking people apart. He escaped from a secure house and we're still not sure how he managed it. Does that tell you anything?'

More than she wanted to know.

'How much time do you think we have to catch him?'

Dan gave a long, bitter sigh. 'I don't know. Not long enough, probably.'

She was about to say something else when she heard the knock on the front door. Annie. Seven o'clock already. Quietly, she closed the door of Dan's room. He was already back to his papers.

'Ready?'

'Come in. You know Ma's going to want to see you, Leading Aircraftwoman.'

Annie blushed. 'Go on, then. Just for a minute.'

Cathy watched her mother make a fuss, and the pleasure on her father's face at another young voice filling the room.

'Where do you fancy going?' she asked as they walked arm in arm up the street. 'Scala? Majestic?'

'How about the Starlight Room?' Annie said. 'I hardly slept after the all-clear last night, and I have to report back at fifteen hundred tomorrow.'

Fifteen hundred. She was definitely part of the Air Force.

'That's fine.' It was only a short walk, tucked behind the Shaftesbury cinema. 'You're wearing stockings. I saw them. Are they real silk? They're ridiculous here. Gone up from sevenpence ha'penny to well over a shilling, if they even have them.'

'Nylons,' Annie said. 'I told you we have those Yanks flying with us, didn't I, the ones who joined the RAF? One of them heard us moaning about stockings. He got a mate to send some over and he sells them to us.'

'Sounds like he has a good little earner. Can you get me some?'

'Don't you worry, your Auntie Annie has already looked after you. There's a pair waiting at home. I meant to bring them tonight. I'll drop them round before I go tomorrow. Brought some for my mam and my sister, too.'

'I'll pay you.'

'Buy me a drink, that'll take care of it. Now, what's this about your brother being here?'

Thursday, a quiet night. A couple of gin and tonics, shuffling round the floor whenever a man worked up the courage to ask one of them; mostly it meant plenty of chance to natter. All the gossip about the WAAFs and the air crews. Mucky but fun. More enjoyable than a band that couldn't have swung if their lives depended on it, a singer who tried to sound like Al Bowlly and failed, and a crowd that mostly looked as if they'd rather be somewhere else.

'You have someone up at the airfield?' Cathy asked. Annie had never been one to last with a man. Two, three dates and that was enough.

'No. The flyboys are fun, they flirt with us. Same with the Yanks.' Her mouth turned down. 'But when they take off, you never know if they'll come back. What about you? Does Tom have any leave due soon?'

'A few weeks.'

'You're not going to have one of those rushed marriages while he's home, are you? If you don't invite me, I'll never speak to you again.'

Cathy roared with laughter. 'Not a chance. Do you want another drink?'

Well before half past ten they were strolling back down the ginnel, still chattering away, laughing and happy in each other's company.

'A promotion,' Cathy said. 'I'm proud of you. Who'd have thought it?'

'Give over. It's not just you who can do it, clever clogs. I've earned it. Plenty of hard graft. I'm proud of that badge.'

'You should be.'

Another giggle. 'At this rate I could be Air Vice-Marshal by the end of the war.'

They were laughing loud enough to wake the neighbourhood. Annie always had that effect on her. After this week, it was exactly what she needed. No knowing when they'd be out together again; there was no rhyme or reason to Annie's leaves and passes. At the corner of Brander Grove they hugged each other, and Cathy smiled all the way home.

A thick frost covered the roofs. The grass was white and crisp. It was bitterly cold on the tram, and Cathy gazed enviously at the conductress in her trousers. She'd owned a pair for two years but hadn't summoned up the courage to wear them yet. Instead, she was in the old tweed skirt she'd made over one long winter, with the hem below the knee, a warm flannel petticoat and wool stockings. She knew she'd be grateful for them later.

On the way out of the house, she'd picked up the small bag she'd packed.

'You can't be going away,' Dan said. 'Not when we're in the middle of a job.'

'Don't be silly,' she told him. 'Sandwiches and a flask. Friday is my firewatching night.'

In the office, a message was waiting on her desk: *Ring your inspector*.

'When did this come in?' she asked.

'About five minutes ago,' Terry replied. 'She said it was important.'

She pressed the receiver to her ear, holding her breath as she waited for Inspector Harding to answer. Her voice was brisk and formal, the sound of a woman trying to juggle three tasks at once.

'You left a picture with WPC Rains yesterday. She showed it to the others at the start of shift this morning, and WPC Barker believes she's seen him. Rains said you needed to know as soon as possible.'

Cathy felt a shock through her body. Every nerve tingled. She glanced around at the others; they were talking casually to each other.

'Where was this, ma'am?'

'You'd do better to hear the story from her. Barker's on the market beat today.'

'Thank you, ma'am.' She swallowed as she lowered the receiver. Was Minuit really here? Cathy picked up her headscarf and handbag. 'I need to pop out for a few minutes,' she said.

She dashed across Briggate and Vicar Lane, then down into Kirkgate market. Every nerve was jangling. This could be what they needed, a way for the hunt really to begin.

The place was alive with shoppers, sellers bellowing out their wares and raising their voices over each other. Cathy watched for a dark blue police cap.

She pushed through the people, hurrying up and down the aisles, beginning to feel frantic as she moved out into the open market. Then . . . off to the right, talking to a woman running a second-hand clothes stall.

Daisy Barker was small, just a couple of inches above the height to qualify as a copper, but with a quick, sharp gaze and piercing intelligence. She smiled as soon as she spotted Cathy.

'I hear you have something for me.' Her heart was beating so hard she thought it was going to fly out of her chest.

'I think I do, Sarge.' She frowned. 'Betty showed us that photo and I think I saw him on my way in to work this morning. I'm pretty sure I did.'

She drew in a breath. Maybe they really were coming closer to Minuit. 'How sure?'

'I can't be positive. It wasn't much more than a quick look from the tram, but it looked very much like him.' She lowered her head and blushed. 'Actually, Sarge, I only noticed him because he was quite handsome. A couple of other lasses were staring, too.'

Daisy had always had an eye for the men, Cathy thought. For once it might help them.

'Go on.'

'After that, I started to wonder why someone like that wasn't already in uniform. He was big. A strapping bloke.'

That fitted with the way her brother had described Minuit. 'Was he clean and shaved or more like he'd been on the tramp?'

Barker narrowed her eyes, reliving the scene. 'It was only a few seconds, while we picked up a passenger. He was clean,' she decided. 'He had to be. It would have registered otherwise.'

'What was he wearing?'

'A dark overcoat. I could see a shirt and tie. A trilby in his hands.'

Good observation. Now the big question. 'Where was this?'

'Kirkstall Road, right by the viaduct that goes up to Armley.'

'What was he doing?'

'He looked as if he'd stopped to glance over his shoulder. I think he might have started to walk as we pulled away, but I can't be sure.'

'Walk?' She leapt on the word. 'Which direction?'

'Out towards the old abbey.' Cathy's heart leapt into her throat. The road that would take him to Kirkstall Forge.

'That's excellent work,' she said. 'Really good. Very keen eyes.'

'Thanks, Sarge.' Barker glowed with pride.

Cathy took a breath. 'Now, this is really important. I need to ask again: how sure are you that the man you saw was the one in the photograph?'

Barker took her time. 'Like I said, I can't be *positive*, but as soon as Betty showed me the picture, I thought it was him. If it's not, they could be brothers.'

That was enough. It had to be Minuit; there couldn't be two like him in Leeds. This was the piece of luck they needed. He was here and now they knew it. For the first time since Dan had told them about the spy, she felt a touch of hope.

'Is he really a deserter and a criminal, Sarge?'

'He is. Not your type, believe me. You carry on with your beat. I need to tell my squad and get after him.'

'I'm glad I could help.'

'Our spy might be in Kirkstall,' she announced and suddenly the office was silent.

The air crackled as she told them what she'd just heard, all of them alert, rapt. Except Bob Hartley.

'A half-second glimpse from a tram.' He snorted. 'The dozy cow probably imagined the whole bloody thing.'

Cathy rounded on him, sick of his sniping. 'I've worked with WPC Barker for a long time. She's observant and steady.' Her words blazed. 'If she's convinced it was Minuit, then there's an excellent chance it was.'

'Bob.' Faulkner kept his voice low. 'Have you come up with anything on our spy?'

He muttered his reply. 'Not yet.'

'Then we're going to follow up on this and be glad we have it. Got that?' He began to issue orders. 'Cathy, Dan, I want you out along the canal towpath. Bob, Terry, show Minuit's picture in all the cafes and shops along that road. Ask if he's been a customer this morning. George, you and I are heading for the Forge. If you find him, you know what to do.' He paused as a thought came to him. 'Did he have an overcoat and hat when he vanished?'

'No,' Dan replied.

'Then he's come up with them somewhere. If he's shaved and washed, it sounds as if he had a bed for the night. The lodging houses would have let us know if he'd shown his face.' He turned to Derek Smith. 'Go round the hotels and guest houses on that stretch heading out towards Kirkstall. We'll meet back here this afternoon.'

SEVEN

Cathy was glad she'd worn the shoes she'd used on the beat. Warm and sturdy, just right for a walk along the frozen, rutted canal towpath. Dan's footwear was made for London pavements, but he'd survive. His face was more cheerful than he'd been when they left home.

'If he really is up here, we should be able to bag him inside a couple of days,' Dan said.

'He's in Leeds,' she told him. 'Daisy Barker's got sharp eyes.'

A smile. 'Then I'm fairly confident. With all of us after him . . .'

'With that overcoat and hat, I wonder if someone's helping this spy. You said—'

'I remember.'

'Eighty per cent sure the Jerries didn't have anyone round here to help him,' she said. 'That's nowhere near definite, is it? We all want him caught, but . . .' The truth was they had no idea what it would take. Cathy glanced at her brother's face and saw the confidence falter behind his eyes. Better to be realistic, even if it hurt.

'Do you think he'll have come this way?' she asked after another minute. Nobody around, but her voice was as hushed as if she was in church.

'It's possible. He'll have studied maps before he was sent.' Another hundred yards before he spoke, changing the subject. 'I was thinking that Dad looks smaller.'

'He's shrinking, more each year.' Inch by inch, their father was becoming tiny, withering away in front of their eyes. Only fifty-six, but he might as well have been an old man. A shadow of the muscled boiler engineer in the wedding picture who marched away to the trenches all those years before. Slowly but certainly, that dose of gas in no man's land was killing him.

Out towards Amen Corner, she picked out a vague shape next to the canal. Her body stiffened as she walked, and she narrowed her eyes, trying to make it out. Finally, as they came closer, she gave a small laugh.

'Mr Yarwood,' she called. 'What are you doing all the way out here?'

'Now then.' He dipped his head and looked at her. 'I'm trying to catch my supper if no lass starts shouting the odds and disturbing the bloody fish.' She smiled at his annoyance. This was the face he showed to the world. Dig beneath the surface and he was a kind old man. 'Who are you, anyway?'

'Sergeant Marsden. Police. Remember?'

He cackled. 'Oh, aye. I know you now. Trying to trick me by not wearing your uniform, are you? What are you doing, checking to see I have a fishing licence?'

'Had any luck?' She used to see him twice a week when her beat took her around the back of the railway station. He'd be sitting with his rod and reel beside lock number one, where the Leeds–Liverpool canal met the river. Grumpy old Arthur Yarwood, happiest when he could moan about something.

'Nobbut a tiddler so far. Not even enough for the wife.'

'How long have you been here?'

He unbuttoned his overcoat and pulled a watch from his waistcoat. 'A bit over an hour. Why? Are you setting a time limit now?'

'Many gone past?'

'One or two, I suppose. It was quiet until you turned up and started bellowing for all you're worth.'

'Don't be so daft,' she told him. 'It's not my fault they're not biting.' Cathy brought out the photo of Minuit. 'How about him? Has he come by here?'

It only took a second before he was shaking his head. 'No. Too young.' He handed it back. 'He looks like a right bruiser.'

'He is.'

'Someone like him, he ought to be in uniform.'

'That's one of the reasons we're looking for him.' She looked at the calm surface of the canal. 'I hope you catch a few.'

'Aye, well. We'll see.'

'You know enough people,' Dan said as they walked on, the dirt of the towpath hard under the soles of her shoes.

'Comes with being a bobby. You meet them on the beat.'

'You seem to have a knack with them.'

She shrugged. 'I enjoy talking and listening. Not as much as this job, but I do. I'll tell you, though, I've never felt prouder than when I made sergeant. I really felt I'd achieved something. Do you have ranks where you are?'

'Not really. More a sort of pecking order.'

Conversation faded and her thoughts wandered. Something from a school lesson about horses pulling the canal boats on these paths.

The gunshot echoed across the sky. Without thinking, Cathy dropped to the ground.

Silence all around. She turned her head. Dan was crouching behind a tree, and he peered through the brush and woods into the valley towards the river below. She felt as though a fist was squeezing her heart.

'Are you all right?' she whispered and saw him nod.

'What about you?' His voice was hoarse.

'I'm fine.' The shot hadn't come from anywhere close. Hesitantly, she climbed to her feet and dusted off her coat. Her breath was still fluttering and her hands trembled. Every muscle was stretched and tense.

'Where was it?' Her breath steamed in the air.

'I don't know.' He gestured towards the valley. 'Down there somewhere, I think.'

Cautiously, she peered. Brush and undergrowth, a field leading to the steady flow of the river, then the old, ruined abbey in the distance, the crumbling tower peering above the treetops. Nobody moving.

Maybe Bob or Terry had found the spy. They both carried sidearms.

'Someone will have rung the police,' Cathy said. A shudder ran through her. 'They'll be out here soon.'

'If Minuit was ever around, that will have sent him running,' Dan said. She heard the frustration in his voice. 'It was probably just a farmer.'

'Let's keep going,' she decided finally. It had to be better than standing here, worrying and imagining. Still, as they walked, she kept looking back, skittish at the slightest movement, the tiniest noise. A bird starting to sing nearby was enough to startle her.

No conversation, both of them lost in their silences.

'See the Forge over here?' Dan asked finally. 'The other side of the railway lines.'

It was impossible to miss. Sprawling, ugly, a mix of stone and metal, wreathed in smoke from its chimneys. They were still a good quarter of a mile away, but Cathy believed she could feel the heat from the furnaces and taste the raw tang of metal in her throat.

'We need places like this. They're the ones that are going to help win us this war,' he said.

As long as they could keep it safe from the bombers and saboteurs, Cathy thought as she studied her brother's face. Determined. Scared.

'How do we get in?' she asked.

'A couple of days ago, their security needed work.' A dour smile. 'Want to see if the army's improved it yet?'

They circled around, searching for weaknesses in the fence. Any spot to squeeze through. After twenty minutes of scrambling among brambles and hawthorn, she gave up. They marched along the railway line, and presented themselves to an astonished guard. Cathy brandished her SIB identification.

Another soldier escorted them to the security office.

Faulkner and George were studying a plan of the site with an army captain. The men looked up as they entered.

'Who—' the officer began.

Faulkner cut him off. 'They're with me.'

'You've done a good job on the fences,' Cathy said. 'But with enough time, someone could still work his way in.'

'We've barely started,' the captain told her. 'Assigned to this place yesterday.'

'Make sure there are regular perimeter patrols,' Dan told him. He had the steel of authority in his voice.

'Already in hand. Who are you?'

'MI5.'

'Any sign of him?' Faulkner asked.

'No, but there was a gunshot.'

'What?' He shouted the word. 'How long ago was this? It's too noisy to hear any damned thing in this place.'

'About twenty minutes,' Cathy said. 'We couldn't tell where it came from.'

'Just one?'

'Yes.'

It only took a moment for him to make the decision.

'Let's see what we can find out about that. Maybe . . .'

'It's never what you wish for, boss,' George sighed. 'You ought to know that by now. Never.'

Sitting in the back of the Humber as they drove along Kirkstall Road, Cathy felt the small aches from throwing herself to the frozen ground. She watched from the window: no police vehicles.

All very curious.

'We need to find out who fired that damned shot,' Dan said.

Faulkner put down the telephone receiver and gave a snort. 'Turns out it was a bloody smallholder. He had an old gun from the last war.'

'What the hell was he aiming at?' Bob Hartley asked. 'We could hear it from the road. Everybody stopped for a second.'

'According to the constable who arrested him, he'd been drinking.' He raised his eyebrows then shrugged. 'Taking a potshot at something eating his winter cabbages. Weapon's been confiscated, and he's facing a fine.'

'Throw him behind bars for a few days.'

'No joy in the shops?'

Hartley shook his head and lit a Capstan with quick, jerky movements, blowing smoke at the ceiling.

'If he's out that way, he's not been ducking in anywhere and spending money,' Terry Davis added. He packed his pipe and struck a match.

The men vanished to the canteen for dinner. Cathy stayed in the office, reading through Minuit's interrogations once more. Maybe there was some tiny hint in there, something they'd missed. Even the smallest thread that she'd overlooked.

Nothing. Too many people would have already picked the words clean.

It was the same with the handler's notes. The spy presented

a calm face to his captors, Underneath that, he'd been planning, simply waiting for the right opportunity.

Frustrated, she pushed the papers away and examined the photograph again. She'd seen it so many times his face was imprinted on her brain. Where was he? If Daisy Barker said she'd seen him, Cathy believed he was in Leeds somewhere.

Where?

EIGHT

Not long after six and town was growing quiet. Trams and buses still going up and down Briggate, but the flood of people had become a thin trickle.

Cathy paced a small circle on the roof of Matthias Robinson's department store, bundled up tight as the hard chill made her body hunch in on itself. She gazed at the sky. At the opposite corner, Brenda Lambert was doing the same, a cigarette cupped out of sight in her hand.

This was her Friday night duty, every week until half past ten, watching in case the Germans dropped incendiary bombs. They'd finished pulling the tin hats and the stirrup pump and buckets from the cupboard, and now came the boredom. A quarter of an hour and they'd retreat inside. If the sirens sounded, they'd be out again.

Fish paste sandwiches wrapped in greaseproof paper and soup heated up and poured into a flask; her mother prepared the same thing every time. Brenda worked on the counter at Woolworth's; she brought food from the canteen there. A pleasant woman in her fifties, she was a widow with a son overseas in the army. Doing her bit and filling another empty night in the calendar.

Two months of this and they'd had no emergencies yet, thank God. But the possibility always lurked, the need to stay alert. Catch an incendiary as soon as it landed and it was easy to extinguish. That was the theory, what they'd been taught when they started. She just hoped she'd never need to put it to the test.

The duty was worth it for the view over Leeds. All around town others were doing the same, waiting, ready for the worst; on clear nights she sometimes saw their silhouettes on the skyline.

After her third week, she realized she'd been in Matthias Robinson more often as a firewatcher than a customer. The prices were too rich for her blood. She had a steady job, a good rank, but the police were poorly paid, women less than the men. Even a sergeant didn't earn much and half of that went straight to her mother to cover board and a bit more.

She had plenty to occupy her thoughts tonight. How were they going to find Jan Minuit? They'd been looking at Kirkstall Forge, as if they believed it was the likely target, but what if he was setting his sights on the Avro factory? Disrupting the production of bombers would have a disastrous effect on the war. It was something to discuss in the morning.

She poured herself a cup of soup from the flask. Still hot, warming. A bite of a sandwich.

'Dead again,' Brenda said.

'Let's hope it stays that way.'

Sometimes they talked all through their shift. But tonight seemed to be a time when they both needed quiet.

Dan . . . The picture of him kept shifting. Each new fact she learned about him forced her to rearrange all the things she'd believed about her brother. This job he'd been handed . . . it seemed like an impossible task. No wonder his face looked haunted.

'You're miles away,' Brenda said. The woman was standing beside her, handbag tucked under her arm. Was it that time already? 'The night shift will be along in a moment. I've filled out the log, not that there was anything to write. You'd best get yourself shifted.'

The wish of a quiet night when the men arrived to take over until morning, then hurrying along the dark streets to catch the tram. Bouncing up and down along York Road, and finally the walk to her front door.

The house was dark and silent. Cathy crept upstairs, completely exhausted, closed the blackouts in her bedroom, suddenly cheered as she saw the packet of stockings on the bed. Annie hadn't forgotten.

The siren sounded late in the night. Only a short alert, but enough to ruin her sleep and leave her downhearted when she looked out of the window at Saturday morning. The cold had gone, but a steady rain was coming down.

Standing at the tram stop, she was grateful for her galoshes, the stout policewoman's shoes, her rain hood and the lined raincoat she'd bought from C&A years before. She didn't look elegant, but she was dry. Better than Dan; he stood hunched and uncomfortable, huddled under his umbrella.

'Quiet on your watch?' he asked.

'Thankfully. Any idea where we can look today?'

'I'll talk to our man up here, see if he's heard anything more.' His mouth turned down. 'Apart from that . . . no.'

Yesterday's hopeful moment had turned to dust.

One-Eyed Sam stood in his wooden booth on Kirkgate, selling his newspapers, offering more about the British victory over the Italians in Libya. She bought a copy for later.

The squad all looked bedraggled by the rain, quiet as they settled at their desks and lit cigarettes. Terry Davis filled his pipe, taking two matches before he was satisfied with the way it drew.

Dan had hurried off as soon as they stepped down from the tram. Now they were sitting and waiting for him, hoping he'd found some crumbs they could follow.

Faulkner glanced at her, inclining his head. Down to the canteen, sitting among the clatter and noise with two cups of weak tea.

He lit a cigarette and asked: 'Do you have any idea where we should be searching?'

'I wish I did.'

'That constable of yours . . .'

'Daisy? She wouldn't have said it if she wasn't pretty sure.'

He nodded. 'But not absolutely certain.'

'She seemed convinced, so I am, too.'

Faulkner laughed. 'Enough to lay into Bob about it. Feminine intuition?'

'Don't you start,' she warned with a smile. 'Copper's intuition.'

He was grinning, ready to reply when they heard feet running down the stairs. Terry Davis, worried and looking around for them.

'That inspector of yours just rang. She said the WPC who gave you the information yesterday has been taken to the infirmary and you should get over there as soon as possible.'

Cathy nodded. Within a moment she was on her feet, dashing up the stairs, pulling on her coat and hat, grabbing handbag and gas mask case before she hurried out on to Briggate. Still raining, but the sting had gone out of it, not much more than drizzle now.

Only one reason Inspector Harding would want her there: whatever had landed Daisy Barker in hospital had something to do with the spy.

All manner of dark thoughts flashed across her mind as she hurried along the streets. Just her imagination, she told herself as she tried to push them away. But they refused to leave.

Finally, she burst through the doors of the infirmary, pulling out her warrant card and trying to catch her breath as she approached the desk. The clerk sent her to the accident department.

Cathy knew the way all too well; she'd brought plenty of people here over the years. Some battered and bloody, others too drunk to stand properly. But never one of her own constables.

Daisy Barker was lying on a bed, curtained off from everyone else. Tape over her nose, dried blood crusted round it, cotton wool poking from her nostrils and bruises starting to form around her eyes. Cuts to her face, uniform smeared with dirt, ladders in her stockings.

A broken nose and a few grazes. Thank God it wasn't anything worse. Still, for a moment, Cathy couldn't speak, feeling the anger rise in her body. Someone had done this to one of *her* constables. She'd make him pay. She stared until Barker tried to smile and winced.

'Sorry, Sarge.' She closed her eyes for a second. 'It hurts.'

'I bet it does. What on earth happened to you?'

Her voice was thick. 'I was on my beat this morning and I saw that man again—'

'The deserter? The one in the photograph?' She brought a copy of the picture from her handbag. 'This one? That's twice in two days.'

'Yes. That's him.' She tried to nod; pain made her stop. 'I followed him, I thought you'd want to know where he was going.'

'Did he do this? Where did it happen?' The words rushed out. Her heart was pounding and her hands gripped the metal bed frame so hard her knuckles turned white. 'How long ago?'

'I'm not sure. It could be an hour, might be more now. I lost track. I saw him turn into a ginnel off Wellington Street, just past King Street and I thought I'd see where he was going. I gave it a few seconds, but he was waiting for me as soon as I turned the corner. Dragged me out of sight and hit me a couple of times before I could do anything, kept throwing me against the wall until I must have passed out. When I opened my eyes again, he was gone.'

She reached out and squeezed Daisy Barker's hand. 'I don't know how much they've told you, but he broke your nose and you're going to have a right pair of shiners.' If he'd pummelled her hard enough to black out . . . Cathy smiled. 'It's a day or two on the sick for you, Constable.'

She managed a weak smile. 'Yes, Sarge. I'm sorry. I let you down.'

'Don't be so daft. You were up against someone very dangerous. Make sure you do everything the doctors tell you.'

'Honestly, I didn't think he'd noticed me. But it was the man I'd seen from the tram. I'd swear on the Bible. Same overcoat, everything. Grey trilby.'

'It's hard to hide in a uniform. Get yourself off home when they give the word and let Inspector Harding know. When you're up to it, send me a report. Something else might come to you. No hurry, don't push yourself.'

'Yes, Sarge.'

In the telephone box Cathy put a penny in the slot and the dialled the number for the office. She was quick, precise.

'No doubt?' Faulkner asked.

'None,' she replied. 'Who else could it be? Wellington Street is the start of the road that leads out to Kirkstall.'

'Come back here,' he told her. 'Your brother's returned and he has some news, too.'

Dan was pacing around the room, scarcely looking up when she entered. Nobody talking, just a murmur of voices from the rest of the building.

'I've talked to our agent again,' he began. 'I told you he has sources, good ones.' A pause. Cathy saw his Adam's apple bob up and down as he swallowed. 'They've confirmed Minuit's in Leeds.' A small pause. 'They believe he has a contact here, too.'

'Who is it?' Terry Davis spoke quietly through the pipe smoke, but his question sounded like an accusation.

Dan shook his head. 'We don't know.'

If it was true, it meant that someone in Leeds was helping the Germans. A traitor. The grimmest thought she could imagine.

'What exactly does that mean: believe he has a contact?' Faulkner looked up from the notes he'd been making.

'That they have no proof. But if this contact exists – *if* he does – then he's a well-kept secret. Nobody's heard anything about his existence before today.'

'Or her,' Cathy said, and her brother turned quickly towards her, mouth wide. He hadn't considered that. 'Minuit's handsome, he'd attract women.'

'Or her,' Dan agreed after a moment. 'My agent is pushing everyone he knows. The staff at headquarters are sifting through every scrap of paper for any possible reference.'

Haystacks, she thought. Needles.

'If Minuit has a bolt hole . . .' Dan continued. He didn't need to say more than that. It would make their job almost impossible.

'He knows someone's on to him now,' she said, and explained what had happened to Daisy Barker. 'He's going to be even more cautious.'

'If this Minuit has a scrap of sense, he'll go to ground for a while,' George Andrews said. 'Leave us to chase our own tails.'

Dan was shaking his head. 'I don't see how he can. He escaped to come here and do a job. The man's certainly not a fool; he's already shown that. He has to know we're going to catch him sooner or later.'

'We've all been assuming he's going after the Forge,' Cathy said. 'But this shadow factory would be the real prize, wouldn't it?' She glanced around the faces. 'Not just the physical damage, it would shatter morale.'

'If anything like that happened, the news would never get out,' Dan told her. 'The government would slap a D-notice on the papers. None of them could report it.'

'Give over. People who live over that way would see it. They'd know. You can't stop them talking.' No answer, because her brother knew the truth of it. 'If you had to go for one, which would it be?'

'We don't have the numbers in the squad to protect both places,' Faulkner said into the silence. 'Not if we're going to search for him, too. All we can do is make sure the security they have is up to snuff.'

'The Forge is improving, but we've seen they still have a way to go. Minuit could get in there.' She gave them time to digest that thought. 'What we need is a plan.'

She saw Faulkner studying Dan's face.

'What are the odds of your man here and his sources coming up trumps?'

A brief hesitation, then: 'Slim,' he admitted.

'Then we're on our own. Cathy's right; we'd better work out how we're going to find our friend.'

'Alive if possible,' Dan told them. 'We can make him talk and find out who's been helping him.'

Alive, if possible, she thought bleakly. But people were dying in their hundreds every single day. Soldiers, civilians. It was difficult to feel any sympathy for someone like Minuit.

'Well,' Cathy said brightly, 'which of you lot has a plan up his sleeve?'

Faulkner paired her with George Andrews. From the day they met she'd liked his dry humour and nasal Liverpool accent. He was burly, almost ready to burst out of his suit, teeth yellow after years of smoking; the type who looked as if he lived for a scrap. but George wasn't a brawler. He was a real family man, with a wife and two young daughters in a Liverpool suburb. Whenever he had a couple of days' leave, he was home to them like a shot.

'Do you reckon there's much to learn here?' he asked as they began to stride along Wellington Street. At least the rain had stopped. 'He'll be long gone.'

'This is where Daisy Barker spotted him. He was around here for a reason.' And they had nowhere better to begin.

She found the ginnel, a small, dark opening between buildings. For a moment, she could imagine the WPC taking a deep breath before turning the corner to follow Minuit.

'Nothing,' George said after a minute. He'd been examining

the ground, poking at matchboxes and empty cigarette packets with the toe of his boots. 'You said it happened just after she stepped in here? I think we're wasting our time.'

'Maybe you're right.' She'd hoped for . . . she didn't know what. A clue, a hint. Anything at all. The spy had given one of her constables a beating. She wanted her revenge for that. A few yards along, another ginnel ran off to the left. Poky and dark and easy to miss. They were here; they might as well look. Cathy started down into the gloom. 'What's that door? The metal one?'

'No idea.'

She tried the knob. Locked. When she tapped it with her knuckles it felt solid.

'Must be the back entrance to something on the main road,' George said.

'Probably belongs to this one,' he said as they stood on the pavement ten yards beyond the ginnel, staring at a sign that read *The Glory Club* in bright scarlet letters. The paint looked so fresh that it had to be new. *Music Nightly. Dancing.*

'I've never seen it before.' She racked her memory and came up empty. 'I couldn't tell you what it used to be.'

She could see him thinking, turning his head to look along the road. 'Which way was he going when that lass of yours saw him?'

'Out from City Square.' Towards this place.

Now it all made sense. Half the clubs were owned by crooks. Put together on the cheap, they were a quick way to make money from soldiers on leave. After a week or two the complaints would begin, the police would raid and close them down. A fine, maybe a few weeks in jail for the manager, and a few days later they'd be back in business. New name, different person in charge. Andrews narrowed his eyes as he gazed at the sign again. 'Of course, by itself that doesn't mean much.'

'Of course not,' she snorted.

Cathy waited as George rang the office, watching him speaking and gesturing in the telephone box, the cigarette in his hand waving up and down. Minuit spotted a few yards away didn't necessarily signify anything at all.

She tilted her head. The building had two floors above the club. The perfect place for a wanted man to keep himself hidden.

'You're not going to believe this,' George interrupted her thoughts. 'The paperwork for the Glory Club was filed a month ago. It's been open for three weeks.' He began to grin. 'Want to take a guess who owns it?'

'Who?' The pulse was throbbing in her temple. 'Come on.'

'Dennis Graham is the name on the licence. We all know what that means.'

'Well, well,' she said. 'One of Jackie Connor's lieutenants.' That was no fluke. She ran her tongue over her lips. 'Look up there.'

A short glance and he understood.

'What did the boss say?' she asked him.

'We're to go back to the office.'

Her mind tried to arrange the jumble of thoughts as she walked. Minuit had made a slip when he attacked Daisy Barker. If he'd simply vanished, nobody would have thought much of it. Instead, he'd drawn them here. Now it looked as if they had the connection nobody had suspected before.

Jackie Connor. The spy's contact in Leeds. A traitor.

NINE

'I'll have my men there at quarter to eight,' Chief Superintendent Johnson announced. His mouth curled into a smile. 'I guarantee we won't have any trouble.'

Every bobby in Leeds had heard about his raids. Johnson had a hand-picked crew of big coppers, all of them rugby league players on the weekends. Brutal and thuggish, every one of them loyal to him. The rumour had gone round that he'd persuaded them not to enlist in the forces.

The squad had no choice but to bring them in. Clubs and rackets were their territory, and the superintendent knew judges who'd sign a warrant for him without question. The Special Investigation Branch didn't have that kind of clout. This way, everything stayed legal.

A tall, heavy-set man, Johnson seemed to suck the air from the SIB office, looking primed for a fight.

'We want the upper floors,' Faulkner said, and Johnson nodded.

'That's fine with me, laddie. The meat I'm after is downstairs anyway.'

The superintendent had a worn, fleshy face that didn't suit his thin, Clark Gable moustache. His sparse sandy hair was held down with pomade. Johnson had a reputation as a tough detective, one who forced confessions to fit his ideas, never mind guilt or innocence. It was probably true, Cathy thought. The one thing she did know was that he believed women had no place in the police; he'd made that clear to her one afternoon in a corridor.

'There's a back door,' she said. 'Made of metal.'

'Opens into Atkinson's Walk,' he replied, voice dismissive. 'I'm aware of that, Sergeant.' He glared, then turned to Faulkner. 'I don't care if she's one of yours, I won't have a lass on any operation I'm leading.'

He stared calmly back at the chief superintendent. 'There will almost certainly be women in there. I want Sergeant Marsden available to question them.'

The tension seemed to build between them. For a second, Cathy wondered if it would erupt into an almighty argument, then Johnson nodded.

'That's fine,' he agreed finally. 'It'll have to be at Millgarth police station, mind. Out of the way of people doing proper work.'

A concession of sorts, the best they were likely to get.

'All right.'

After he left there was a long silence before Faulkner turned to her.

'Sorry.'

She smiled. 'That was mild. You should hear him when he's in a proper strop.'

He nodded. 'There's not much for you to do right now. Why don't you slip off home and report to Millgarth at half past eight? It's likely to be a long night.'

'Looking to get rid of me?'

'There's plenty of filing if you're that eager to stay . . .'

'Only kidding.' She could do some window shopping, a hot meal at home, maybe time to catch forty winks. 'Do you think we'll find him up there?'

'No. But we might come up with something useful.' He chuckled. 'Let's hope, eh?'

The alarm sounded and she stretched, warm in her own bed. A large slice of Woolton pie had filled her, then a doze that felt like a luxury, time stolen while others were working. She dressed in her warmest clothes, remembering that the interrogation rooms at Millgarth were always like ice.

A few minutes to eight. The squad would be gathered and ready, waiting for the signal. She'd have loved to be part of it, but with Johnson in charge, there was never a hope in hell. Questioning the women was better than nothing. The consolation prize.

Her mother was snoring in her chair, eyes closed, but her father turned his head as she opened the living room door.

'I'm on my way,' she said quietly.

'Look after yourself,' he told her in his wheezing rasp. 'Saturday night. You know what that means.'

Drinking, dancing, laughter, loud voices, fights. She'd seen enough of that in uniform.

'I won't be anywhere near that. Don't you worry.' She kissed the top of his head and darted out into the chilly February night.

The skies had kept clearing during the day. The temperature was falling; her breath steamed in the air. They'd have a thick frost later, probably ice, too. The moon was bright enough to pick out the barrage balloons and the long curve of Quarry Hill flats as she walked past the bus station. The biggest block in Europe, some writer had claimed. It seemed to stretch around and back for miles, like another small town inside Leeds. All kinds of modern innovations inside. The tenants loved it.

Cathy didn't.

She'd watched it go up, and from the start it had seemed terrifying to her, a dead-eyed warren of a place. An entry arch like a gaping mouth, ready to swallow anyone who came close. Endless grey concrete walls. Very modern, with all sorts of acclaim and awards. But it didn't appear much better than the streets it replaced.

She'd grown up back in there, in a damp house on Billet Street that should have been torn down years before it was finally demolished. She didn't miss it, not one tiny bit. Just a shame something more attractive hadn't taken its place. Did Dan ever think of that old house when he was sitting in London? Not if he had an ounce of sense.

Plenty of people in uniform in the bus station. Khakis, all the different shades of blue. Land Army women in green. More she didn't recognize. England had become a country of uniforms, so many of them on the move. She strode on, crossed George Street and through the sandbagged doors into Millgarth.

Waiting grated on her nerves. Pacing around the cold interview rooms, glad she'd worn her overcoat, she willed the minutes away. All the usual sounds of a police station on a Saturday night rose around her: yelling from the cells, the chatter of voices, a lone voice singing off-key, and someone pecking out a report on a typewriter.

In the corridor she paused to examine the framed photograph

of Chief Constable Tom Harper, MBE. Retired when Cathy was still a nipper and dead for three years now, he'd run this division before the last war. As working class as her and supposed to have been a very different policeman from Johnson. One the men had all liked and respected.

Half past eight came and went.

It was almost nine before she heard the van draw up outside. Three women were marched in and seated on the old wooden chairs.

'I'll keep a watch on the door,' a bobby offered. 'In case there's any problems.'

Cathy studied the faces waiting for her. All young. One looked defiant, glaring through smudged make-up and dyed blonde hair. The second wore a frightened gaze. The third was someone Cathy knew well, a woman in a shiny frock that didn't reach her knees. No slip, no jacket or coat.

'Hello, Deirdre luv, why don't you come with me? We can have a nice chat.'

She'd lost count of the times she'd arrested Deirdre Thomas for soliciting. At least seven over the years. Five minutes in court, ten days in Armley prison. A day or two after release she'd be on the streets again.

'You remember me, don't you?'

'Maybe.' With trembling hands, she brought a packet of Woodbines and matches from her handbag. As she sucked in the smoke, she seemed to relax a little.

'You ought to. I'm Sergeant Marsden. I've hauled you away more often than you've had hot dinners.' A pause, long enough for the woman to recall. 'You're going to catch your death dressed like that.'

The woman gave a vague smile and shrugged.

'It's what they want.'

'What were you doing in the Glory Club?'

'I'm a cigarette girl.' Not much of a job, going from table to table with a tray of cigarettes, selling them at high prices to the clientele, pocketing a bit from each sale. She probably wasn't even scraping a living.

'Pick up a few customers for yourself, too?'

The woman gave another uninterested shrug. 'Here and there.'

'Who runs the place?'

'Mr Graham. He's the boss. I've only seen him a couple of times.' After a moment, she added: 'The place is still new.'

Dennis Graham. Listed as the owner. Jackie Connor's man.

'If he's not around, there has to be a manager to look after things.'

'Mr Rawlings. He sets up when we open, closes at the end of the night, handles any trouble.'

Cathy scribbled down the name and the duties. She turned over the photograph of Minuit.

'Ever see him in the club?'

Deirdre reached into her handbag again and brought out a pair of spectacles.

'No.' She shook her head, quite definite. 'Never. What's he supposed to have done?'

'Bad things. Who uses those two floors above the club?'

'They store stuff upstairs. Booze, fags, things like that. Top floor, I don't know. I think it's empty.'

The woman didn't know much. She probably didn't care beyond her next prospect and a drop of gin. But Cathy believed she genuinely didn't recognize the spy. Free to go after she'd given her address.

The sullen one was called Evelyn Wilton. A waitress who claimed she was twenty-one but looked closer to seventeen. She said she'd spent the last year shifting from job to job as clubs opened and shut their doors. For someone so young, she'd developed a hard face that tried to stare down the world, as if she'd already had too many bad experiences.

'Identity card?' Cathy asked.

She scowled. 'Do I have to?'

'Yes.'

Reluctantly, she passed it over. Eighteen.

'Any idea who owns the club?'

'Mr Graham.' She slouched back on the chair, bored. 'Not seen him much, mind.'

'When was the last time he was in?'

She had to think about that. 'I don't know. It could have been Wednesday. I'm not sure.'

'Does he ever have people with him? Men?'

'Once. I don't know who they were.'

Cathy had a photograph of Jackie Connor, taken when he was arrested a few years before the war. 'Seen him?'

'I don't think so.'

'What do they do with those two floors above the club?'

'We keep things in the one right above. Bottles, cigarettes, like that. You know, storage.'

'And the one at the top?'

'No idea. I think it's empty.'

Finally Cathy passed her the photograph of Minuit.

'What about him, Evelyn? Has he been around at all?'

Evelyn stared at it for a long time. 'Someone who looked like him. I think it was Tuesday night. As soon as he came in, Mr Rawlings took him into the back.'

Cathy felt goose pimples rise along her arms, pulse beating faster.

'How sure are you?' She tried to tamp down the urgency in her voice.

'He looked like that picture. Nice-looking bloke. Big.'

That sounded like a match.

'What was he wearing?'

'A suit.' The girl thought, then blinked. 'I remember I was surprised he didn't have a coat or hat because it was perishing out.'

'Did you see him again?'

She shook her head. 'Never thought about it. People came in and I was busy. Why, who is he?'

'Someone we want to find.'

They had a real sniff of him now, beyond any doubt.

'You're a minor,' Cathy said as she finished. 'Under twenty-one. I can't just let you go. Do you live with your parents?'

A nod. 'Me mam. Worse bloody luck.'

'I'll have someone escort you home.'

The third girl had nothing to offer. She was close to tears, terrified at being in a police station. Her name was Polly Barlow. She had a full-time job at Burton's, sewing army uniforms, and she'd seen an advertisement for waitresses at the Glory Club. She'd done the work before; it seemed a good way to make some extra money a couple of nights a week.

Her face crumpled. 'I only started there last night. I'd just begun when the police turned up.'

It all sounded reasonable and the girl appeared earnest. But there was something behind her eyes.

'Let me see your identity card,' Cathy said.

'I lost it.'

'Then I'm sorry, but I'll need to keep you until we can be certain who you are.' She nodded to the bobby at the door. 'Find somewhere safe for her. I'll be back in the morning.'

Half past ten. It felt much later as she rushed up the street, a fast rhythm of shoe soles on the pavement. Cathy had a warm glow of satisfaction in her chest. The Market Tavern, the pub everyone called the Madhouse, was quiet, not a peep behind the blackouts and the sandbags. No lock-in for once; they must have run out of beer.

Terry, George, Derek Smith and Bob Hartley were all in the office, looking weary.

'Any sign of Minuit?' Their faces held the answer before she'd finished the question.

'Someone's been camping out on that top floor,' George told her. 'There's a mattress, a cup with cold coffee at the bottom, and some food wrappers. Impossible to tell who it was, though. Plenty of fingerprints to check.' He snorted. 'The men we took in have no idea, of course.'

She laughed. 'Of course. How many did you hold?'

'Twelve.'

'Any of them named Rawlings? I don't suppose you netted Dennis Graham?'

'No sign of Graham, but we brought in Rawlings,' Hartley said. 'The boss and your brother are grilling him. We let the others go, they were just customers.'

'Where do they have him?'

'The bridewell under the town hall.'

'Can we get a message over there?'

'Why?' Smithy asked. 'Did you come up with anything interesting?'

She told them, watching the way they suddenly became alert.

'I'll go and tell them myself,' Terry offered. 'Fancy coming along?'

Cathy smiled. 'Yes. I would.'

Terry Davis was a big man, a full head taller than her. Another large, bulky copper. He'd been on the force in Leicester for a full decade; almost thirty, still single, the type who was happy to float through life. But for a big man he was quick on his feet; she'd seen him chase down a few criminals.

They talked of nothing much as they hurried through the streets. In the blackout, the brooding bulk of the town hall was just a deeper darkness, the shape of a barrage balloon bobbing nearby. An entrance beside the front steps led them past the policeman on duty and into the bridewell, the jail. Inside the door, the bright lights and tiled walls came as a shock to her eyes.

It had the same stink as every jail she'd ever entered, the sickening mix of piss and sweat and fear. They showed their identifications for a second time and a guard led them to an empty room.

'Depressing, isn't it?' Terry said as he glanced around. 'Still, it's always a pleasure to see the faces when I shove a criminal in a cell and lock the door. It's the way something goes out of them.'

Five long minutes before Dan and Faulkner appeared, listening intently as Cathy explained what she'd learned.

'The woman is positive it was Rawlings who greeted him?' Dan asked. His face was flushed, tiny hints of Leeds speech creeping through the careful elocution.

'She told me without any prompting. And she said Minuit wasn't wearing an overcoat or hat when he arrived. He had them when Daisy Barker saw him.'

Dan was pacing, rubbing his chin. 'When did this woman claim she saw him?'

'Tuesday night. That would fit. And Graham turned up the night after.'

He walked around for a few moments more, flexing his hands, then looked at Faulkner.

'Why don't you leave Rawlings to me for a while?'

Cathy studied her brother's face. She'd never seen that expression on it before. Like granite. She knew how much hinged on him finding the spy. Now she'd handed him a wedge and he was going to use it to extract every scrap of information from Rawlings. No matter what it took.

'All right,' Faulkner agreed after a long moment, and turned to Cathy. 'I'll give you a lift home.'

'Does he want me out of the way?' she asked once they were settled in the car.

'All of us. Rawlings is our big chance and he hasn't given us anything yet. Your brother wants to ask some questions without any prying eyes around.' His eyes flickered towards her, away from the road. 'You know what I mean.'

She did. Dan intended to crack him wide open. Someone had taught him how to do it, and he wasn't going to be squeamish about getting to the truth.

Exactly who had he become in MI5? Cathy sat with her thoughts as Faulkner eased the car along York Road, keeping to the strict safety of the twenty mile an hour limit. Just as they turned off by the Shaftesbury cinema, the sirens began to wail. She thought of Dan, in the jail under the town hall. One bomb and he'd be buried . . .

'Do you want to share our Anderson? It'll be a bit of a squeeze.'

'Thanks, but I'll take my chances.'

'What do you think?' she asked. 'About what Dan's doing?'

'Honestly? I'd probably do the same in his shoes. This is too important for chivalry. Even more so for your brother. Go on, get yourself safe.'

Her bed looked so tempting, but between thinking about her brother and the alert, Cathy knew she'd never sleep. She picked up the Georgette Heyer novel and joined her parents in the shelter. Tea already made, hurricane lamps lit, a little heat from the Primus stove, all cosy except for the threat of bombs.

'Daniel didn't come home with you?' her father wheezed.

'No. He's still working. He'll be at it all night.'

The only noise was the fast click of her mother's knitting needles and her father turning the pages in his book.

It gave her more unwelcome chances to think.

TEN

Sunday and Leeds was quiet as Cathy strode up Kirkgate from the tram stop near the Parish Church. No bells to announce the services; those would only ring for invasion or victory. All the shops were closed, the market empty for the Sabbath. But no day of rest for the Special Investigation Branch, not in the middle of an operation like this.

She was dressed for the cold again, only a royal blue beret at a sharp angle to give a hint of style. Quite rested, even with an hour in the shelter before the all-clear sounded. Leeds had been spared once more. But they were living on borrowed time. Soon enough . . .

She quickened her pace, eager to know what had happened with Dan's interrogation.

He never came home and it didn't look as though he'd been back to the office. Coats and hats were draped over chairs, but the place was as deserted as the *Marie Celeste*. The moment passed as the squad returned from the canteen, balancing cups of tea.

They barely had time to settle before Dan arrived. His suit was rumpled, he had a ring of grime round his collar, and his hair was uncombed, flying all over. Everyone looked at him expectantly.

She was the first to speak. 'Did Rawlings talk?'

'Eventually.' His mouth twisted into a slow smile. She saw the grazes across his knuckles.

'What did he have to say?'

'He admitted Minuit had been there, staying on the top floor.'

Faulkner broke the short silence that followed his words. 'Who arranged it?'

Dan turned his head to face him. 'Jackie Connor.'

'Bastard,' Smithy said.

'He's the German contact up here. Not just a deserter and a racketeer, he's a traitor, too. That puts him in my sights, as well as yours. Rotten as they come. He passed word to Rawlings on Monday to expect the man, so Minuit must have contacted him right after he escaped. It looks like everything was in place before he ever reached England. It was Connor who arranged money and false papers for Minuit.'

She felt the hollowness in the pit of her stomach. God Almighty . . .

'What orders did Connor give Rawlings?' Faulkner asked.

'Said to help him, make sure he got whatever he wanted.'

'And what did this spy—' George Andrews spat the word '—ask for?'

'A place to stay. A coat and hat. Money. One hundred pounds, all in real bills, nothing counterfeit that could bring questions.'

Cathy drew in a breath. A hundred pounds. That was a small fortune. Enough to bribe people, to buy most things.

'There was something else,' Dan said. 'He wanted a pistol, an automatic, and two full magazines.'

'Did Rawlings provide it all?'

'He didn't want to admit it at first, but yes, he did.'

Minuit was armed. She saw the men look at each other, anxious and worried.

'What name was Minuit using?' Smithy asked.

'Rawlings claimed he didn't know and I couldn't shake him on it. Minuit said it was safer like that; he couldn't give it away.'

'How long did he stay?' Faulkner again.

'Until yesterday morning. By the time Rawlings showed up at the club yesterday afternoon, Minuit had already gone. He'd taken everything he had. Not that he was carrying much, it seems.' He looked at Cathy. There was something unnerving about the intense gaze of his eyes. 'It must have been after his . . . encounter with your WPC.'

'No indication where he was going? No note?'

Dan shook his head. 'Nothing. Rawlings had already decided it was best not to ask too many questions.' He paused and bit his lower lip for a moment, thinking. 'I'm sure he was telling me the truth.' A tight smile. 'That's all. I rang my office last night, but I still need to write up my report.'

'Make sure we have a copy,' Faulkner told him. He looked at the squad. 'With all this, we've let Connor slip. We need to find him and bring him in. He can lead us to Minuit. I'll contact the council when the offices open tomorrow. They can give us a list of every property that Graham owns. That other lieutenant of his, too: Eddie Moore. And Jackie, if he's stupid enough to have anything in his own name.'

Dan had managed to learn a lot, she thought, and none of it was good. Whatever name he was using, the spy had money and he was armed. He was growing more dangerous by the day.

'Where's Rawlings now?' she asked. 'What's going to happen to him?'

Dan glowered at her, as if the question was an annoyance. 'Some people from the Service took him away. A quick trial well out of the public eye and then behind bars for the rest of the war, where he can't go talking to people.'

Cathy said nothing. Somehow, that didn't feel like real justice.

'Jackie bloody Connor.' Bob Hartley enunciated the name slowly and clearly, staring down at his notepad. 'Got his finger in everything, hasn't he?'

'This is beyond crime,' Faulkner said. 'Didn't you have a lead from that petrol tanker driver Smithy questioned?'

'I haven't had chance to follow it up properly.'

'Do it. It's another way to Connor. Once we catch him, he'll hang.'

'We've hardly had much luck putting him behind bars so far, have we?' Hartley's voice became a frustrated shout.

'Then we'd better make sure we succeed this time. He's a traitor now.'

They could go round and round all morning. In the meantime, she had somewhere to be.

'Let's run through this once again,' Cathy said. 'You say your name's Polly Barlow.'

'It *is* Polly Barlow,' the young woman pleaded. 'I told you. It really is.'

She'd been scared when they'd brought her in from the Glory Club. After a night in the cells, hearing the drunks and the brawlers, she was petrified. She looked even younger than before, close to tears as she sat drawn into herself in the drab green of the interview room.

'But you don't have any identification. No card—'

'Please, I told you: I *lost* it.'

'And you won't say where you live.'

The woman's voice was small. 'I can't.'

That was all it took. Just those two words and Cathy understood. 'It's your father, isn't it?'

Only a moment before the tiny, reluctant nod. It was like a tap, turning on the tears.

Herbert Barlow wrenched the front door open and looked at his daughter.

'Where the bloody hell have you been, staying out all night?' He turned his gaze to Cathy and George Andrews. 'Who the—?'

Cathy held her warrant card in front of his face. She knew the neighbours would be lurking, watching through net curtains.

'I'm Sergeant Marsden, Leeds City Police, sir.' Loud and clear. Let everybody listen. 'That's Corporal Andrews, Special Investigation Branch. Now, do you want the whole street to know your business or shall we go inside?'

She'd deliberately parked the Humber in front of the house on Seaforth Terrace. No other cars around; any kind of vehicle would be a rarity in Harehills. It was less than a minute before a swarm of boys and girls arrived, eager to inspect the car. This was why she'd asked Faulkner to borrow it for a few minutes. To be noticed, to impress and intimidate. And remembered.

She'd brought George Andrews with her. Silent, big, and useful in case of any problems, he loomed in the doorway, keeping watch as Cathy asked her questions.

Through her crying, Polly had told a story Cathy had heard far too often. The mother dead or run off, the father expecting his daughter to provide every service he'd known before. Beatings if she didn't. In Barlow's case, more blows if she didn't turn over her wage packet from Burton's every Friday, too. The job at the club was to give Polly a little money for herself.

The man was a bully. Cathy read him the riot act, threatened him with court and prison, and told him she'd be keeping an eye on the family. It didn't need more than that. No uniforms on show, but word would already have flashed around that the coppers had brought Polly home. People would be talking. The family secret would leak out. No shame for the daughter, but Herbert Barlow would be a pariah. If he tried anything else, the people on the street would find their own justice. That was how things worked.

'You won't have any trouble with him now,' Cathy told Polly as they stood on the doorstep.

'Thank you.' Her eyes still had a dazed look, as if she couldn't believe everything that had just happened.

'That club won't be reopening. If you want a second job, try somewhere else.'

A dull nod.

'And get yourself a new identity card tomorrow.'

'I will.' Polly gave a wan smile. 'I promise. Thank you,' she repeated.

'I hate men like that,' George said as he guided the Humber back to town, past St James's Hospital. 'Cowards.'

'He's not a real man,' she said. 'Not in my book.'

'Did you find that a lot?' he asked. 'When you were on the force. We never had to deal with it even when I wore a uniform. Not men, you know.'

'Trying to take care of it is part and parcel of being a woman copper.' The small spark of satisfaction was fading. Time to look at other things. 'What are we going to do about this spy?'

He didn't take his eyes off the road. 'Find him and kill him. Then we hunt down Jackie Connor and make sure we squeeze out everything he has. When we've finished, we throw him in a bloody dungeon and lose the key.'

'What traitors deserve?'

'Better than hanging or a firing squad. No mercy for them.'

'Done with your charity work?' Hartley's moustache bristled. Trying to needle her.

Cathy felt her hackles rise. 'It's police business. I'm still on the force.'

'I thought you'd been seconded to us. We have a more important job to do, or had you forgotten that?'

A warning look from Faulkner halted her reply.

'Minuit won't be coming back to the club,' he said. 'We can

take that as given. He left nothing behind.' He sighed. 'He's out there somewhere.'

'Think Connor is still helping him?' Smithy asked.

'Yes.' He turned his head. 'Dan, what do you say?'

The fire was burning in her brother's eyes. The hunt had really begun. 'Connor's already up to his neck in it. He'll know about the raid, and he'll have guessed that Rawlings talked. That means he knows what's ahead when we arrest him.' He gazed around the faces. 'At this point, he's got nothing to lose, has he?'

'We're going to spread the word about him helping a spy,' Faulkner told them. 'I know it's Sunday, but I want you out in the pubs and clubs, passing that around. Remind them that anyone who helps him will be looking at charges of treason. Plenty of crooks are going to have family serving in the forces. This might turn them away from him.'

'I'll follow up that lead on the tanker,' Hartley said.

'Minuit knows we're on to him. He's going to be feeling the pressure. He's been here since Tuesday, long enough to scout out some places.'

'What if he's decided to fly solo?' Cathy asked. 'Cut his ties with Connor.'

The man was clever, sly. It seemed perfectly possible.

'Then we'd better start praying for some luck.'

If she went into the pubs on her own, men would think she was on the game. Much simpler to let the others handle that side of things.

'Your brother did a good job on the interrogation,' Faulkner said as they ate Sunday dinner in the canteen. All on the ration: curried carrots, a tasteless sponge pudding and weak tea. At least it was hot and filling.

'What do you think Connor will do?' she said.

'If I had to guess, I'd say he'll go quiet for a while. That's good – it gives us a real chance to crack down and break up his empire. I don't see too many of his men sticking with him once it becomes general knowledge that he's helping the Jerries. Some of them might decide to talk to us. I've already contacted Kirkstall Forge and the Avro factory. They're both going on to high alert.'

'What about me?'

'Play your angle. You know all sorts of women around town. Tell them what Connor's done. Show that photo of Minuit and ask them to keep their eyes open. It's all going to help.'

'Which place do you think he'll try to hit?'

He ran a hand through his hair and gave a long, weary sigh. 'I wish to God I knew. I really do.'

'What about Dan?'

'I'm going to send him home. Did you see his face? He's dead on his feet.'

The best thing for him, Cathy thought, as she gathered her coat and beret from the office and went out into the bitter cold of Briggate. Maybe things were beginning to move. It had already taken too long.

ELEVEN

In the Sunday quiet she could move quickly around Leeds, starting at the Market Tavern for a word in the back parlour with Doris, the landlady. Her clientele was a mix of criminals and coppers from Millgarth police station at the bottom of the street, sizing each other up, sometimes exchanging tips. Almost neutral territory.

'I won't insult you and ask if you know who Jackie Connor is.'

'Then I won't have to offend you by saying I've never heard of him.'

'We have evidence that he's helping the Germans.'

'Is that right?' Her face showed nothing as she took a Gold Flake from a cigarette case on the table and lit it. 'Easy enough to say. What proof do you have?'

'I can't tell you. But have I ever lied to you?'

'No,' the woman allowed after some thought, 'I'll grant you that, luv. But we've never talked about him before, have we?'

'You'll have to trust me.'

Doris laughed. 'You've got a right cheek on you, Sergeant. Don't you know trusting people is a good way to go broke in this business? No credit, nothing on the slate. That's my rule.'

Cathy pulled Minuit's photograph from her handbag. 'We're looking for him, if he should come in.'

'Wanted?'

'Yes.'

'Then he'd be daft as a brush to show his face in a place full of coppers, wouldn't be? Is he connected to the other thing you just mentioned?'

Cathy gave her a sweet smile. 'Now why would you think that? But some of your customers might be interested to know what Jackie's doing.'

No prostitutes walking the streets; it was far too early for them to be parading their wares. They operated best in the anonymity of the blackout. But she passed the word in a couple of the discreet, private clubs they used, among the cramped courts off Lower Briggate.

A unit of the Home Guard was drilling outside the town hall, putting on a display for a few spectators with little better to do.

Cathy cut across to Woodhouse Square. The fancy metal railings that once surrounded the elaborate central garden had disappeared to build Spitfires and Hurricanes, and a deep pond had been dug in the grass to make an emergency water pool. She carried on up the street, to the back door of a quiet house, where Hettie Williams ran her brothel.

After that, as the afternoon edged away from her, another half dozen places where she knew women. Someone might turn on Jackie Connor and tell her where to find him.

Meanwhile, she could sense the clock ticking loudly in the hunt for Jan Minuit. Every time she thought about him, Cathy felt her chest tighten. They had to catch him before he was able to act.

Two minutes in Park Square to watch women from the ATS raise the barrage balloon as darkness fell. Then back to the office.

Faulkner was busy at his desk, scribbling out a report.

'Where is everyone?'

'Bob's following up on that tanker lead, and I hope he cracks it very soon. We could do with something positive to gee us up. The others are probably still passing the word about Connor in the drinking clubs.'

Tiny, illegal places that had sprung up all over town, staying open long after the pubs shut. Stocked with black market booze.

'Do you think all this will help us catch Minuit?'

'We'd better pray it does. But there are only six of us to do everything. Seven with Dan.'

'It just seems like I should be doing more.' She felt she'd been rushing around all over town and achieving absolutely nothing. Occasionally she wondered if Bob Hartley was right, and she shouldn't be part of this outfit at all.

'What?' Faulkner blinked up at her. 'If you can come up with something you should be doing, by all means go ahead and do it. But you'd better remember that if it hadn't been for you, we'd never have discovered Minuit was in Leeds or his connection to Jackie Connor. Does that sound like skiving to you?'

She smiled, flattered. Maybe she had been useful. 'I suppose not.'

'You keep finding things. You're good and you're lucky. Sometimes that's more important. Don't imagine we haven't all noticed. Even Bob.' A smile. 'Now, get yourself home.'

As the tram trundled away up York Road, its bell jangling, Cathy turned and looked back at Leeds. Moonlight glinted silver on the forest of barrage balloons that had grown over the city and she tried to recall the way it used to be, before it became a place of water tanks in the middle of the street, of blast walls and sandbags and tape on every window. Before the war.

She realized that she couldn't. Try as she might, it was all a blank, as if Leeds hadn't existed before September 1939.

So many things were going badly for Britain while Germany rolled on. Ships lost, defeats, and only a few small victories to lift their heart. The future looked dark, bleak. But she still believed they'd win in the end. She *had* to believe it, just like everyone else. It was the only hope they had. So far, the only bright spots were the pilots who'd won the battle for the skies and the threat of invasion by the Germans that had receded. And those felt like bitter comforts.

At least she'd met Tom. By the time he had some leave, this Minuit business should be done. It would be spring, warm enough to walk together, maybe talk about the future. They'd never really discussed that. The idea seemed too fragile while war was raging.

Her mother was busy in the kitchen, making a pot of tea.

'Where's me dad?'

'He's in bed, he's been having a poorly day. I rubbed some embrocation on his chest, but I don't know if it helped that much. I'm worried about him, Catherine.'

'I'll pop up and have a word.'

'Would you?' The woman looked relieved as she handed her a tray with three cups. 'There's one there for your brother, too. I heard him moving around a few minutes ago.'

Her father was sitting up, the covers pulled around his body, flannel pyjamas buttoned all the way to the neck, wearing a muffler and a dressing gown tight across his body. He looked frail, almost transparent, but he'd seemed that way as far back as she could recall.

'Not so good today,' he told her with a gentle smile. 'Nowt more than that. You know your mother; her world isn't right unless she has something to fret about.'

'Don't be so daft. She does right to worry about you. She loves you.'

'I know she does, bless her.' He studied her face. 'You get some rest yourself, lass. You look tired. Whatever you and our Daniel are working on must be important for them to work you like a pair of blooming pit ponies.'

'It is, Dad.'

'And him just a civil servant, eh?' He winked. 'Go on, away with you.'

Her brother had his thick jumper over his shirt, paper and pen on his lap.

'Cuppa,' she said.

'Did you find anything today?'

He nodded from time to time as she recounted it all.

'You surprised me,' she said as she finished.

'What do you mean? The way I interviewed Rawlings? I've been trained.'

'Trained?' She raised her eyebrows.

'Trained.' He didn't offer an explanation. 'I scared him enough to give me everything.'

'Still think we'll catch Minuit in a day or two?' she asked.

He gave a long, low sigh. 'We have to. He's running and we don't have time on our side.'

Still in her overcoat, Cathy sat in her cold bedroom and started another letter to Tom. After a few lines her mind wandered back to Dan. A couple of times since he'd come back to Leeds she thought she'd caught glimpses of the boy she'd once known, but she wasn't sure she'd ever understand the man he was now. He'd developed a hardness at his core. Maybe that was what he needed for his job. MI5, knowing how to interrogate. This bloody war had changed all of them. Perhaps him more than most.

Another cold morning.

'Italians defeated at Jilib,' One-Eyed Sam the newspaper seller called out. 'Expeditionary force for Greece. Come and read about it.'

Cathy handed over her penny and folded a copy of the *Daily Sketch* under her arm. Some good news for later, if she had chance.

Not even eight o'clock and everybody was in the office.

'How are things with the tanker?' Faulkner asked Bob Hartley. 'Are we any closer to recovering it?'

'Moving along quickly,' he said. 'Connor's men aren't happy with him helping the Jerries. Another day might do it.'

'Well done. A result by tomorrow would be perfect. So we all know, Dan's going to be in charge of the hunt for Minuit. Terry and Smithy will be with him. George, you're with me and Cathy. We're going to broaden our outlook. Not just Connor; we'll stir things up and start hunting Dennis Graham and Eddie Moore. Think of it as attacking on all fronts.'

'We've never had much luck finding them before, boss,' George reminded him. 'We've been trying for a while.'

Faulkner smiled, baring his teeth. 'We bloody will this time. We have a very good reason. Let's go out and press every informer we have. Tell them we'll turn a blind eye to a few of their sins if they give us Graham and Moore.'

'Do you mean that?' Cathy asked. Did he have the power to make those promises?

'I do. Not forever, and not for everything, but a short amnesty. Let's give them a reason to help us.' He raised his voice. 'We'll all meet back here at six.' He gave her a meaningful glance. 'It's time to play dirty.'

By eleven she was weary. She'd repeated the same words, the same sentences, so often that the ideas had slipped away from her.

'You're not lying?' Barbara Trott asked sharply. 'You'll let things go?'

'We will.' Cathy felt her heart start to beat a tiny bit faster. The woman had to be asking for a reason. Her husband Frank was an artilleryman who'd never reported back to his unit from leave. A deserter. He fancied himself as a gangster, dressing in suits from the cheap tailors along North Street and trying to look like he'd just stepped out of a Hollywood film. But he was a tiddler in a big pond, barely pulling together a living. Frank ran some gambling and protection, while Barbara handled three prostitutes for him. Most of the time he was hiding, but his wife always knew where to find him. 'Just for a short while, mind.'

'Why do you want them?'

'We're after Jackie Connor. Turns out he's working with the Germans.' She saw the woman's eyes widen. 'Finding Moore and Graham is a way to get to him.'

'Dangerous business, hunting Jackie.' She stared. 'I'll need to have a think about it.'

'I'll come back later today. If you haven't made up your mind by then, the offer's gone.'

That was the closest she'd come to success. Hardly a surprise, she thought as she sat in the British restaurant under the town hall. Barbara Trott was right: get on the wrong side of Connor and you might as well paint a target on your back.

But all it took was one good hint . . .

No more joy during the afternoon. All over the place, taking trams here, there and everywhere. The gathering cold and thin wind sliced across her cheeks. She waited until after five to return to the Trott house on Francis Street. Her final stop of the day. She made her way along the pavement, only a faint rumble of traffic from the main road to disturb the stillness of houses hiding behind their blackout curtains.

Cathy took a deep breath and knocked on the door. Nothing. She tried again, hammering louder, then a third time.

Nobody at home. That was her answer. She turned away, striding furiously towards Chapeltown Road and a tram back to the office. So much for those hopes. Maybe one of the others had been luckier.

She was twenty yards away from the shops and the rumble of traffic on Chapeltown Road when someone slid alongside her and reached for her wrist. A man; she could smell his sweat and the smoke that clung to him. Cathy pulled away, ready to fight.

Rough fingers pushed something into her hand. Then the figure was gone, footsteps receding in the blackness. She closed her fist, sensing the crinkle of paper. Her pulse was thudding fast. Perhaps she'd been wrong; maybe there was more to Frank and Barbara Trott than she'd imagined.

Off the tram at New Market Street, past the stink of stale beer from the General Elliot. Up to the top of Kirkgate, and finally the explosion of people all along Briggate.

In the office she shrugged off her coat and put the hat on her desk before she sat and caught her breath. Cathy flattened out the paper. The name Eddie Moore and an address, carefully printed in pencil. Worth a fortune to them.

'That's the place?' Dan asked.

They were all crammed into the Humber, parked thirty yards from a small workshop on Pontefract Road, close to the street that ran down to Thwaite Mills. The air was thick with smoke. Cathy rolled down the window to let in some cold air and the linseed smell of putty drifting from the mill.

'It's the address I was given.' She could feel a pulse start to twitch in her neck.

'Do you think it could be a trap?'

'Anything could be.' Faulkner was seated behind the wheel, staring straight ahead, watching and listening. 'We need to be careful. We don't have time to recce the place first.'

The others had brought back scraps of information on Moore and Graham. But no addresses. He was right; they needed to strike now, go in without the luxury of observation. Faulkner turned his head and spoke to Hartley.

'How are things looking with the tanker?'

'Tomorrow still looks good. That information about Connor made all the difference. I'm meeting them at ten.'

Silence returned.

'What about the police, boss?' Terry Davis asked from the back seat. 'Have you told them what we're doing here?'

'Nothing to tell,' he replied stonily. 'This operation doesn't exist. Eddie Moore's boss is helping the Germans. In my book, that means he is, too.'

'It comes under MI5.' Dan's voice was flat. That trumped everything.

Her brother had been quiet since she'd passed on the information. That dark, intent look was back on his face.

'I'll help you question him if you like,' Bob Hartley offered.

'We'll see.'

Cathy peered at her wristwatch. Half past eight. No traffic had gone past in the last quarter of an hour. No trains on the nearby tracks. No sirens, thank God. Just the stillness of the night. She could hear the constant churn of the River Aire and the weir a hundred yards away.

'It's time,' Faulkner announced. 'Remember, we don't know who's in there. Stay alert and keep your weapons close. But you don't fire unless you're under threat. Understand that? We don't have a cat in hell's chance of keeping this quiet if a gun goes off.'

Cathy stayed back, letting the others go first, two of them covering any back entrance. Dan was going to lead: he was the one in charge of the search for Minuit.

She stood in the cold, feeling the chill biting at her face. She'd been on other raids with the squad, standing with the men, waiting, running.

But this felt different. It was more dangerous. Deadly. Too much depended on the information the Trotts had passed to her. She hoped to God they hadn't sent her on a wild goose chase.

Her body was taut, stretched like wire. Just the long, aching pause until everyone was in position. The soft whistle, almost lost in the air, was the signal.

Suddenly the night became noise as the doors were kicked open and the squad was inside. Shouting. Ordering.

A moment, a deep breath, and she followed, pushing the door closed behind her so no light leaked into the night. The last thing they needed was an air raid warden turning up.

Two men were standing, wrists cuffed in front of them. It was easy to pick out Moore. Sleek, with an expensive suit, good barbering and a charming, self-satisfied smile across his face.

'You lot must know I have friends in CID—' he began.

Hartley cut him off. 'We're not the police.'

The man beside Moore was big. Nervous. He was the one to watch, she decided. Dressed like a cheap imitation of his boss. Eyes shifting around, gauging the distance to the door. The smallest chance and he'd try to bolt.

Cathy waited. She felt a drop of cold sweat slide down her spine. Soon; he'd go very soon.

All the men were focused on Moore. He'd been pushed down

on to a wooden chair. Dan was slowly pacing around him, taking his time and saying nothing, long enough for a shadow of worry to cross Moore's face.

The other man found his moment. He moved like lightning, before any of the squad could react. Straight towards the door.

She saw it in his eyes. He was building up speed, planning to run right over her. He probably thought he was large enough to intimidate, that she'd back away at the last second. Cathy smiled; not a chance of her doing that. She was a good size herself. Big-boned, her father called it. Plenty of heft to her body, all of it muscle from those years on the beat and breaking up fights. She breathed, then charged into him from the side. It brought him up hard; panic filled his face and he began to lose his balance. As he flailed, struggling to stay on his feet, Cathy brought her knee up between his legs. A gasp and a whimper, eyes widening as he crumpled to the floor, legs drawn up tight against his chest with the tears starting to form. No need to worry about that one for a while. She gave a smile of grim satisfaction as she looked down at him.

Dan brought his face close to Moore.

'I have some questions. You're going to answer them.'

The man spat. Cathy watched as her brother took a handkerchief from his breast pocket and wiped the phlegm from his face.

Patiently, he shook his head. 'I'm going to give you a word of advice. It's time to stop believing you have any value. I don't give a monkey's what you did for Connor. You need to realize all of that is in the past. It happened in another life. You're just someone who'll be eager to tell me everything by the time I'm done with you.'

Simple, straightforward, but the way he spoke chilled her. Dan sounded as though he relished what was going to happen. He nodded for Hartley to stay, then turned to Faulkner.

'Three hours.'

'All right.'

'What about this other one?' George nodded towards the man curled up on the floor.

'I saw a storeroom at the back,' Terry said. 'We can lock him in there.'

* * *

The engine in the Humber didn't catch. With a sigh, Faulkner pulled out the screwdriver. A few seconds of work, then it fired.

'We need to get that bloody thing mended.'

None of them said another word until they were in Hunslet. She could feel her legs beginning to shake. Her part was done. Then the air raid sirens began to scream.

'Here we go again,' Smithy said. 'The Luftwaffe know how to ruin a good night.'

'Probably nothing,' George told him.

'We'll see.' Smithy glanced towards Cathy. 'Good move back there. Very clever. Poor sod's going to feel it for days.'

She felt a flush of pride. She'd reminded them what she could do. The man had been solid and her shoulder was aching. But she'd put him on the floor. He definitely wouldn't forget her. 'What's going to happen to Moore and his friend when Dan's finished?'

'Probably the same as Rawlings,' Faulkner told her. 'Gone for the duration.'

'There's a war on, remember,' Smithy said bitterly. 'Jackie Connor and his people are traitors. You think they deserve any sympathy?'

'No. But—' She stopped, hearing the rattle of the ack-ack guns somewhere off to the east. She turned her head and saw searchlights piercing the sky. The bombers were coming.

'But what?' he continued. 'Finding a spy is too important to worry about the niceties.'

Sabotage. People dying as the bombs fell. But . . . she couldn't put the feeling into words. Not yet.

'Your brother's good at his job,' George said.

'Apparently so.' He didn't notice the irony in her tone. 'That's why he's here.'

Dan had given her another glimpse beneath the surface.

'I'll drop you off at home,' Faulkner told her. 'Get yourself safe in the shelter.'

TWELVE

The bombs came. She heard the explosions off to the east and south. Most landed away from the city; only a few came close enough to shake the ground, leaving her mother clutching her father's hand. In the wavering light of the hurricane lamp, Cathy watched the terror in his eyes, helpless as he relived all the bombardments of his own war.

Then, just as the furore seemed as if it would never end . . . silence.

The guns were stilled and the night turned still. Was another wave on the way? Every muscle in her body was so taut she thought her bones might snap. It wasn't until the all-clear sounded that she began to relax.

'Come on,' Cathy said. 'Let's go inside where it's warm.'

She helped her father up to the bedroom. He sat, looking grateful and embarrassed that he couldn't do it by himself.

'I hope our Daniel's all right,' Mrs Marsden said. 'That was a bad one.'

'I'm sure he's fine, Ma. We might as well try to sleep now.'

She settled in the bed, sheets icy against her skin. Her mother was wrong; that hadn't been a bad raid. Not in Leeds, at least. Another reminder of what would be coming their way sooner or later. Enough to keep them all on edge.

The bombs wouldn't have distracted Dan. His mission was too important. Terrified at the scale of what he had to do, so much depended on him, but enjoying it, too. He was driven, and would make sure he pulled every tiny sliver of knowledge out of Eddie Moore. As the bed warmed around her, Cathy's thoughts began to drift.

The next thing she knew, the alarm clock was ringing.

A brisk walk up to the tram stop of York Road. Like all the other passengers, she craned her neck to try and spot any destruction. Rumours flew around: Wakefield, Morley, Tadcaster, the airfield at Church Fenton.

Where Annie was stationed. She listened carefully, hoping to hear more details, but the conversation had moved on.

No sign of her brother in the office. Everyone was sitting, reading the paper or quietly staring into space.

'Bad night everywhere, according to the reports on the radio.' Faulkner spoke into the subdued silence. 'Sounds as if we were lucky up here. Not much damage. London got a pasting again.' He glanced across at George. 'Liverpool, too.'

'What about your families?' she asked.

'We wait and see,' Andrews said emptily.

'I'll ring home later,' Faulkner told her.

How must it feel to be away, she wondered, not to know? To be unable to look after them.

Cathy changed the subject. 'Anything from Dan?'

'He's with his local MI5 man, making arrangements for Moore and his friend.'

She looked at Hartley. 'Did the two of you discover much?'

'That brother of yours is very persuasive.'

The telephone rang. Smithy lifted the receiver, then held it up. 'It's for you,' he told her.

'This is Sergeant Marsden.'

'It's me.' She could barely make out his voice; it was almost lost in the noise. Crowds, railways engines and the hiss of steam, the loud shriek of a whistle.

Tom. She smiled. Hearing him was exactly what she needed right now. The comfort of his voice. Did he have leave already? Was he on his way home? 'Where are you?'

'Standing with my kit bag, keeping an eye on the platform, and getting evil looks from the queue behind me. They're shipping us out.'

'What?' She swallowed. 'Now?'

'Final orders came through last night. We're going immediately. I'm sorry. No chance for any leave first.'

'Where? Can you say?' Her heart lurched; she felt a clutch of desperation. Stationed in the Midlands, training mechanics, she'd known he was safe—

'Nothing official yet.' He chuckled. 'But we've had an issue of shorts and long socks. People are saying it's all a bit bizarre.'

Bizarre. Bazaar. North Africa. His joke. Tom enjoyed a bit of wordplay. A clever way of evading the censors everyone said monitored phone calls.

She could hear someone shouting at the other end of the line, then Tom said, 'I'm sorry, I've got to go. I'll write as soon as I can. I'll miss you.'

'I—' she began.

'I love you,' he said. Before she could reply, the line went dead.

As she replaced the receiver, she felt numb. In shock. Cathy was suddenly aware of the others staring at her as she replaced the receiver on the cradle.

'My bloke,' she said. 'He's being posted overseas. No warning. It sounds like North Africa.'

'Sorry,' George murmured. 'That's rotten luck.'

What could she say? All over the country, women, families, were facing the same emptiness in their hearts, the same terror. Any feeling of safety was an illusion. This was what war did.

When Dan finally arrived, he looked drained. His expensive suit was rumpled, skin pale, and his hair needed combing. But the fire still burned in his eyes.

'Moore and his friend won't be seeing much of the outside world for a long time. As far as anyone's aware, they've just dropped off the face of the earth.' No satisfied smile, just that intent, haunted gaze.

'Did he tell you where to find Minuit?' Faulkner asked.

'No. He doesn't know. He *really* doesn't know, I'm absolutely sure of that.' He glanced at Hartley. 'Wouldn't you agree?'

'Definitely.'

'But he did tell us where to find Dennis Graham. My local man has someone watching the place now. We might be able squeeze a few more answers from him.'

'Does he know his boss is helping the Germans?' Terry asked.

'At first he claimed it was all news to him.' Dan paused. 'He changed his mind pretty quickly.' A look of disgust crossed his face. 'He admitted he knew about Minuit. Claimed Connor told him someone had paid them to help. Another bloody traitor.'

'Did he say where we could pick up Jackie?'

'He says Connor gets in touch when he needs him.' Another pause. 'He wasn't lying.'

She could seek Faulkner eyeing her brother.

'Keep that watch on Graham. We'll take him later today. Connor's really going to flounder when his lieutenants vanish. He won't have a clue what's happened to them. The police don't know about any of this so his contacts there won't be able to tell him anything.' He turned to Hartley. 'Things still looking good with that petrol tanker?'

A nod. 'This morning, all being well. I'll take Terry. If it works out, we'll deliver it to Carlton Barracks. You'd better warn them.'

Cathy tried to concentrate, but her thoughts kept slipping back to Tom. He'd be on the train now, heading for the south coast and a troop ship. She traced the route in her mind, imagining it laid out on a map. At sea the real danger would start. German planes and U-boats waiting in the Atlantic, more in the Mediterranean. Battling the German army across the desert.

Stop. She had to stop. She was turning into a worrier. Was this how her mother felt when her husband had been ordered to the trenches? She needed to concentrate on work. What they were doing was important.

'. . . as soon as it's dark,' Faulkner said. 'We'll haul him straight off. That way Dan can take his time with the questioning. Fine with you?'

Her brother nodded. 'We should probably have done it that way last night—'

'—but we took what was there. An empty room, isolated. We made it up as we went along.' He rubbed the back of his hand across his chin and looked at Dan. 'That's the way we've always done things here. But we still need Minuit and Connor.'

'We're isolating them. Your friend Jackie Connor's world is already collapsing. He's going to be scrambling around and trying to save himself. That's going to leave Minuit with nowhere to turn. He's going to be completely on his own.'

'We hope he is,' Cathy said. 'We don't really know, do we? What if there's someone else your service doesn't know about? Consider this, as well: if he's on his own, he might be even more dangerous.' She paused to the let words penetrate, surprised by the anger suddenly bubbling to the surface in her. At Dan for plunging them into this world of spying, at the war for taking Tom away from her. At the bombers that came in the night. 'He's still armed, he has money. We have no idea what else by now. Do we?' She looked around at the faces.

Her brother answered. Calm, reasonable. 'We can only go by the information we have. You know that. When we have more, we amend our tactics.' He turned to face Faulkner. 'Connor is going to feel even more alone if Bob steals that petrol tanker back from him.'

'I will.' He looked at his watch. 'I need to go.' He slipped into his overcoat and hurried out, Terry Davis right behind him.

'We're putting pressure on him and Minuit.' Dan again.

'See what your sources bring you on Minuit,' Faulkner said. 'They seem to be doing a good job right now. We'll focus on Jackie Connor.'

'Remember, you were told to give me every assistance.'

'I haven't forgotten,' Faulkner told him. 'But hunting criminals is what we do best, and these are connected.'

'Very well,' Dan agreed and gazed around the faces. 'You need to be aware of something I was told when I talked to my case officer this morning. This is a decision that's been made at the very top.' He emphasized the final words. They all knew what it meant: Downing Street. 'When we find Minuit, we kill him. Those are the new orders.'

'But—' Cathy began.

'It's not up for discussion,' Dan said. 'This is for the safety of the country.'

Nobody said another word.

Kill him. Small words, but they seemed far too big for the room.

Kill him.

Her skin was cold.

It was going to be an execution.

Cathy closed her eyes for a moment, grateful again she didn't carry a gun. She'd never have to decide whether to pull a trigger. The others . . . she glanced around the others, seeing the troubled faces. They were army, they carried weapons. But scratch the surface and they were all coppers. Going out there to kill went against the grain.

'We need to put on our thinking caps,' she said. 'How the hell are we going to find either Jackie or the spy?'

* * *

The Humber purred past Lawnswood Cemetery and out into the countryside. Everything looked quiet here, tape on the windows of shops and houses the only stark reminder of the war.

Cathy saw the entrance to Golden Acres. Gates closed, paintwork weathered down to bare, rotting wood. She and Annie had come out here a couple of times when it was an amusement park. They'd ridden the little railway inside, walked round the lake and enjoyed the attractions. Sunbathing, buying bottles of lemonade and ice creams from the café. Summer days when life was carefree. It had gone broke and closed a year before the war. The fancy hotel just down the road probably billeted workers from the Avro factory now.

No matter which way she turned, there was always a memory. Small ghosts of herself scattered across Leeds. No surprise; this was her history. She had to hope it would be her future, too. Another string of defeats and that could be in doubt again.

'Thinking about your boyfriend?' Faulkner asked.

She shook her head. 'Remembering a place that used to be out here. Go on, you might as well say it. So many men going everywhere and doing their bit, and Tom will probably come through it all just fine.'

A faint smile played across his lips.

'I hope he does. My youngest brother is out there. The middle one's in India. I know what it's like.'

'I'm sorry.' He'd never mentioned any brothers. But he'd talked very little about himself, no more than a few mentions of his wife; perhaps he found it easier to keep his life separate from the job.

'Makes what we do seem cushy, doesn't it?' she said.

'Going to kill a spy, you mean?'

'Would you? Kill him, I mean.'

He said nothing, gearing down and turned left. All the signposts had been removed to try and confuse any invading Germans, as if they wouldn't carry maps.

After a few miles, Faulkner stopped the car at the top of a small rise.

'Over there. Take a look.'

She'd never seen the shadow factory before, never even heard of one until a few days ago. It was far bigger than she'd imagined, rising like a hill with no peak, flat, as if someone had neatly sliced off the top. The sides were covered with turf and grass.

'What are we doing all the way out here?' Cathy asked. She was in no mood for distractions. 'We should be hunting Jackie Connor.'

'You'll see.'

He drove on. A tall wire fence marked the factory's perimeter, a gatehouse where a soldier from the RAF Regiment checked their identification and directed them towards the building.

'I thought you should see Minuit's other target.'

A chill rippled up her spine as she gazed at the size of it all. To think of that as twisted metal and fire . . .

'We can't allow him to get anywhere close to this,' Faulkner continued.

'How do we stop him? There's plenty of open country out there.'

'And camouflaged patrols all over the place.'

'Thank God for that.'

'Keep your eye open for any flaws or gaps.' She knew he must have seen the look on her face and sighed. 'I know. But I needed to visit anyway. And killing in cold blood isn't what we signed on to do. I'm not any happier than you about it. I doubt if any of us are. But we have our orders. Your brother's right about one thing. Everything's riding on us. Everything.'

Up on the flat roof, shivering against a bitter wind, she agreed with the foreman showing her around that it was impressive. Inside, the factory was huge, stretching further than she could see. Acres and acres of ground. Lancaster bombers in different stages of completion. Up here she had a better sense of the size. From thousands of feet in the air, the foreman assured her, this would look exactly like the landscape all around. Convincing enough to fool a pilot or navigator. There were even large model farm animals, cows and sheep, that were moved around each morning.

'The boffins who came up with the factory thought of everything,' he said proudly.

Had they? She gazed around, able to see for miles in the chilly, clear sky. Most of the way to Pool Bank, far off the distance.

'What's that?' she asked. Something caught her eye. It wasn't a bird.

'It looks like someone's flying a kite.' The man frowned as he peered towards the horizon.

'Is that allowed anywhere near here?'

'No. A patrol will be checking. Come on, it's a good chance for you to see them in action.'

She held on for dear life as the Land Rover bumped through gates and across rutted fields.

Cathy watched the bobbing kite. She kept trying to swallow; her mouth was dry. Could it be Minuit, testing how effective the defences were? She could feel every rapid beat of her heart.

'Off to the left.' Ahead of them, a soldier took her by surprise as he emerged from behind a bush, rifle aimed at them. 'Pull up over there,' he ordered. 'We'll go and see what they're doing.' He turned and grinned at Cathy. No more than eighteen, she guessed. Young enough to make her feel ancient. 'You all right, miss?'

'Don't you worry about me.'

'Some rubber boots on the floor next to you. Going to be too big, but . . .'

'I'll survive,' she told him. 'Watch out. Just in case.'

'Always careful, miss.'

She hoped that was true.

'A pair of schoolboys,' Cathy said in the car on the way back to Leeds. 'Couldn't have been more than ten years old.'

'The soldiers must have given them a shock.'

She had to laugh at the memory of the boys' faces as the men appeared, brandishing their rifles. 'They'd been skiving off school. The soldiers took them back. I imagine their hides are well tanned by now. Then their mothers will be at them later.'

'I was with the captain in charge of security when he received word about the kite,' Faulkner said. 'Took it all in his stride. They're on top of things.'

She could believe that. It had been a worthwhile visit, not just something to divert her. At least now she knew what they were protecting, both in Kirkstall and here. But it didn't bring them any closer to finding the spy.

'Bob should have pulled off his tanker trick by now,' he continued. 'That will hurt Connor.'

'That and one of his top men gone.'

'Especially after the other one vanishes tonight.'

'Bob's been very quiet about it all.'

'You know what he's like. Always plays things close to his chest.'

Probably scared of someone else taking the credit, she thought. That sounded like Bob Hartley, bristling with anger and resentment. 'Where are we going now?'

'Back to the office. See if your brother has any good ideas and prepare for tonight's raid.'

'Did you talk to your wife?'

He nodded and the relief flooded across his face. 'Everyone's well.'

'I'm glad about that.'

'I'm sure your boyfriend will be fine too.'

'I wish I was.' She gave him a small, wan smile.

'He's a mechanic, isn't he? Behind the lines.'

'Yes, but . . .' She'd be devouring every piece of news until she had a letter saying he'd landed safely.

Faulkner found a place to park on Commercial Street, round the corner from Briggate. 'Let's see if Bob has come up trumps.'

Hartley preened himself and swaggered round the office. Let him, Cathy thought; he'd earned it. The tanker was at the barracks, the fuel untouched.

'That's a remarkable job,' she said. 'How did you manage it?'

Bob tapped a finger along the side of his nose. His secret. Of course. Fair enough, she thought; they all had their private sources. No matter; the result was a solid victory for the SIB. Something niggled, though, and she finally understood what it was. It had happened too easily, too smoothly.

'As soon as Dan shows his face, we'll make our plans for this evening's snatch,' Faulkner said.

She ate her dinner in the canteen and spent a few minutes window shopping along Briggate, but every thought turned to Tom. On the Headrow a crowd had gathered, staring off to the east. She looked, gazing far past Leeds to pick out an aeroplane in the sky. So far away, hardly bigger than a speck. Lazily circling, dark smoke rising. She felt people holding their breath around her. Everyone was looking, wondering.

'What is it?' a man asked finally. 'Can anyone tell?'

A boy stood, hand shading his eyes. 'I think it's a Mosquito. Probably a training plane. There should be two people on board.'

Cathy couldn't move. They were all rooted, mesmerized, needing to know the ending. Others joined them. Traffic had come to a standstill on the road, drivers clambering on their bonnets for a better view.

Suddenly, everyone seemed to let out a sigh. Something blossomed in the sky. A parachute opened. The aircraft continued to spiral down. It appeared to be falling in slow motion, dipping gently towards the ground. Then a second chute appeared, bobbing down to earth. They'd both managed to bail out. Suddenly people were chattering, as if life had stuttered and started up again. The pilots were safe, that was what mattered. The plane vanished beyond the horizon.

The excitement had passed. Only the boy was still gazing.

'Dennis Graham's in a house in Cross Green,' Dan said. 'As far as our local people can tell, he's on his own.'

'Back-to-back or through terrace?' Cathy asked. That was important. A back-to back was hemmed in on three sides by other houses, with only one way in or out. A through terrace had front and back doors, a way to escape.

'Through. There's a small yard with an outdoor toilet, ginnel behind the houses.'

They all knew the drill. They'd gone into places like that a few times.

'Usual plan,' Faulkner told them. 'Three at the front, two at the back, one to keep watch. 'Half past seven, as soon as things are quieter. In and out as fast as possible, before the neighbours realize what's happening. No shooting.' He glanced at Dan. 'No more word on Minuit from your man?'

'Nothing yet.'

He nodded slowly, the frustration hidden at the back of his eyes. 'It's almost two now. We'll meet back here at five.'

Action. Pushing ahead and bringing them closer to Connor. This was their war. Just like the men in uniform, there was no room for defeat.

The spy was still out there. Eluding them. What was he doing right at this moment?

THIRTEEN

'Get him to the hospital. Fast.' Faulkner threw her the keys to the Austin Seven he'd commandeered, while the others dragged Dennis Graham from the house and pushed him into the Humber.

Derek Smith was sprawled across the Austin's back seat, grunting to dull the pain as he struggled to find a comfortable position.

'How bad is it?' Cathy put the car into gear and started down the street.

She heard him try to laugh; it came out half-strangled. 'I'd scream if I thought it would help. Christ.' She sensed him grit his teeth. 'It's never like this in the bloody films.'

'We'll make sure the cameras are rolling next time. Hold on.'

She followed Upper Accommodation Road through Burmantofts, jaw clenched in concentration. She drove as fast as she dared in the blackout, willing herself to the hospital. Every sense was jangling. She wanted to speed up, but it was impossible with only black and white stripes on the kerb and the telegraph poles to guide her. Her eyes kept darting to the mirror, watching Smithy try to cover his pain. Something slipped across the road right in front of her, caught in the slitted headlights, and she stood on the brake, slapping the steering wheel, swearing and drawing a deep breath afterwards. But never stopping. She felt the rush of urgency in her veins. Along dark streets she barely knew, aiming for the barrage balloon that hung over St James's hospital.

'Bloody come on,' she yelled at the gear lever when it didn't want to settle in third. The car was another piece of rubbish, just like the Humber. Her nerves were in shreds. But finally they were there, bumping through the gate and parking outside Casualty.

'Only a moment now.' She turned her head and smiled at him. 'Promise.'

Her warrant card brought a nurse and a doctor on the run. An orderly with a trolley bustled Derek through the doors and into the bright lights.

It seemed like a straightforward snatch. Everything had been set beforehand: the squad would haul Graham off to the MI5 safe house. She and Dan would stay to check and collect any papers. A simple plan.

Cathy had felt her pulse throbbing as Terry Davis broke open the front door and the squad rushed inside. Graham was in the kitchen, making a pot of tea. He threw the kettle at them. It crashed harmlessly against the wall, and they were on him. Wrists cuffed in front of his body.

Less than thirty seconds before they were marching him out. Quick, everything according to plan. In the hall, Graham turned. Then Smithy began to clutch at the wall before he collapsed with a cry. His leg gave way and the blood flowed.

Hartley battered Graham to the ground, stamping on his hand until his fingers released the knife. Terry Davis dragged the man upright, pulled him outside and threw him against the Humber.

Cathy knelt by Smithy. His face was pale. He was starting to go into shock. Plenty of blood on the floorboards, but it wasn't spurting. Not an artery. He wouldn't die from this.

Her heart kept thudding as she yanked a cloth from the table and wrapped it round and round his leg. In seconds the blood started to seep through.

'Let's get you on your feet. Can't have you spending all night lying around.' She tried to sound cheerful. But it was a thin, useless mask. So quick, so easy . . . it could have been any of them.

Very carefully, Cathy eased him to his feet, taking his weight as she draped his arm over her shoulders. Faulkner supported the other side.

'All right?'

A stiff, strained nod was his reply, biting down hard on his lip. They stretched him along the old, cracked leather of the back seat and Faulkner tossed her the keys.

'I don't care who you are. You'll have to wait with everyone else.' The hawk-faced ward sister wasn't going to give an inch.

Cathy had taken part in enough of these battles to know she had no hope of winning.

Nothing to read but yesterday's newspapers or old magazines about country life before the war. She glanced through the articles; fox hunts and county balls, a far cry from anything that people round here knew. Would a world like that ever exist again?

Nothing left but the persistence of her own thoughts.

Dan and his interrogations. An order to kill. Cathy felt as if everything had spiralled far out of her control. But what could she do? Retreat to the safety of a uniform? Could she still do that, the same routine each day? Would she really want it?

She knew the answer before she asked the question.

What would her brother say if she told him how she felt about all these things he was doing? Would he see it as a betrayal?

Every other minute she was back to Tom, on his way to the desert. Still feeling the wrench of his phone call. When would she see him again? He trained the people who repaired vehicles; he wasn't a real soldier. Would he need to fight and kill? She sat in the waiting room, her mind suddenly overwhelmed, head in her hands, surprised to find tears rolling down her cheeks.

'Are you all right, luv? Is that your bloke with the knife wound?'

She looked up and saw a young nurse staring at her with a kindly expression.

'No. We're on the same squad.' She couldn't begin to explain it all to a stranger. It would seem horrific, unreal even in wartime.

She must have fallen asleep. When she blinked her eyes open, a doctor was towering over her. Straight-backed, grey hair. Past retirement age, she thought, and persuaded to stay on. At least he gave her a smile.

'It's not a dangerous wound, but Corporal Smith has lost a fair amount of blood,' he said. 'I'm going to keep him overnight for observation. I don't expect any problems, so all being well we'll be able to discharge him after rounds in the morning. He's lucky it wasn't a lot worse.'

We all were, Cathy thought. 'Can I see him?'

The physician shook his head. 'Let him rest. I've given him something to make sure he sleeps.'

She could do with something like that herself, she decided as she drove slowly back to Cross Green. A long, dreamless sleep far away from the world.

Dan had everything waiting in a large cardboard box that he placed on the back seat on the drying blood.

'How is he?'

'In until tomorrow, then a few days to recuperate and he should be right as rain, thank God.'

'Back there,' he began, then hesitated. 'You were all so quick.'

'We're used to working together. Between us we have years of police experience.'

'I didn't know what to do.'

'Staying out of the way was probably best,' she told him.

'Maybe you're right,' he agreed quietly and stared at the ground for a moment. 'We'll drop this off, then I'll go and interrogate Graham.'

'Find much?'

'Nothing to help me. Probably a few things for your squad.'

His hands were bunched into fists, resting on his thighs.

'I'm sorry about your boyfriend. George Andrews told me.'

She wanted to speak but couldn't. Just a small nod.

The others were waiting as they bustled in. Cathy saw relief spread across their faces as she gave them the news. Even Bob Hartley was smiling as he lit another cigarette.

'Nothing more for us tonight,' Faulkner said, then turned to Dan. 'Unless you want someone with you.'

'No.' She heard the darkness rising in his voice. 'Not this time.' He picked up the keys to the Austin. 'I'll tell you more in the morning.'

'Then the rest of us might as well all go and have a good kip. With a drop of luck we'll be busy after we go through these papers tomorrow. We're going to be short-handed for a while.'

She glanced at her watch. Quarter to eleven. How could it still be so early? Barely more than three hours since they burst through the door of the house. It felt like another age.

'Lift?' he asked.

Cathy had been too exhausted to open the letter from Tom that was waiting on her pillow. The day had overwhelmed her. As she closed her eyes, she kept hearing the order to execute, then reliving the stabbing until sleep finally dragged her down.

She woke with the envelope still clutched in her hand, smoothing it out as the tendrils of bad dreams drifted off into the early morning. It had been sent before he knew about his deployment, gossiping about some of the men in his section and complaining about the work the army expected them to do. She could almost hear him, and his words banished the bad thoughts, enough to make her smile as she dressed. He would be somewhere at sea now. Somewhere at sea. Please God, keep him safe for me.

Frost on the roofs again. Her thickest stockings, the wool skirt she'd stitched from a pattern, a fleecy liberty bodice under the bulky Aran jumper her mother had knitted. The shoes she'd worn to walk the beat; not fashionable but practical and warm. Toasty.

The Austin was parked outside the house; she'd never heard Dan arrive during the night. He came down to breakfast shaved and sharp, looking pleased with himself.

'Have a productive evening?' she asked.

'Very,' he said. Nothing more. She saw the inquisitive look her mother was giving them both. Safer to cut her off before the questions began.

'Work, Ma.'

The iron tang of blood hit her as she opened the car door, the stains across the back seat; she lowered the window for the drive into town. Dan was silent, as if he was crowded by his own thoughts. At least he looked like he'd had a few hours' sleep. He'd been wild-eyed when he left the office last night to question Graham. She saw the fresh grazes across his knuckles to join the ones just starting to scab over. He'd unearthed a broad streak of cruelty inside himself, she thought. It was probably something that would carry him a long way in the Service.

Faulkner waited until they were all settled, cups of tea from the canteen on their desks.

'The good news is they're discharging Smithy this morning. I'm going to pick up some clothes from his lodgings and collect him at nine. He's heading home on sick leave for a week. Back next Monday, all being well.' He held up a buff envelope. 'This is the list of the places Moore and Graham own. Took the council forever to put it together. Eight of them, and we need to check every single one. Our spy might be there.'

'What about Connor?' Terry asked.

Faulkner shook his head. 'Nothing under his own name. Dan, what did Dennis Graham tell you?'

'Very little for a while, but then he was very forthcoming. He knew all about his boss aiding a spy. He didn't seem to mind too much as long as some of that Nazi money ended up in his wallet.'

'Where's Minuit?' Hartley asked.

'He doesn't know.' A small hesitation, a flicker of a smile. 'He honestly doesn't. I made absolutely certain about that. Our spy is playing things very carefully.'

It was the way he said it, stroking the words, that gave her a chill.

'Connor?' Faulkner asked. 'Where can we find him?'

'He said the man moves around. He gave me a couple of addresses—' Dan tore a page from his notebook '—but he doesn't know how current they are. I got plenty more out of him; I'll write a report. But those are the highlights.'

'Enough to keep us going.' Faulkner thought for a moment. 'Cathy and I will look at these addresses for Connor. Bob, Terry, George, take the Austin and start working through that list of properties. Meet back here at noon.'

'Do you know these places?' Faulkner asked as they sat in the car, looking at the addresses Dan had handed over. Derek Smith was on his way home. Pale, using a crutch and looking forward to a few days with his wife.

'Millwright Street?' She frowned as she tried to place it in her mind. 'The only one I know is very poky, runs between Regent Street and Mabgate. Doesn't look as if it's changed much in about a hundred years. All little workshops. No houses that I recall.'

Faulkner snorted. 'Sounds like a perfect place to hide. No nosy neighbours to pay attention. Not just for Connor. Minuit could keep out of sight there. But if they are in one of these places, we're not going to do anything heroic. Understand?'

'Yes.' She wasn't that much of a fool.

The street was as dark and gloomy as she remembered, a road of old cobbles and broken flagstones for the pavement. Garages with mechanics working on small lorries and vans, small businesses where the welding equipment sent bright sparks into the air. Someone had *Workers' Playtime* blaring from the wireless; she picked out Charlie Chester's grating voice.

They walked on.

'Which one is Connor's?' she asked.

'Number four.' Faulkner looked around. 'Why don't we show Minuit's photo around first? You never know.'

No luck. But these were men who immediately made them for coppers, the type who were never likely to tell the police much. She saw one or two slip quietly out of the back door. Deserters, maybe. Not worth the chase.

'Let's see if Connor is at home today,' Faulkner said.

'How are we going to do it?'

'I'm sure he won't mind if we walk straight in.' With a small flourish, he produced a set of lock picks. 'Very useful. Confiscated them when I was a young detective constable.'

Two doors, one of them a double, designed for a cart. He chose the other.

But the lock was reluctant to cooperate.

'Out of practice?' Cathy asked.

'Yes, but someone's beefed this up.' Another minute of patient work before she heard the click and the door was open. She began to step forward, but he raised his hand, holding a Colt automatic. A soft whisper next to her ear: 'Careful. We don't know what's waiting.'

Faulkner slid cautiously inside, eyes searching around, gazing up the steep flight of wooden steps ahead. He put a finger to his lips and indicated the door that went off the small entrance hall.

Cathy nodded, hardly daring to breathe. She gave him a chance to start his climb, then stood protected by the wall and reached round to turn the door handle and push it open. She swallowed hard. What would happen?

No shot, no rush of sound. Just a deep sense of emptiness.

She eased through, into a room with bare brick walls, the floor swept clean. Too tidy. Someone had been using this for storage.

Light poked through the gaps in the double doors, enough to see there wasn't a newspaper or empty paint pot left behind.

No sound from above. But she was still slow and careful on her way up the stairs, grateful for thick-soled shoes that landed silently as she walked. The door hung open, and daylight poured through the open shutters.

Living quarters. A small fire was burning low in the hearth, a full coal scuttle off to the side. Cigarette smoke hung in the air, a pile of dog ends stubbed out in an ashtray. Cathy reached out and wrapped her fingers around a half-drunk mug of tea. Still warm. He must have escaped just before they entered. How? The stairs looked to be the only way in or out.

Then the other thought slammed into her: who was it? Connor or Minuit?

Two rooms. This one was a fair size, big enough for a bed, a table and hard-backed wooden chair, and an old easy chair near the fire. A sink with a man's safety razor resting on the rim, a primus stove for cooking. Toilet and bathtub in the other room.

No luxury, no telephone, not even a radio. But this was somewhere for a person to hide out. Gone now . . .

Faulkner appeared behind her. 'Take a look over here,' he said. He opened a door that sat flush with the wall and she saw a steep flight of steps. Raising the gun, he clattered down. She waited, tense. If someone was hiding down there . . .

Not thirty seconds before he was back, wearily shaking his head.

'It opens on to a ginnel that looks like it leads through to Mabgate. He's already off somewhere.'

A handful of papers sat on the table. She scooped them up and shoved them in her handbag, moving around, hurriedly searching the room. Nothing else worth taking.

'Find a telephone box,' he told her. 'Ring the office. Ask your brother if Minuit smokes cigarettes. After that we'll try the other address he managed to wring out of Dennis Graham.'

There was fire in his eyes, copper's blood surging now the hunt was on.

'Minuit loathes cigarettes and pipes,' Cathy said as she returned. Faulkner was pacing outside the building. He slapped the palm of his hand against the wall.

'It was Connor. We were this bloody close to him.' He turned, face red with fury and frustration. 'This bloody close. And he managed to get away. How did he know?'

She glanced at the windows above and spotted it. A small mirror set in the wall at an angle that would let someone watch the front door.

'That's your answer.'

'Bastard.' Faulkner took off his hat and ran a hand through his hair. The anger was flowing off him. God help anyone who stepped in his way now.

'We need to give the place a proper going over,' Cathy told him.

'We don't have *time*,' he said. 'We're right behind him. We can't let up now.'

Less than a quarter of a mile to Connor's second bolthole, but no guarantee he'd have run there. She glanced at Faulkner's face. He was hoping. Praying. Jaw set, sensing that he *had* to be right.

The Humber wouldn't start. Faulkner fiddled with the screwdriver. Still nothing. He grew angrier with each attempt.

'Bloody piece of junk.'

She turned her head as a hand tapped on the window. A mechanic from one of the garages along the street.

'You've got a broken wire in there, mate.' He smiled. 'Give me five minutes and I'll have you right as rain.'

Only three until he turned the key and the engine started smoothly. Faulkner put a pound note in the man's hand, thanked him and drove away.

'Worth every penny,' he said.

Connor's other property lay on the other side of Regent Street, one house in a street of back-to-backs awaiting demolition in the Leylands. Old, frayed posters covered the gable end of the block, a mix of English and Yiddish; this area had been home to the Jewish immigrants who'd flocked to Leeds near the end of the last century. Many still lived here when she was a kid, barely a stone's throw away from her home on Quarry Hill. She'd walk over with her friends, feeling like an explorer when she heard the strange language and looked in the windows of the little shops at items she didn't recognize—

Faulkner broke into her memories. 'What do you think?'

It looked abandoned, boarded up just like the other streets around it.

'I suppose he could have knocked through to the house behind or on either side. Who would have heard? Why here, though?'

'Think about it. No need for a mirror on the brickwork here to warn him someone's coming,' Faulkner added with a wry smile.

'Let me take walk around,' Cathy said. 'See what I can spot.'

Not a soul to be seen. It was eerie; the city centre was just a few hundred yards away, with all the roar and rumble of people and traffic. Yet here it was quiet, fragments of the past that would soon be rubble and dust. She looked about her. If the Jerries dropped a bomb on this place it would save the council some money.

She reached the end of the block, examining each door and window for a way inside, but they were all tightly covered with plywood. Her mind began to wander. When this was all over . . . how many times had she thought that since the war started? But that seemed too far in the future. So much could happen before that. To Tom, to her . . . to the country. As she turned the corner at the end of the block, Cathy caught sight of a man, no more than twenty yards away, striding towards her. Anonymous in a dark overcoat and a cap, staring down at the ground, hands bunched in his pockets. He must have sensed something, pausing and raising his head. For a split second, he stood completely still. Then, in a flurry of motion, he turned and began to sprint hell for leather down the hill towards Regent Street.

Jackie Connor.

She shouted, hoping Faulkner would hear her and come.

FOURTEEN

Connor was fast; fear was giving him speed. But those years of walking a beat had given her powerful legs.
She was starting to gain on him. As the ground began to flatten he risked a glance over his shoulder before skidding round on to Bridge Street.

She watched his legs pumping hard, pulling away again. An aching burst of speed and she narrowed the gap once more. No more than ten yards between them now.

Still too far.

Her chest was on fire. Every breath felt like needles flaying her lungs. She ignored the pain and kept running, eyes fixed on the man ahead of her. A few more seconds and he'd reach Eastgate. The traffic there would slow him.

But he judged his timing well. Slid into a gap behind a lorry, then dashed in front of a bus on the other side of the road; it barely kissed his hip as the brakes screeched and the driver cursed a blue streak. Connor never stopped or slowed down. He didn't need to; he had the devil's own luck carrying him.

Cathy had no choice. She'd come too far to give up now. She had to follow, plunging between the vehicles and hoping for the best. A pause, then another rush of speed, heart in her mouth.

Her feet hammered against the pavement behind Millgarth police station. No coppers on parade. Never around when you needed them. Across George Street and into the bustle of the open market.

The crowd jostled close as Connor tried to force his way through. Cathy knew how to deal with them. Squeezing past, jabbing with an elbow, making a path with a small push or a sharp shoulder. She was gaining on him again. He turned to look, eyes widening in panic as he saw her drawing close.

Only a tiny gap now, but he dodged and slid, then vanished into the covered market.

At the door, she stopped, bent over, gasping for air and

clutching the metal frame for dear life. Damnation. Not a snowball's chance in hell of catching him. Too many different aisles and ways in and out of the building. In front of her, a maze of faces.

Her throat burned. Her lungs were ready to burst. Every breath hurt. All she could do was stand until she could breathe properly.

But it was far more than her chest that hurt. Connor had been too fast, too sly for her. He'd beaten her.

She'd failed.

Finally, shoulders slumped, she made her way back towards the Leylands. Only a short distance, but it stretched out like miles ahead of her.

George summed up the morning. 'We found three of Moore's men in those properties.' 'Interrogated them, then let the bobbies arrest them.' He grinned. 'They can deal with the paperwork and the bumf. Small fry. They knew about black market stuff, nothing more.'

'This is all well and good, but it's not bringing us any closer to Minuit,' Dan said. His voice snapped in the air. 'My agent up here hasn't heard anything from his contacts. He seems to have vanished.'

'We know he had a hundred pounds,' Cathy said, her eyes moving around the squad. 'That can keep him going for a long time. But we've taken away every safe house we know about—'

'Shame you didn't catch Connor this morning.' Bob Hartley stared into her face. 'He'd have been able to tell us more.'

She felt the prickling on the back of her neck, ready for battle. But Faulkner stepped in, his voice placid and friendly.

'We came close twice. The first time it was me who just missed him.'

An hour after the chase her chest still tingled whenever she drew a breath. She could still feel twitches and tremors in her legs. Far more than that, the desolation of failure.

Dan had a point: how were they going to find Minuit? Every minute he was out there he became more of a threat. No leads, and they were down a man while Smithy was recuperating.

'Is there any chance at all that these XX people of yours would let us have another man or two?' George asked.

Dan shook his head. 'I've asked. We don't have anyone spare. Nobody at all. Look, it's rotten, but we're a tiny organization; everyone's already doing two jobs.'

'We have no idea where to look,' Faulkner said. 'That's what it boils down to. But he's been relying on Connor, and Jackie's not going to be much help now he's desperate to keep his own head down.' He counted the events off on his fingers. 'Both his lieutenants have vanished without trace, Bob took back that petrol tanker, and those places where he thought he was safe have gone. He's got nothing left.' A glance at Hartley. 'I know he's not in custody, but he's going to be very rattled. I had a word with Detective Superintendent Johnson. They're going to start mopping up his men. That's Connor's business gone and his income with it. He won't be in any position to help Minuit. At least we've managed that.' He chuckled. 'Speech over. Let's look at this afternoon. Terry, you and Bob go to that place in the Leylands. It's a cert that Connor was heading there. Find out which house it was, get inside and bring back whatever you find. George, I want you and Cathy in that place on Mabgate. Give it a thorough going over.'

'I already have the papers we took from there,' she said.

'Then you stay here and go through them.' He considered for a second. 'Two lists: one about the black market, the other with anything relating to Minuit. George, you've got me for company instead. I'll enjoy tearing the place apart. Dan?'

'I need to talk to my office, then go with our local man to see some people.'

Connor had cramped, awkward writing. She had to puzzle words out, sometimes guess at the spellings. He might not have had much education, but he was clever. Quick, too. He'd bested her. That was going to rankle and fester for a long time.

She'd gathered more papers than she'd thought. Plenty in them, too; Connor had rackets they knew nothing about. He'd just started a little factory in Holbeck that produced hooch by the case. Genuine bottles and labels, but inside was raw alcohol, diluted, flavoured and coloured to pass as whisky, brandy or gin. Cheap to produce, a handsome profit. But dangerous. Sometimes deadly. That was one to pass to CID.

Another curious thing: Connor had taken a stake in a demolition company, money he'd invested just the month before. An established, legitimate business. She pursed her lips; it was a move that seemed out of character for him. Maybe his Jerry friends had warned him about big raids coming. There'd be good money in cleaning up the rubble. Bringing down buildings. Then Cathy felt her heart stop as she realized. Demolition . . . explosives. Dear God. She grabbed her coat and hurried out.

'Aye, that's right.' John Hardcastle took his pipe from his pocket, unhurriedly tapped down the tobacco with a finger, struck a match and started to puff. Everything smooth, without thought.

He had the air of a man who took his time over things. Not impulsive. Hardcastle had a worn, craggy face, his silver hair Brylcreemed flat under a cap. The skin on his palms was thick, and looked as hard as stone.

'How did Connor come to put money into your business?' Faulkner asked. George had wandered away to poke around the yard. Cathy stayed close, listening.

A mound of scaffolding was piled against one wall. Wooden planks, all carefully stacked. The yard was protected by a sturdy fence and strong gates. A faded sign warned that a dog guarded the site at night. It stood beyond Seacroft along the York Road, out in the country, spread across a few acres. Land was probably still cheap out here.

'I were reckoning to expand,' Hardcastle answered. A genial voice, but one she could imagine turning furious in an instant. 'That meant I'd be needing more equipment, and owt like that's expensive these days with everything going to make tanks and the like. Still, it stands to reason that the Jerries are going to give Leeds the drubbing they're giving everyone else. Terrible, but someone's going to have to clear it all, and if I can make a bob or two while I do that . . .'

'Did Connor come to you?'

'He did. I'd mentioned the idea to a pal of mine, and I'd just started putting together some figures before I made an appointment with the bank manager. Connor rang me out of the blue one day, said he'd heard I been looking to grow bigger, and he had a little money that was doing nowt.'

'How quickly was the deal made?' Cathy asked.

He turned to her. Dark blue eyes, she noticed, a clear, steady gaze.

'Same day. On the blower in the morning, handshake and cash in the afternoon. I'm not used to working that fast, but he seemed like a man in a hurry. Dun't know a jot about this business, mind.'

'What did he want from it?' Faulkner said.

'Just a fair return on his money, that's what he told me. No contract, said he believed a man's word was enough. That was fine by me. We've been in business for sixty year, my pa started it. Never cheated anyone yet.'

'Did he have any men with him?'

'Aye, a couple. Nasty looking bug—' He glanced at Cathy and corrected himself with a cough. 'Blokes. But they didn't make no trouble.'

'Do you keep any explosives here?'

'Some dynamite.' He drew himself up. 'Part of the trade. Everything's properly licensed and registered, and it's all under lock and key, if that's what you're suggesting. I know how to use it.'

'Did you show it to him?'

A nod. 'Course. He wanted to put his brass in, so I gave him the full tour.' Suddenly the man looked worried. 'Why, what's he done?'

'Deserter, criminal,' Cathy began. 'Traitor. You name it.'

Hardcastle frowned. 'I didn't know none of that.'

'It doesn't matter now,' Faulkner said. 'The notice says you have a guard dog.'

'Ah.' He sucked on his pipe again. 'We did, but after he died, I never got around to finding another one. Not had any trouble this far out.'

'Mr Hardcastle,' he said, 'could we see where you keep the explosives, please?'

A stone shed with a thick door and two strong locks. Hardcastle selected the keys from a large ring.

'No one's going to break in here,' he said with pride.

'Would you check the dynamite?'

A locked metal cupboard. Inside, a large fireproof box with

its own padlock. Good precautions. The man bent over, looking. When he straightened his back, his face was pale as ice.

'Oh Christ, there's eight sticks gone. I—'

'What about fuses?' Faulkner asked.

The man's hands were trembling as he unlocked another metal cupboard that was bolted to the wall.

'We keep them separate, see. Safer that way.' The door opened with a deep groan.

'They took two rolls.' His voice was empty. 'A hundred feet.' He hung his head.

'I don't understand how he did it,' Hardcastle said. His skin was grey, he seemed lost as he looked from face to face for some kind of answer. 'I've got the best locks money can buy on everything, the gate and the shed. You've seen it.' He chewed his lip. 'I'm going to have to report it to the police, aren't I?'

'I am the police.' Cathy produced her warrant card. 'When did you last check in there?'

'I don't know.' The man sounded small, defeated. 'Probably when I showed it to him. Not needed any since.' He shook his head. 'I don't understand. He seemed like a decent lad. What do I do if he comes back?'

'I don't think you'll see him again,' George said. 'I wouldn't worry about him wanting his money back, either.'

They were halfway back to Leeds before Cathy spoke.

'Minuit's armed, he has money, and it's a pound to a penny that he's the one who has the explosives now.'

'We wouldn't have known anything about the dynamite if we hadn't gone after Jackie Connor,' Faulkner said. 'Remember that.'

'Connor's not a threat any more,' Andrews said.

'We *hope* he's not. As long as he's still out there we can't write him off.'

Cathy gazed out of the window. York Road library and baths, the stonework turned black by generations of soot. A couple walked past it. He was in his khaki army greatcoat, forage cap on his head. The woman wore her own thick coat, a defiant, brilliant red, a bright floral headsquare covering hair in curlers. A sight to make her smile. At the bottom of the hill, the ugly, brooding shape of Quarry Hill flats.

'They must have been planning this for a while,' George said. 'Connor put money into that business a month ago. Then he opened that club with empty floors above. Started setting things in motion well before Minuit turned up in England.'

'Which means he's been in touch with the Jerries for quite some time,' Faulkner said.

'He probably stayed in contact until we put him on the run. They know the spy escaped.'

'And we still don't have any leads on Minuit,' Cathy reminded them.

'Your brother's going to need to pull a rabbit out of his hat,' George said to her.

'As long as he does it soon,' Faulkner added. 'With these explosives, it just became a lot more urgent.'

She could hear the clock ticking in her head.

FIFTEEN

'You might as well go home,' Faulkner told them a little after five o'clock. The subdued conversations in the office had trickled to silence, leaving them with their imaginations. A dangerous place to be.

Dan still hadn't returned.

Cathy finished writing her report on the chase and placed it on Faulkner's desk as she left. Until they had some small thing – a tip, a lead, even a rumour – they had nowhere to search for Minuit. Back to haystacks and needles.

A long day, she thought as the tram jostled and jangled over the tracks on York Road. If she tried to take a deep breath, her lungs still ached from running. The fear for Tom lurked at the back of her mind.

Where the hell was Dan? They desperately needed whatever scraps this local man of his had managed to unearth, and he'd disappeared.

She walked down Brander Road beside Mrs Rafferty from number seventy-six, on her way home from the shops and full of complaints about the food ration.

'It's not enough to feed a skeleton, never mind my George. Well, you've seen him. He'd eat me out of house and home if I gave half a chance. He's always hungry.'

Her son was sixteen and growing; at that age every boy was a bottomless pit. Still, the war wasn't going to end soon. The army would be feeding him in a couple of years.

A letter was waiting for her on the stairs. Another one from Tom. Her heart leapt. She tore it open and skimmed the pages. Written on the train and posted just before they embarked for overseas.

'Did he have much to say, pet?' her mother asked.

'Not really. This and that.' Her mouth curved into a smile that she didn't feel inside. Where was he now?

'He's a good lad,' her father said with a nod. 'Steady.'

Husband material; that was what he meant. Trying to marry her off.

Her mother put the plates on the table and her father poked at the food with a fork.

'What is it?'

'Vegetable goulash,' she announced.

'Oh aye?' He sounded doubtful.

'It's from that Ministry cookbook they sent out last year. The butcher at the Co-op let me have a few scraps of beef, too, so I put them in. Mind you, I'd been queueing the best part of an hour.'

'It's not too bad, I suppose,' he said as he tasted it. 'Better with a little sauce.'

Cathy exchanged a quick grin with her mother; it was the same phrase he used about almost everything.

'I was at Edna's on the parade this morning, too,' Mrs Marsden said. 'Got my hair done.'

'It looks very nice, Ma.'

'She told me she's rushed off her feet. Can't hire a junior to work in the shop for love nor money. They're all in the factories, where the real wages are. She'd give her eye teeth to have Annie back.'

But Annie was wearing air force blue at RAF Church Fenton. Leading Aircraftwoman Ann Carter.

Later, wrapped up warm in her bedroom and sitting with the eiderdown over her legs, she could take her time to sink into Tom's letter.

> We've been sitting in a siding for over an hour. No idea where or why, nobody gives us an explanation, of course.
> A senior officer issued an order to simulate a gas attack, then those below him to write reports about it. Pointless stuff. Something to pass the time and cut the boredom, I suppose.
>
> It was wonderful to talk to you, even if it was only a moment. To hear you and know you're real, not something I dreamed up one night. What I told you about has been in the works for a week or more. That was the rumour, but no confirmation until about three hours before we left. We

all thought we'd have a few days of leave first. Best laid plans, eh?

I was looking forward to coming home, seeing Mum and Dad, and you, always you. One of the chaps here has parents who are knocking on and his mother's had to go into hospital. He applied for compassionate leave, but it was turned down. Now he's spending all his time growing frantic.

We're on the move again. I'm going to try and get a little kip. Sleep whenever you can seems to be the army motto. I know a couple of blokes who can do it standing up.

I miss you so much, you know.

All my love,

Tom

She finished reading, a warm ache inside. The words on paper helped make him real. Then she opened the writing pad and began her reply.

She'd nearly finished the first page when she heard the front door and the murmur of voices downstairs.

Cathy opened the bedroom door and watched her brother hurry up the stairs.

'Get dressed,' he said. 'Wear dark clothes. Faulkner's waiting outside in the car.'

'Why?' she asked. 'What's happened?'

'I'll tell you as we go.'

'Two minutes.' She slid on her heaviest jumper. Her hair looked awful; she jammed a black beret on top. Skirt? The hell with it. A bitter night in February, she was going to wear her trousers. The men could say what they liked; she wanted to be warm. Her police greatcoat and a final grab for a pair of gloves.

A glance at the clock as she turned out the light: five past ten.

The rest of the squad was crammed into the Humber, the air already thick with the smells of tobacco and beer. The car started as soon as Faulkner turned the key. He followed York Road into town.

'Where are we going?'

'My agent had a telephone call from one of his sources,' Dan explained. 'Minuit rang him.'

She felt goose pimples rise on her arms.

Dan went on, 'He's panicking a bit, wants to know what's going on. He hasn't been able to get hold of anybody. He said Connor's disappeared, along with his two top men. The three of them are his contacts in the gang.'

In the faint glimmer of light from the dashboard, she saw Faulkner smile.

'The contact said he'd try to find out. Minuit pressed him, said he needed to meet tonight.'

'Have they ever met before?'

She felt him shake his head in the darkness. 'Their only contact has been on the telephone. No,' he added quickly, 'I don't trust it an inch.'

'Minuit probably wants to see if he's been betrayed.'

'Right now he'd be a fool if he didn't suspect everyone. And we'll be there instead of his contact. This is the first chance we've had to catch him.'

'If he turns up.'

'We have to take the chance,' Faulkner said.

'When's it supposed to happen?'

'Midnight,' Dan told her. 'That gives us plenty of time to set up out of sight.'

'Where?'

'Woodhouse Moor, by the Queen Victoria statue.'

It was only a few years since they'd moved the old queen there from the front of the town hall. Cathy had been part of the guard for the unveiling in its new location. Bushes around for cover; good for them, but also for Minuit. The man had obviously learned his way around Leeds in the last few days.

'Who's going to be the one who meets him?' Standing out there, exposed and waiting. A target.

'I am,' Faulkner said. 'He's never seen me, and I've been given the code word he'll use.'

'There's too much that can go wrong,' Cathy warned.

'Of course there is,' Dan snapped. 'But do you have any other ideas?'

They were caught in a cleft stick.

'He's armed,' she said.

'So are we,' Bob Hartley said from the back seat. 'Most of us.'

She bit her tongue. No point in a flaming argument right now.

The barrage balloons bobbed over the city. They passed the university and turned down Clarendon Road, the moor an empty black expanse to the right. Her mouth dried as they parked.

'We need to be very careful,' Dan ordered. This was his show; he gave his orders in an urgent whisper. 'Dead quiet, no talking at all. No smoking. It only needs a glowing cigarette tip to give us away. Spread out in a circle. Get as close to the statue as you can, but stay out of sight. Remember, Minuit's a professional. He's thorough. There's a fair chance he could be there already. But he's worried, he doesn't know what's going on, and that helps us.'

'If he turns up,' George said.

'He will.' Was that certainty or hope? she wondered. 'He needs to know. He may not be waiting out in the open, but he'll be there. Once he appears, we'll have him.'

'Last thing: don't fire unless you have no other choice,' Faulkner said. 'There's plenty of cover round there. Use it.'

A few minutes before eleven. It was going to be a cold wait; she was glad she'd decided on the trousers, and shoes with a thick sole. The squad melted into the darkness, going very slowly, little more than groping their way along.

She'd barely covered fifty yards when the air-raid siren began its banshee howl. Cathy froze for a second, closing her eyes. No bomb shelter out here. They were going to have to take their chances.

Two more minutes and the first searchlights pierced the sky. A clear night, with the stars glowing; perfect for a raid. Away to the east, she head the rattle of anti-aircraft guns, then the deep drone of the bombers. Fear gripped the pit of her stomach. The Luftwaffe was close. The noise grew and grew until it seemed to blot out everything else.

Out of sight behind a tall laurel bush, she gazed at the heavens. The lights picked out the aircraft. It was the first time she'd seen the enemy, the stark, brutal shapes in the sky. On the other side of the moor, little more than two hundred yards away, one of the ack-ack guns began to fire, louder than she'd imagined. Shells burst around the planes in harmless puffs of smoke.

The first bombs landed in Hunslet. A few seconds, then she picked out blazes rising from the valley. More explosions, creeping closer and closer. Flames caught and rose. Marsh Lane railway station must have copped it again. Too close to home, and for a tiny moment she felt guilty for not being in the shelter to look after her parents. But this was her job, her duty.

The bombers peeled away, dropping their final loads. She picked out another sound. Higher, insistent, furious. For a second a beam picked out two fighters bearing down on the Germans, tracer bullets flashing colour in the sky.

It became a battle of the guns as the planes headed back towards the coast. Cathy realized she was holding her breath.

Fires were burning bright where the bombs had landed. Just a small raid. Not much more than a hit and run. A taste. One more warning for the future.

Around her, quiet slowly returned to the night. Only the faint creak of a barrage balloon nearby as it twisted against its cables. The occasional vehicle that crawled along Woodhouse Lane. The snuffle of an animal in the undergrowth.

She didn't risk a glance at the illuminated hands of her watch. Patience.

The others had their guns. Cathy held a branch she'd found. Hard, solid, with enough weight to do some damage. A weapon she hoped she wouldn't need. But it gave some small comfort.

How much time had passed since they left the car? An hour, perhaps? Off beyond the horizon, the blazes were burning high and fierce; the Luftwaffe had done damage. The light breeze carried the stink of the bombs' destruction.

Finally, something caught her attention. The clouds parted and she saw Faulkner stroll to the statue. Hat pulled down, shoulders drawn in and hands in his pockets to make himself appear smaller.

Approaching midnight. Was Minuit close?

Her fingers tightened around the wood. Eyes searching, trying to pick out any shape or movement in the moonlight. Alert for the smallest sound.

Nothing.

She waited.

A stone bounced and rattled against the base of the statue. Cathy tensed. She saw Faulkner arc his head around.

And then . . . nothing. It was an old trick, Minuit checking to see if he'd raised an alarm. He was somewhere around here.

Faulkner kept pacing. Back and forth, back and forth.

Cathy sensed something behind her, the sudden warmth of breath on her neck. As she turned, from the corner of her eye she saw something coming down towards her. She swung the branch with all her strength, and knew she'd caught him just right when she heard a pained grunt and felt the sweet snap of bone.

Then emptiness.

SIXTEEN

She came around in the Humber, stretched out along the back seat, covered with a smelly, scratchy army blanket.

She blinked. Nothing would come into focus. She felt she knew the faces peering at her, but they were watery and blurred. For a second she tried to sit up, but pain shot through her skull and she let herself sink back, stomach churning, lying quiet until the feeling passed.

'Have a sip of this,' George Andrews said, wrapping her fingers around a hip flask. 'Just a little one, like.'

Bracing herself, Cathy tilted her head, slowly, very slowly, wincing at the thunder booming round her skull. A few drops of liquid burned on her tongue and she spluttered. Brandy. A little more and the warmth began to spread through her body. It helped.

'What happened?' she asked, her voice thick and slow.

'Minuit hit you on the head. You were spark out for about three minutes,' George told her.

'I . . .' She exhaled and rested her head back on the seat.

'Can you remember any of it?' Faulkner asked.

She needed a little time to find all the pieces and arrange them in their proper order. Cathy could recall being in the bushes, then the bombs, the smell. The quiet that followed. Finally, sensing someone there, and—

Her hand moved to the top of her head, mouth tightening as her fingertips stroked the tender spot. No blood, but even the lightest brush of her fingers sent pain jolting right through her.

'He must have used the butt of his gun,' George told her. 'Fetched you a fair old whack. That beret you were wearing spared you the worst of it. As soon as you cried out, we began to move. Your brother and Terry and Bob have gone after him. He can't be more than five seconds ahead of them.'

Another fragment clicked into her memory. Her eyes snapped

open. She stared hard, until she could make out the faint shapes of eyes and mouths. Cathy swallowed, the taste of brandy still in her mouth, grimacing as she lifted her head off the seat.

'I hit him,' she said. 'I had a branch.' She curled her fingers as if she was still holding it. Her proper voice was returning, stronger now, steady. 'I heard a bone break.'

'Where?' Faulkner asked urgently. 'Where did you hit him?'

'Wrist,' she remembered.

'Which wrist? Do you know?'

She frowned as she relived it, hearing the bone snap once more. 'I swung round. The branch was in my right hand . . . it must have been the left. Yes. It was definitely his left wrist.'

Even in the darkness, Cathy picked out his smile. 'You did very well. Come on, let's take you down to the infirmary. I want them to take a look at you.'

'No,' she said. Not a hospital. She'd spent too much time there recently, first with Daisy Barker, then Derek Smith. There was no need. It was only a bang on the head. Her father always told her she had a thick skull. She'd suffered worse than this on patrol and been back on duty after a few minutes. Not much choice when you were a sergeant. 'I'm fine. I—'

'No, you're not. You might have a concussion,' George told her. 'How many fingers am I holding up?'

'Three.' She was certain. 'If I have a problem tomorrow, I'll go to casualty then.'

It was the best she was prepared to offer.

Faulkner sighed. 'Have it your way. I don't have time to argue. We have other things to do.' He tossed Andrews the car keys. 'Drop me near the office then take her home.' She saw him looking at her. 'Day off for you tomorrow. That one is an order.'

She wanted to keep her eyes open, to see how badly the bombs had hurt Leeds. But once she settled on the passenger seat, the next thing she knew was George shaking her shoulder.

'What?' They'd stopped moving. She felt comfortable; she didn't want to open her eyes.

'You're home.'

Reaching the front door took forever, walking through the bitter night. Then the slow, aching climb up the stairs.

In her room she shrugged off her coat and shoes and settled under the blankets.

Wherever she looked, everything was sharp, snapping straight into focus. No problem with her vision. Her head hurt like the devil, and she gasped as her fingers outlined the spot where Minuit had hit her. She was tired, but not exhausted the way she'd expected. Cautiously, Cathy sat up in bed, then stood. For one moment she felt groggy and uncertain, but it passed. A glance at the clock; after nine. She'd slept late. It felt wonderful. It felt . . . sinful.

Cathy peered in the mirror. Her skin was pale, no colour on her cheeks, and deep shadows under her eyes that no make-up would hide. She took her compact from her handbag and tried to hold the mirror to examine the top of her head.

In the bathroom, she dissolved two headache powders, making a face as she drank them down. Washed her face and brushed her hair carefully and tenderly. The liberty cut was meant to be easy to take care of, but the last week had played havoc with it. What she had now sprang out all over her head, a million miles from the glamorous look Annie had given her. She was more like the witch in a children's storybook.

Dan's door was still open. Bed made, blackouts closed.

'Have they given you the day off?' her mother asked as Cathy came into the kitchen.

'Yes, Ma. We were working very late.'

'I heard you come in.' She made it sound like an accusation. 'Your brother wasn't with you.'

'No.' She sat at the table and lifted the teapot. Plenty in there. She poured a cup and swirled it round her mouth, revelling in the taste, a balm on her tongue. 'He was still busy.'

Had they caught Minuit? They must have done. He'd had no start at all, and three of them haring after him. But . . . she felt a shiver of panic race through her body.

'We've barely seen him since he came back.' Mrs Marsden stopped. Hands on hips, she stared at her daughter. 'You're looking very peaky, Catherine. Has something happened?'

'In the wars a bit, Ma, that's all,' she admitted. Better to say it than have her mother ferret out the lie. 'Honestly, it's nothing.'

She felt the gaze, the one she knew all too well, the one that seemed to see straight into her heart. 'Honest.'

'She's a grown woman, Edith. Leave her be. She knows if she's poorly,' her father said quietly.

Five minutes of sitting by the fire, trying to read the Georgette Heyer novel, and she knew she couldn't spend the day like this. She forgot the words as soon as she read them, going back over the same page a dozen times and none of it sinking in. Her head was throbbing. Cathy knew she should go back to bed and rest.

But she needed to know.

Her mother was in the kitchen, frowning as she prepared dinner from one of the new wartime leaflets.

'Potato suet paste,' she said doubtfully, 'What do you think?'

'Put some sauce on it and dad will be happy.' She kissed the top of her mother's head. 'I need to go to work.'

'You just said you had the day off.'

'Yes, but there's a war on.' The words had never felt so true.

Only Faulkner in the office. He looked at her for a moment as she came through the door marked Special Investigation Branch, then shook his head.

'I don't know how the hell the bastard managed it, but he slipped away from us.'

She dropped into her seat, untying her headsquare. All the way into town, as she gazed out from the tram at some of the damage from last night's raid, she'd managed to convince herself that it was over. That they'd captured him. He'd been right there. She'd felt his breath on her skin. The memory sent a chill creeping up her spine.

Cathy didn't want to believe what she'd just heard. How? But the bitterness on Faulkner's face said it all.

'What did he do?'

A long, exhausted sigh. 'I wish to God I knew. Vanished into thin air. Everyone's out beating the bushes.' He rubbed his chin and lit a cigarette. 'How are you feeling?'

'I'll be fine.' When she was in uniform she'd learned to never show any weakness. The first sign and men pounced on it. No chink in the armour.

'What about your head? No indications of concussion? Because—'

Cathy gave a little shrug. 'It hurts, but no blurred vision, nothing like that. I'm fine. I came down because I had to find out.'

He nodded. It was an explanation he understood.

'Your brother's frantic. Minuit is—'

'Smarter than the rest of us.' She saw Faulkner's eyes flash but ignored him. 'Better trained, too. The Jerries did a thorough job of preparing him. They've put a lot of time and effort into him. Face it, we're a bunch of amateurs in comparison.'

'We're police,' he said, then sighed. 'We have to work out how to use that to our advantage. It's all we've got. And Dan . . .'

'What about Dan?' she asked. 'What is he? I certainly don't know. He makes out he's a civil servant who ended up in all this by accident. But he's not, is he?'

'No,' he agreed. 'But right now he's probably even more terrified than the rest of us. Minuit's not likely to trust anyone now. He'll stay out of contact. We're back to square one. It's not just your brother's neck on the block with this. It's the whole country.'

'Haystacks and needles.'

'Something like that.'

'But he's hurt. His wrist . . .'

'No record of him going for treatment. We checked.'

She sighed. 'Since I'm here, I might as well make myself useful.'

'I'd rather you turned around and went home. But I don't suppose you'll do that.'

Cathy grinned. 'Not on your nelly.'

'Then go up where it happened last night. Show his picture around. He had to be familiar with the place. He must have spent some time scoping it all out.' He paused, stubbed out his cigarette and lit a new one. 'Not just in the daytime; very likely in the dark, too, or he'd have been stumbling around like us.'

'There are a couple of pubs up there that the students from the university use. We might get lucky.'

In the grey February daylight, Woodhouse Moor didn't look threatening. Just blustery and cold, with hardly a soul on the paths. A young woman with a baby in a pram shook her head as soon as Cathy produced Minuit's photograph. An older couple apologized for not being able to help.

She edged around the statue of Victoria, moving into the undergrowth until she found the place she'd stood the night before. The grass was trampled. A thick branch lay on the ground.

The pounding in her head grew more intense; she felt her body shake and had to close her eyes, taking shallow breaths. Cathy knew she'd been aware of everything, senses sharp, but Minuit had still managed to creep up behind her. A professional. She stiffened, certain she could feel the breath on her neck again, as if he might have stepped out of a nightmare. She jerked her head around, but there was only the shock of pain screeching round her brain.

Why hadn't he killed her? It would have been so easy to do. A snap of the neck, a slice of a blade. Over in a moment and without a sound. Nothing to it for a man with his skills.

Time to walk away. No backward glance in case the ghosts were still lurking.

Across the road and into the Pack Horse. Groups of students sitting around the tables, deep in discussion over their drinks.

'What'll it be, luv?' the woman behind the bar asked.

'Just a glass of Tizer,' Cathy replied. A gin and tonic would hit the spot, but right now it might finish her off. She brought her warrant card and Minuit's photograph from her purse. 'Have you ever seen him in here?'

The barmaid gazed at the picture before shaking her head.

'No.' She sounded absolutely certain. 'I only work dinnertime, mind. You want to talk to Lou. Wait a minute.' It was more like five before a man appeared, smoothing down his hair and straightening his tie.

'I'm Lou. The landlord.' A wry, flirting little chuckle. About her father's age, the type who probably fancied his chances with every woman he saw. Fleshy, with thick lips and a bulbous nose.

'I'm Sergeant Marsden, sir.' Hearing the rank wiped the charm off his face. But he didn't recognize the spy. She went around; nobody in the pub had seem him. It was the same down the road in the Eldon. An exercise in frustration.

Tiredness crept through her body on the walk back into town.

She was empty, completely drained. Faulkner was right; she should have spent the day at home. But last night Minuit had turned it into a very personal battle. In her own way, she was probably as bad as Dan. At least it stopped her worrying about Tom.

Even now, when she knew the sensible things was to catch a tram back to Gipton, curl up again in her own bed and sleep, her feet refused to obey her.

'Nothing.' The same from George and Terry. Bob Hartley shook his head and lit another cigarette with angry, jerking motions. Finally, Faulkner turned to Dan.

'Has your agent managed to come up with anything more yet?'

'No.' His answer was flat and empty. 'I think last night was a test, to see if he could trust anyone. Now he knows he's on his own.'

That made him even more dangerous, she thought. Why was he waiting? He had the explosives. She swallowed two more aspirin with the dregs of her tea to blunt the headache before it could take shape.

'That broken wrist is going to limit what he can do,' Cathy began as a thought began to take shape. 'He won't be able to climb, or do anything where he needs both hands.'

'If you really broke it.' A dig from Bob Hartley.

She stared daggers at him. 'I heard the bone crack.'

'Go and think about that. All of you.' Faulkner sounded weary. 'Any answers would be very welcome in the morning.'

'I still don't understand how he got away,' Dan's voice was strained and raw as they walked down Harehills Lane, through the ginnel and into the Gipton estate. The better part of twenty-four hours since it happened and he was still bewildered. 'Especially if his wrist was broken. There were three of us after him.'

'He must have had a plan. Would he have arranged a meeting without making sure he had a way out?'

'No,' he replied. 'He's like a chess player.'

'How do you mean?'

'Thinking five moves ahead, anticipating his opponents. He had a set in his room. His handler said sometimes he'd play against himself or work on chess problems. We thought it was just a way of passing the time.' Dan snorted. 'It seems he was handing us a clue right there.'

'Didn't you enjoy chess when you were young? Weren't you good at it?' She had a faint memory of him receiving a trophy.

'That was years ago. I was all right, nothing better than that. I haven't played since I left Leeds.'

'Maybe you need to try thinking that way again. It might help.' As they turned on to Brander Road, she began to yawn. 'I'm dead on my feet.'

'He gave you a good crack. How are you feeling?' The first time he'd asked, but she knew he was wrapped tight in his own problems.

'Like the devil's banging a set of drums in my head.'

With Connor running and his lieutenants gone, Minuit had nobody to help him. No one they knew about, she corrected herself.

As she opened the latch on the front gate, Cathy asked: 'How are we going to do it?'

'Catch him? I don't know,' he told her. 'I just don't know.'

The first truly honest answer she'd heard from her brother since he returned to Leeds.

Later, settled under the covers in bed, she heard the radio playing downstairs. Forces radio, the soft melody of 'Begin The Beguine'. She hummed it under her breath. Her father would be reading a newspaper, her mother would be snoring gently in her chair. So ordinary and wonderful.

Cathy turned off the light and settled into the darkness.

SEVENTEEN

Dan was up and out before she woke. By the time she arrived at the office, he'd already left. Cathy put her bag with her packet of sandwiches and flask of soup in the drawer. Friday night, firewatching once more. They were hunting a spy and chasing the clock, but the routines of war persisted. Routines . . . she shook her head. Every horror and loss had become normal.

Cathy wore her trousers again, feeling more comfortable and confident in them now. Let people think what they wanted; she was going to be warm when she spent the evening standing up on the roof of Matthias Robinson's department store.

Her scalp was tender, but the throbbing pain had dulled overnight to no more than a persistent ache. Two aspirin pushed it further into the background. It wouldn't give her any problems.

'Minuit hasn't shown up at a hospital or doctor's surgery anywhere round here to have his wrist treated, and MI5 has no idea where he might have run,' Faulkner announced. 'The Forge and the Avro factory are both on high alert. Dan's chasing down a few possibilities, but they're faint. Until we have some kind of lead, we're stymied.'

'What do we do now, then?' Hartley asked. He drew down smoke from his cigarette, exhaling a perfect ring and watching with satisfaction as it rose.

'We take down Jackie Connor. He might be able to lead us to this spy.'

'The last I saw of him, he was disappearing into the market,' Cathy said. She felt a tingling in her lungs at the memory of the chase. 'Have we heard anything since then?'

'No,' Terry Davis said. 'Remember, though, his lieutenants have both fallen off the face of the earth. None of the people he knows will be able to tell him what's going on. Since this is our operation, his contacts in the police can't give him any information. He's as much on his own as Minuit.'

'We came within a whisker of catching him. He's probably looking over his shoulder all the time, thinking we're a lot closer than we really are. Let's try and really give him something to worry about.' Faulkner gave a weak little smile. 'At least we'll be doing something. Maybe it'll pay off and he'll lead us to Minuit. At the very least, we put him behind bars and it's a big feather in our caps.'

'As long as this bloody spy doesn't blow up half of Leeds before we have a chance,' Hartley said.

Faulkner gave him a look. 'It was Connor who supplied him with that dynamite. He's certainly going to know things that can help us. The sooner we question him, the sooner we can end this whole business.' He looked around the faces. 'Off you go. Come back with answers.'

Cathy saw people nod when she spoke Connor's name. But none of them had seen him for a few days. Vanished without trace, just like the spy.

'He'll be around somewhere. Always is,' Jean Finch said. She sipped a cup of tea; they were in the café at the market, upstairs, looking down on the stalls. Jean was one of those women who kept turning up, working in different shops. One of life's sharp-eyed drifters, unmoored yet content to float through life. Cathy had met her years before, not long after she began walking the beat. This morning Cathy had spotted her at a stall, selling a scrappy collection of vegetables. No fruit, just a handwritten sign with the old song title 'Yes, We Have No Bananas'. The joke of rationing. 'You know he has a girlfriend.' She frowned and coughed as she lit a Woodbine. 'Had, any road.'

'Does he?' She tried to sound casual, but her mind was racing. She'd never heard of Connor having anyone special.

'Dottie Chambers.' She cocked her head. 'You know her?'

'I don't think so.' The name meant nothing at all. 'Where can I find her?'

'Last I heard, she was pulling pints at the Cross Keys over on Water Lane. Been a while, though.' She shrugged. In Jean's world, people shifted from job to job, never staying anywhere for long.

'How long's she been with him?'

'Don't know. Dottie's the one who told me. You know Jackie,

keeps things very quiet. The less people know about him, the better he likes it.'

'I'm sure.'

Two o'clock, just as Dottie Chambers called time and put the towels over the beer pumps, Cathy showed her warrant card in the public bar of the Cross Keys.

'Do you think we could have a quiet word?'

She'd arrived with Faulkner twenty minutes before, and barely sipped at a gin and tonic as she watched the faces in the bar. Friday, payday for some, and the place was busy. But by closing time at the top of the hour, most of the crowd had drained away.

'Go through to the back. I'll be there in ten minutes. Need to clear up a bit. That bloke with you will have to wait outside, though.'

The woman settled at the table with a sigh, took a Park Drive from a tarnished cigarette case and blew out a trail of smoke.

'That's better,' she said. 'Now, what do the rozzers want with me, as if I couldn't guess?'

'Jackie Connor.'

Chambers snorted. Her face consisted of tight planes, a bitter mouth with stained teeth, hair brittle and crumbling from being bleached too often. Rings on some of her fingers, Cathy saw; all cheap, imitation jewellery. 'You're behind the times, luv.'

'What happened?'

'He gave me the heave-ho.' She sounded resentful; it must have been fairly recent. 'Bloody men. They promise you the moon, but as soon as push comes to shove, you're out on your arse.' She took another deep drag on the cigarette. 'Do you have a fella?'

'In the army.'

A shrewd stare. 'Overseas?'

'On his way.' No harm in saying that much.

'Watch out he doesn't come back riddled with . . . you know.' She stubbed out the cigarette and lit another.

'Jackie kept quiet about you.'

She snorted. 'That were part of it. I wasn't allowed to talk about him. I started to feel like I was a piece on the side. How would you like that?'

'I wouldn't stand for it,' Cathy said.

'Me neither. I told him and we had an argument about it one night. He turned around and said he'd had enough. Didn't need a bunch of grief. That were the end of it. I'd heard that people are looking for him. Your lot?'

'Yes.'

'Then I hope you find the bastard and lock him away for years.'

It was the perfect opening, a gift; the wound was still raw and festering. 'You might be able to help us do that. Do you know he's been helping the Jerries?'

The woman narrowed her eyes. 'I didn't, but I wouldn't put owt past that bastard if there was a shilling in it for him. That, though . . . you're not lying, are you?'

'No. It's true.' She sighed. 'Very true. Any idea where I can find him? We tried the places off Mabgate and in the Leylands.'

'How about the one in Woodhouse? He loved that little house, took me there quite a few times.'

'Isn't there something about a woman scorned?' Cathy asked as they walked back towards Leeds Bridge.

'Hell hath no fury,' Faulkner said. 'A place in Woodhouse, eh?'

'Crossfield Street. Just the other side of the main road from the Victoria statue on the moor. It's probably only a hundred yards away.'

'Minuit could dash over there in no time.' He chuckled. 'We'd have had no chance of finding him. Perfect place for him to vanish.'

'He'll have moved on.'

'I'm sure he has.' He tried a grin. 'Still, we can hope. And there's always Connor. He'd be a big enough fish to land.'

'Friday,' she said bitterly. 'I have firewatching duty.'

'Probably for the best. I'd have kept you out of it anyway.' She opened her mouth but he shook his head. 'That bang on the head. You're not fighting fit yet. It's not just for your safety. It's everyone.'

She wished . . . but she knew he was right.

'My Bobby's in hospital,' Brenda said as they took a turn around the roof, keeping a lookout for enemy aircraft. They were both bundled up in coats and scarves, tin hats perched on their hair.

Bobby, her son, in India with the army. Without thinking, Cathy turned, held out her arms and gave the woman a hug, feeling her stiffen at the unexpected contact.

'What happened? How is he?'

'I don't know. They won't tell me.' She sounded at the end of her tether. 'All they're willing to say is it didn't happen in any type of action and he's not likely to die.' Her eyes flashed. 'What does that mean? They won't even let me know exactly where he is. Just that he's over there somewhere.'

'Can I do anything?'

Brenda shook her head. 'No, pet. Nobody can. It's the War Office. When the telegram arrived, I thought . . .' Of course. The worst. It would be the same for anyone these days. A pause as Brenda gathered herself again. 'I have to wait until I hear from him. God knows when that might be. The post is likely to take forever. Meanwhile, I'm stuck here, quietly going mad.' She paused. 'I'm sorry for burdening you, luv. It's not your problem.'

Before Cathy could reply, Brenda strode off to the other side of the roof, looking north towards Sheepscar and Meanwood. Cathy stared out towards Hunslet and Knostrop, downstream along the river, where most of the bombs had landed the night before last. It must have been terrifying to all the firewatchers, like hell opening up in from of their eyes. Thick clouds tonight; there wouldn't be a repeat of Wednesday, thank God.

War . . . it was holding Brenda in limbo, tearing her into pieces as she was forced to wait. It was pushing and pulling at them all.

She checked her watch. Still two hours of her shift to go. The cold bit into her bones. Cathy took couple more aspirin to silence the low, throbbing headache which still hadn't completely gone. By now, the squad would have gone into the house on Crossfield Street. Minuit wouldn't be there; he was too sly to stay anywhere long. But they'd taken another bolthole away from Connor.

Faulkner had gone up to reconnoitre the place. A quick walk by, front and back. To see it and fix it in his mind. She'd offered to go. If she couldn't be on the raid, at least she could do that. But he refused.

'Connor's seen you. You chased him, remember? He's not likely to forget your face.'

Time passed slowly. No sirens likely in this weather. She went back into the warmth downstairs to drink her soup and eat her fish paste sandwiches. A chance to pace, think and wonder.

It was a quiet shift, and it took no more than a minute to fill out the log when they'd finished. The watchman unlocked the front door of the department store and Cathy came out into the night, Brenda right behind her.

'I hope you hear something soon. Some good news.'

'I'm not sure what good news is any more,' she murmured, then gave a wan smile. 'I really am sorry about earlier. I didn't mean to . . .'

'It's fine. Honestly.'

A nod and Brenda walked away. Cathy breathed in the night, the petrol, the soot, everything that hung in the air. She darted across Briggate. Only fifty yards to the Ministry of Works offices, the solid front plastered with cinema posters. *The Maltese Falcon. How Green Was My Valley. Shadow Of The Thin Man.* Up the stairs, through the quiet building to the SIB office. Excitement racing through her, anticipating the tale.

Empty.

Nothing new on the desks.

Dan was facing the wall, the blankets pulled up to his neck. Gently, Cathy shook his shoulder. She gasped as his hand shot out and gripped her wrist.

'What do you want?' His voice was thick with sleep. But his fingers were tight, pushing into her flesh.

'What happened tonight?' she hissed.

'Nobody there.'

'But . . .' she began, then realized she had nothing else to say.

Dan grunted. 'Tomorrow.' He opened his hand and she pulled away.

Last night's thick quilt of clouds was still there in the morning, but she swore she could feel a hint of warmth in the air. The first of March; maybe spring was taking a tentative early step. But it was much too soon to trust the weather. She still dressed in a warm woollen skirt and the raspberry-coloured jumper her mother had knitted when she was in her teens.

Cathy felt rested. Dan, though, was downcast, shoulders slumped as they began walking up to York Road.

'Well?' she asked.

'I told you last night: nobody was there.' His voice was dull.

'That's it?'

He glanced over his shoulder to be sure no one could hear. 'We didn't find any trace of Minuit. A few things that belonged to Connor. It didn't look as if he'd been there recently. Bob Hartley was keeping watch overnight in case anyone showed up. Terry Davis should have taken over by now.'

'I'm sure Minuit must have run there after he . . .' Her fingertips stroked the lump on her head. Smaller now, but still tender.

'I'm certain of it.'

He'd probably been standing inside, laughing at them all blundering around in the dark. A thought that had arrived somewhere in the night came back to her.

'Have you tried talking to his handler again? He might have something more than can help us.'

'She,' Dan said. A single word, but the way he spoke it made her turn and give him a sharp, questioning look. 'She's been suspended from duty. The inquiry is already underway. It's standard procedure.'

'But you've talked to her?'

He nodded. 'There are people waiting for the tram.' Her brother straightened his back. 'Let's drop it for now.'

Plenty to chew on in those few words, so much of it from the things he hadn't said. Her brother had a girlfriend in the service, one who was likely to lose her job for letting the spy escape. Another reason for him to hunt the man.

He broke into her thoughts. 'At least you had a quiet night for your firewatching.'

'I'd never expected to say it, but this war's made me grateful to see clouds.'

Idle, neutral chatter that kept them going all the way to the office. As she passed One-Eyed Sam's newspaper kiosk, she saw the headlines: **Allies take Somaliland. Exmoor sunk off Lowestoft**. Victories and defeats.

They all needed something more to give them heart. Something big.

Faulkner grabbed the phone as soon as it rang.

'SIB.' He listened, then passed the receiver to Dan. 'For you.'

They waited, watching his face. Not many of them in the room: Hartley had gone home to sleep and Terry Davis was watching the place in Woodhouse.

'I'll be there as soon as I can.' He replaced the receiver and buttoned his overcoat. 'I might have something for us.' His eyes rested on her for a long moment, then he was gone.

The house was neat. Everything ordered. The pots had been washed and dried, dishcloth hanging over the tap, bed made. Not the actions of someone who was abandoning the place, she thought. Faulkner had sent her and Andrews to give Connor's house a thorough going-over in the daylight.

No cigarette ends, and the ashtray had been wiped clean. Connor was a smoker; Minuit hated it. Bottles of booze placed on the sideboard. She unscrewed the caps and sniffed: the real thing, not the rubbish Connor sold to others.

A few papers in a neat pile on the table. She collected them to take back to the office.

'Not a single hiding place that I can find,' George called from upstairs. Cathy had come up with nothing in the kitchen, no rolls of bank notes hidden in the flour jar or at the back of the larder behind the tins. But no fresh meat, no milk staying cold on the windowsill; it didn't look as though anyone had been there for a day or two.

Only the outside toilet at the back of the yard to search. She wrinkled her nose as she opened the door. The same dirt and stink she remembered from growing up in Quarry Hill. A stack of old newspapers on the floor. She poked at it with the toe of her shoe, expecting to see a rat scurry away. Instead, she felt something solid underneath.

A box. She froze for a second. Carefully, with aching slowness she moved to the back door of the house, constantly looking over her shoulder.

'You'd better come here.'

EIGHTEEN

Casually, Faulkner flipped open the lid of the box.
Cathy flinched for a second, half-expecting a booby trap.

Nothing.

'Just some bits of torn-up paper,' Terry said as he peered inside. The box was made of stout, corrugated cardboard, a good eight inches deep. 'Making sure he didn't run out in the middle of the night.' He chuckled at his own joke.

Why would Connor keep some old papers hidden away here? Maybe it really was spare toilet paper.

'Take them back to the office,' Faulkner told him. His eyes moved around. 'All finished in the house?'

'Done and dusted,' George answered. 'Next to nothing.'

'I don't think anyone will be coming back here. Not the way the neighbours have been crowding around.'

'Any word from Dan about . . . ?'

'Who knows? He's still off somewhere.' Faulkner started to walk away, then turned back to Cathy: 'I forgot in all the brouhaha, but your inspector wants you to stop in and see her.'

'Sergeant?' Daisy Barker narrowed her eyes, suspicious. 'Me? It's not April Fools' Day, is it? Did I lose a month somewhere? Are you serious?'

Cathy laughed. 'It's real enough, if you want it, Sergeant Barker.'

She'd worried all the way to Inspector Harding's office, wondering if she was about to be recalled to uniform. But it was nothing more than to have her recommendation for an acting woman police sergeant, someone to replace her until the end of the war, as Cathy was with SIB for the duration. No hesitation in suggesting Barker.

'Why don't you go and tell her, Marsden?' Harding said when Cathy stood in the inspector's office. 'She'll appreciate it from you. Saturday at this time, she'll be patrolling the market.'

Now they were sitting in the café upstairs, wiping condensation from the windows, hearing the cries below: 'Tuppence a pound.' 'Threepence a pound.' 'Three for sixpence and can't say fairer than that, luv.' Daisy still had her black eyes, the other bruises where Minuit had hit her were only just beginning to fade, and the cuts were scabbed over. At least the hospital had straightened her nose.

She look dazed by the news. 'I . . . that's grand, Sarge. Thank you. I don't know what to say.'

'I felt like that when I was promoted,' Cathy told her. 'But you've earned it. Remember, though, it's only an acting rank.'

She grinned. 'I'll keep it warm for you. And I won't let you down.'

'I'm sure of that.'

Daisy would be good, no doubt about it. Clever, plenty of guts. But what would happen after the war and SIB no longer existed up here? There weren't enough women on the force to justify two sergeants.

But that was something for the distant future. They had to beat the Jerries first.

'Where's the boss?' Cathy asked as she walked into the office. Everybody else was in: George Andrews, Terry Davis, Bob Hartley.

'Down in the canteen with your brother,' George replied. He had papers spread across his desk. 'I'll tell you what: Connor's not as smart as people think. Those papers you found in the toilet might be a year old or more, but there are one or two details about his businesses in here that we can use. Stupid devil.'

'Probably thought nobody would look there.'

'He slipped up, then. Oh,' he added as she left, 'Smithy rang. The doctor's given him the thumbs-up. He'll definitely be back on Monday.' A laugh. 'Probably feels he's missing all the fun.'

The squad would be back to full strength. Right now they needed everyone.

Connor, though . . .

She found the two men at a table away from everyone else, heads down as they talked.

'Well?' Cathy asked as took the chair next to Dan. 'Any progress on our friend?'

Shaking his head seemed to exhaust him. 'It was just someone camping in Roundhay Park. A copy of anything like that is always routed to . . . the service these days. I went out there. Turned out it was just some old boy who decided he fancied a bit of nature for a change.'

'It's still bitter at night,' she said. 'He must have been frozen.'

He shrugged. 'Takes all sorts. We checked. He's clean.'

'Which leaves us with nothing,' Faulkner pointed out.

'Where do we go?' she asked, looking at her brother.

Up in the office, George handed Faulkner a small list.

'That's the worthwhile stuff so far from the papers in the box. Not much. Still, not a bad haul from toilet paper.' He grinned. 'Proper bumf. Bum fodder.'

'How old do you think this is?'

'Mostly from last year, boss. I saw a mention of opening another club or two for the men coming back from Dunkirk.' Back in May, Cathy thought. Ten months old. Almost another lifetime. Long before she was part of SIB.

No conversation until she and Dan started the walk down Harehills Lane, as the tram swayed off up York Road.

'What's her name? Minuit's handler.' Cathy asked. They turned into the ginnel, wrapped in the evening.

'Elizabeth,' Dan replied. 'We started with the XX people at the same time.'

'Not that long ago.'

'No.' He sighed. 'No.'

'But the two of you . . .'

He was silent for a few seconds.

'It's strange. She went to a good school, maths degree from Cambridge.' Cathy felt his glance. He gave a tight, bitter laugh. 'Knocks City of Leeds High School and a leavers' certificate into a cocked hat, doesn't it?'

For a moment she felt sorry for him.

'Does she have a surname?'

'Yates.'

'You said you've talked to her since you came up here?'

'Twice, yes.'

'Anything she can add about him?'

'If she could, she would. As soon as the inquiry's done, she'll resign. It's rotten, but that's how it's done.'

'Will you still see her?'

'Who knows? She's already been offered something else. Something up her street to do with numbers. She's better with them than people. Probably not the best choice to be a handler.'

'Is she one of the reasons you're here?'

'Not really.' A long pause. They'd crossed to Brander Road. Soon enough they'd be at the front door. 'I told you, finding people really is part of what I'm there to do. Between that and being from Leeds . . .' She saw him shrug. 'Of course I want to do everything I can to help her.'

Another surprise. Just when she'd pegged him as cold, he showed another side of himself and made her think again. He did have some warmth hidden away. But if she hadn't asked, he'd never have said a word about the woman. She'd have remained another layer hidden under the surface.

'Right,' she said, knowing her voice was too bright. 'Let's see what Ma's cooked with the ration.'

A letter was waiting on the stairs. For a moment her heart leapt, thinking it was more from Tom. Impossible, he was still somewhere at sea. Cathy closed her eyes and took a breath. Please, she thought, keep him safe. Then she smiled anyway as she recognized the loops and wide swirls of the handwriting: Annie.

> Dear Cathy,
> I'm going to be in Leeds on Monday. I'll be on a one-day course about one of the things I do, and I've wangled an overnight out of it. The work should finish about five, so I'll skip all the drinks and pop up to my mum's. See you there about seven if you can make it, and we'll do something.
> Your pal in mischief,
> Annie

Monday . . . the day after tomorrow, still a lifetime away.

* * *

She could feel some life, a small hint of warmth in the Sunday morning air as she waited for the tram. A breeze, but for once it didn't feel as if it wanted to slice open her skin; maybe spring really was in the air. Even a faint promise of blue skies in the moments the clouds parted.

She'd heard Dan leave a little after six. His desperation increased with each passing day. They were running out of time. Minuit needed to act soon, before they caught up with him, and he had to make whatever he did count.

They had to stop him. But they had no idea where to look.

Only Faulkner in the office, but he was almost always there; he might as well have lived in the place.

'Has Dan been in?'

Faulkner shook his head. Footsteps outside and the others arrived in a welter of conversation. She saw Bob Hartley glower at her as the boss brought them up to date. At least he'd be gone once all this was done.

'I know it's Sunday, but I still need you all out there. Let's try and come up with something. Tell people that Connor's been helping the Jerries. Hammer it home. Make them furious with him. Remember, he's been trying to play us for fools. Someone has to know where he is.'

Terry puffed on his pipe. 'What are we going to do about the spy?'

'We'll show his picture, but I don't have much hope. We'll have to see what Dan turns up, unless anyone has a bright idea.' He looked around the faces. 'No? Then we'll focus on Connor for now, until we have something on Minuit. The information's out there.'

Before she could leave, Faulkner said, 'Hold on a minute, will you?' Once they were alone, he rubbed his chin. 'I'm starting to wonder about your brother. You don't know what's going on, do you? We're supposed to be working together, but he's like a ghost around here.'

She weighed how much to tell him. 'He's feeling the pressure—'

'We all are.'

'—and this might be the first thing in his life that hasn't happened easily.'

'He's going to have to learn.' A strained smile. 'Sorry. I had the people from headquarters on the blower first thing, wanting to know how it was all moving. I think they've had the government brass piling on them because of the spy. All the way to the top. The long and the short of it is they want us to move mountains now, if not sooner. Meanwhile, Dan's wandering round Leeds doing God alone knows what.'

'There's something else that's been bothering me,' Cathy said. 'This tanker business. It was all resolved too quickly. Too smoothly.'

'What about it?'

'Doesn't it seem strange to you?'

'We've both been coppers long enough to know that sometimes you have luck. Connor had other things on his mind and he took his eye off the ball with this.'

'Maybe.' She wasn't convinced.

'Are you sure you're not like this because it was Bob?'

'No,' Cathy told him. 'Nothing to do with that.'

'Then be grateful that business is done. We can concentrate on finding Connor. And stop a spy who has dynamite and fuses.'

Dinnertime and she was empty-handed. Sunday and every business closed. Only the canteen in the basement open. Plain food, but at least it was hot and filling; enough to keep her going for the rest of the day.

Nobody around to ask about Connor or Minuit.

Time was too precious to waste like this.

The office was empty. Cathy settled at her desk with the box of papers from Connor's house. Maybe she'd find something that George had missed.

After more than an hour, scribbling a few notes, she wasn't much wiser. Connor would keep the important information tucked away in his head and the safe deposit boxes that no one else would ever see. She turned to the pile she'd taken from the table and was sifting the last of it when Terry and Faulkner returned.

'Nobody was around out there, so I thought I might as well take a shufti at this lot.' She patted the pile in front of her.

'Any nuggets?'

'No. I think we already have everything useful.' Cathy rubbed her eyes with the heels of her hands. At least all the reading hadn't given her headache; she seemed to have fully recovered from the blow. A thick skull; her father had been right. 'What about you two? Anyone spill the beans?'

'We've got the square root of damn all.' Terry packed his pipe and struck a match. The rough scent of tobacco filled the air.

'No sign of your brother yet?'

'Not since I returned—' she looked at her watch '—almost two hours ago.'

Had she really been here that long?

The telephone rang, loud and shrill. For a second, they were stood, frozen, then Faulkner lifted the receiver. Sunday; it wasn't an idle call.

'SIB.' A long pause, then his voice grew serious. 'We'll be up there as soon as we can. Thank you, sir.'

Cathy turned off the Ring Road and started up Weetwood Lane. The daylight was lasting longer, barely a sketch of dusk on the horizon. Ahead of her, the hill rose steeply, fields on either side. Farmland. No chance to go more than a few yards; the road was filled with police cars, a pair of ambulances and the black coroner's van.

A uniformed constable directed her to park the Humber on the verge. She could see Johnson pacing around and smoking, a harassed detective sergeant at his side.

Farther along, a bobby was questioning a woman holding a dog on a lead. Curious, Cathy edged closer to overhear.

'He's normally very good when I tell him to heel.' A crisp, educated voice. 'But this time he kept pulling and pulling. He wouldn't stop, you see. I had to go and look at what he'd found.'

'What did you find, madam?'

It felt as if an age passed before she replied. 'A body. He was dead, that was obvious from looking at him. I sent my husband home to telephone the police. We just live at the top of the hill, you see. I . . . ' She paused and wiped away a tear. The constable looked around, helpless.

Cathy gave him a nod and showed her warrant card. Better to dive in than stand around looking like a spare part.

A female touch might help here. She wanted to know what had happened, why Johnson had called out the SIB. He'd simply said there was a body that might interest them and given the location. Nothing more than that.

'It must have been awful, Mrs . . .'

'Kershaw.' She wore stout country clothes, an old-fashioned tweed skirt with a hem well below the knee, dirty rubber boots and an ancient, tattered jacket. She was in her middle fifties, her grey hair neatly set under an expensive silk headsquare.

'I'm Sergeant Marsden. I'm sure one of the detectives will want to talk to you in a moment. In the meantime, was there anything that stood out? Something that jumped into your mind when you saw the body?'

Cathy had no idea who was dead or how it had happened; she was bluffing her way through. But the questions made her sound official, as though she knew what she was doing, and she might learn something.

'He looked . . . abandoned.' She spoke the word as if it had taken her by surprise.

Abandoned. A very strange word. 'What do you mean, Mrs Kershaw?'

The woman was the type who would never allow herself to be overwhelmed by emotion for long, and had quickly regained her composure.

'As if someone had thrown him away, like a sack of rubbish. We get some of that out here, you see.' Before Cathy could say more, a plain clothes constable took the woman's arm to lead her away.

'The detective sergeant would like to speak to you now, madam.'

The corpse had gone. She watched as the coroner's van made a five-point turn and headed up Weetwood Lane, the tail lights no more than a hint of red through the blackout slits.

Cathy was recounting the brief conversation to Faulkner when Johnson strode over, ignoring her.

'The dead man's name is Frankie Weir. He's been knocking around for a dozen years or so. I've nicked him a few times,' he said with a self-satisfied nod. 'He was nothing much, mind you. Not part of any of the big mobs, not that we know about. It's the way he was killed that made me think it might be connected to your lot.'

'Oh?' Faulkner asked. 'How was that?'

Johnson glanced at Cathy. 'Hands tied behind him, bullet to the back on the skull. Executed, just like in the gangster films. As if someone wanted to make a statement with it. He's probably a deserter. I reckon there's a good chance Connor pulled the trigger on this one.'

NINETEEN

'Does he have any evidence to tie Connor to this?' Cathy asked.
Faulkner pulled his chin against his chest to shield himself from the wind as he lit a cigarette.

'None,' he murmured. 'But if that's how Johnson sees it, that's the way it has to be. Have you ever heard of Weir?'

'No,' But what did that mean? Women police constables had nothing to do with serious criminals. 'What are we going to do about it?'

'Us?' He looked up in astonishment. 'We're not. If the man's really a deserter, I've never heard of him. We'll leave it to Johnson to investigate.' A quick smile. 'Maybe he'll get lucky and stumble over Connor. He asked me if someone from SIB wanted to work with them. Professional courtesy, he claimed. Probably wants to find out what we're up to. Smithy's back tomorrow. I thought he could go over to their morning meeting and find out what they're doing. Something easy, since he won't be up to snuff.' Five o'clock and a sense of creeping darkness. 'Let's go back to the office. This was a waste of time. Maybe your brother's returned.'

The car started as soon as she turned the key, the way it had since the mechanic had worked his magic. Worth every penny Faulkner had paid.

Dan was there, hunched over his desk, writing a report, the pen moving quickly across the paper. The same awkward writing she remembered from when they were young.

'Anything good for us? Terry asked.

Dan rested the pen on the blotter and turned to face them. The circles under his eyes were deep and dark, like a man in torment.

'A possibility,' he said with a sigh. 'Maybe it'll be something. Maybe not.' A weary shrug. 'That's as close as I've managed to come. I don't suppose . . .'

'Not a dickie bird. You look like you need some sleep. Start again in the morning.' He looked around the room. 'The same for all of you. Let's come back to it fresh.'

'I—' Dan began. 'Maybe you're right. I'm not going to learn anything before tomorrow.'

Monday dawned sour, with threatening clouds the colour of old bruises. The air was thick and damp. Yesterday's promise of spring had vanished like a magician's illusion. Instead, the rain felt like it might begin at any time. At least it would deter the Luftwaffe.

She was prepared for the weather: the warm, lined raincoat, umbrella, rubber galoshes folded in her gas mask case. The old wool dress she'd made from a wonderful pattern before she joined the police. Tight in places these days, but she couldn't bear to part with it. No Dan. She'd heard him leave as she was coming out of the bathroom.

But he was there in the office, a hand over the telephone receiver and hissing 'Canteen' as she walked in, before pointing to her desk and returning to his conversation.

A scrap of paper and a name scribbled in pencil: Mrs Benson.

The WVS woman. There was only one reason she'd ring; she'd seen Minuit.

Down in the basement, the squad was gathered around a table, where Derek Smith held court, a walking stick hooked over the back of his chair.

'I'm glad to see you back,' Cathy told him with a broad smile. 'How do you feel?'

He blushed at the compliment. 'I'm mending. Just don't expect me to do the hundred-yard dash for a while. I heard you took a knock, too.'

'Just a bump on the head. Par for the course.'

'Crocks and wrecks are good enough for SIB,' Terry laughed.

She held up the note. 'Anyone fancy a walk to the railway station? It could well be something on our friend.'

Everyone was staring at her.

'George,' Faulkner said, 'you go.'

Only a couple of minutes along Boar Lane to City Square, with its statue of the Black Prince surrounded by air-raid shelters. Then a plunge into the tumult of the railway station. Barely eight in the morning and already packed. The sounds and smells of the engines: steam, smoke, shrill whistles. Service men and women, accents from everywhere, uniforms of all colours, smoking, talking. Some waiting in the kind of wounded silence no one else could reach.

Cathy jostled through to the Women's Voluntary Service desk, waiting while Janet Benson wrote directions to the bus station for a confused Land Army girl.

'I hope she finds it, poor lamb.' Her expression brightened. 'You got my message, Sergeant.'

'I did. This is Corporal Andrews. You have something good for me?'

She glanced at George, committing him to memory. 'That picture you showed me. I saw him this morning as I was coming in to work. A little over half an hour ago.'

'What? Here in the station?' Cathy was astonished. Her gaze moved around the platforms and the people. How could anyone pick out a single face among this crowd?

Mrs Benson shook her head. 'On the corner of Park Row and the Headrow. I'd just got off the bus. He was standing there and staring at something. I brushed right past him.'

'Are you positive it was Minuit? Leeds is always busy in the mornings.'

Her mouth turned down. 'Miss Marsden, you know I remember faces.' It was a gentle reprimand. Janet Benson had a photographic memory. She was famous for it. If she said it was him, he'd been there. She'd needed to ask. But—

'What was he doing?' The pulse was twitching fast in her neck. 'You said he was looking at something.'

'He was standing there, holding his hat and gazing towards the town hall. If he hadn't been bare-headed, I probably wouldn't have noticed him. He had a bandage wrapped around his left wrist.'

When almost every man wore some kind of hat, that would attract a second glance. The bandage . . . that clinched things. It was Minuit.

'How long was he there?'

'I've no idea.' She smiled. 'I could hardly stop and gawp at him, could I? Besides, I was running late. When I looked back a few seconds later, he'd gone.'

'Thank you,' Cathy said, aware of a queue forming behind her, people needing help in a strange city. 'I really appreciate it.'

'Minuit's taking a risk,' George said as they walked up Park Row. At the corner they stood where the spy would have been, and looked in the direction of the town hall. 'What do you think?'

'Blowed if I know,' Cathy said. Maybe he'd simply been staring. 'But he's here. We'd better tell the others.'

With people pouring into town on their way to work, Minuit would have been anonymous. Another man in his overcoat, pausing for a moment. Pure chance that someone like Janet Benson would notice him. Lady Luck had smiled on them for once.

'I'm sure we're grasping at straws,' Faulkner said. 'But I want you all out looking, anyway. We've got nothing on Connor, and the police are hunting him now. Smithy's on his way to be our ears with them. He'll let us know what they find. The rest of you fan out, and for God's sake look at the faces. You've seen Minuit's picture umpteen times. He's out there.' He looked up at the clock. 'It's a bit after eight now. Back here at half past ten.'

It was impossible to read his face. Mouth set straight, eyes showing nothing at all.

'I—' Dan said.

'Unless you have somewhere important to be, I want you out there, too,' Faulkner told him.

The crowds had eased as the work week began. Yet still plenty of people bustling around. She started with the arcades, Queens and Thornton's, both quite empty. Along Queen Victoria Street, where the war made the grand shops look down-at-heel, through Cross Arcade and the fading splendour of County Arcade.

Cathy assessed every man she spotted. Most were too small, too fat, walking painfully with the help of sticks. The bandage should make him easy to spot. After two minutes she only needed a quick look to judge. Very few took a second glance.

No Minuit.

As she walked, her mind wandered. Minuit had his targets. Jackie Connor had made sure he had money, explosives, a gun. Everything he needed. Her thoughts skipped ahead as she crossed Vicar Lane and into Kirkgate Market, letting the noise fill her ears. The spy must be growing desperate by now. He must hear the clock ticking just as loudly as she did.

Up and down the aisles. Past the rows of fishmongers and butchers with their meagre, rationed offerings. Not a soul who resembled Minuit. Down by the doors where she'd lost Jackie Connor, then out into the open market.

She'd known this place her whole life. Where she'd grown up, in that crumbling old house on Quarry Hill, was no more than a stone's throw away. It had been her Aladdin's cave when she was a child. Cathy could find her way blindfold through the stalls.

This time she found no pleasure in looking.

Where was he? The question preyed on her as she walked and glanced at faces. They desperately needed the answer.

Would Minuit still be able to attack the Forge or the Avro factory with a broken wrist? It didn't sound likely, especially with both places on alert. What if he'd come up with another plan? She stopped suddenly.

The others listened as her thoughts tumbled out back in the office. None of them had spotted Minuit, no one had any idea why he'd been standing at the corner of Park Row, gazing down the Headrow.

'You're spouting a load of rubbish,' Bob Hartley told her when she'd finished. 'It's all in your head. Why would he change tack? We know why exactly he's here. He told the interrogator when he was caught.'

'No, she has a good point,' Dan said thoughtfully. 'Minuit's a professional. He's had ample time. If there was an opportunity at the Forge or out at Yeadon he'd have discovered it by now. We were very thorough when we questioned him. We were convinced he was telling the truth. He probably was; the targets he gave us both seemed logical. But they're both pretty tight now, and that broken wrist is going to make them impossible. During the interrogation, there didn't seem to be any reason not to believe him. After all, he appeared to have given us everything else.' His mouth curved into a brief, wry smile. 'Maybe we believed what we wanted to believe. He lied about being glad he was caught and did it very well. I should have realized he was capable of lying about everything else. He's still here for a reason. He has something in mind. We just don't know what it is.'

'What the hell is that supposed to mean?' Hartley barked out the question.

Faulkner glared at him. 'It means we go back to the drawing board and look at everything we can think of as a potential target. Consider how the broken wrist will affect things, too.'

After quarter of an hour of everyone batting ideas around, Cathy slipped into her coat, gathered up her handbag and gas mask case. Faulkner shot her a curious look but she rubbed the bump on her head where she'd been hit. It was a decent excuse.

She needed space for her thoughts. Cathy strode out along Commercial Street, Bond Street. Past Marshall and Snelgrove, the high-class department store with its uniformed commissionaire, and down to Park Square.

All the railings around the grass in the centre of the square had gone. A sturdy air raid shelter filled one corner. But the benches remained. A woman was playing with her young child; they were the only other people there. All too easy to forget that ordinary life continued. The clouds still hung low and the threat of a downpour scented the air, but not a drop yet.

Dan was right: Minuit's broken wrist had changed everything. But since the spy was still in Leeds with eight sticks of dynamite, he must intend to use them. It had to be here, in town. A place that would have real impact and do damage that would be impossible to ignore.

Where, though?

One of the engineering works in Hunslet? The place was chock-a-block with them. She mulled the idea for a moment, then dismissed it. The Luftwaffe was already attacking over there. Another explosion might have an impact, but it wouldn't *feel* big. Not public enough. The same with the Burton's factory on Stoney Rock Lane, where thousands of women made uniforms for the troops. An explosion might affect the war effort, but it wouldn't make a splash.

It had to be something memorable. Something people would see every day and be reminded.

Cathy raised her head and suddenly her heart leapt into her throat. For a second she couldn't breathe.

God.

It was there, right in front of her eyes. It always had been. It was absolutely perfect. Minuit had been looking at it earlier that morning.

Leeds Town Hall.

TWENTY

Smithy was the only one in the office when she burst through the door, breathless.

'Where are they?'

'No idea. I've only just come back, and it was empty. Why?'

Damn. 'An idea.' She sat down and grimaced as she took a swig of tea from the cup she'd left on her desk. Cold. 'Glad to be back? Those few days at home buck you up?'

His face came alive with pleasure. 'Just what I needed. The doctor's pleased with how I'm coming along. I just have to make sure I don't push myself for a few weeks. I never thanked you for driving me to the hospital that night.'

'It's nothing.'

'It was a hell of a lot to me.' He looked around the office. 'Funny thing, though, after two days I started missing this madhouse. Daft, isn't it?'

'It gets in your blood. What do you think of DS Johnson?'

'I've served under a couple like him. They get an idea in their head and neither heaven nor earth is going to shift it. They start building the evidence to make it seem real.'

'Is there any evidence?'

He snorted. 'I'm damned if I can see anything to connect Jackie Connor to the murder.'

'Connor's sly. A cut above most of them.'

He finished writing his report, blotted the page, placed it on Faulkner's desk and stood, leaning on his walking stick. 'Johnson wants another look at the scene out on Weetwood Lane. He said I should go along, get a feel for the crime scene.' He shrugged.

'I hope you like fields. Better dress warm.'

Once he'd gone, she knew she couldn't sit and wait. Her mind was racing too fast to concentrate. She needed to be doing something. To go and take another look at the town hall.

The rain began as she walked up Briggate. Fat drops hammered on her umbrella and Cathy ducked into a shop doorway to pull galoshes over her shoes.

It came down steadily, clearing people from the streets. She turned up the Headrow, past the blast wall that protected the entrance to Lewis's, crossed Albion Street, and down beyond Green Dragon Yard, with its wonderful name.

The town hall. The more she thought, the more possible it seemed. Now it was time to see if she could put some flesh on the idea. Enough to sound convincing when she presented it to the others.

Cathy followed the pavement all around the building. Large and solid, rooted deep in the ground, made to last through the ages. Probably the one building in Leeds that everyone could recognize.

What could Minuit do to it? He had eight sticks of dynamite, but that was nowhere near enough to bring the whole place down. It would take a whole string of Jerry bombs to turn it into rubble.

Doubts began to stab at her. Maybe she'd let her imagination run too far.

Then she looked up, peering from under the umbrella. The clock tower that she'd seen so often in her life. Sitting above it right at the top, the dome. She saw it and she knew. Minuit would go for that. Blow up the dome and you'd change the whole silhouette of Leeds. He'd make his mark.

The brief uncertainty fled. She was right. She could feel it in her bones. As sure as breathing.

Faulkner listened. 'We need to get a bomb disposal expert in, anyway,' he said. 'Someone who can tell us exactly what dynamite can do.'

'You don't think it's all airy-fairy?' Cathy asked.

'I think it's a possibility,' he replied cautiously, 'and we'd be fools not to investigate.'

'I agree,' Dan said. 'We need to check.'

She beamed, feeling the thud of her pulse. They both believed she might be right.

'Another thing,' her brother continued. 'He could probably manage it with a broken wrist.'

'Workmen must have access. The dome is above the clock.'

Faulkner was muttering into the telephone receiver. 'The Royal Engineers will have a lieutenant here at four,' he said when he'd finished.

'First of all, let me give you a few basics,' Lieutenant Robins said. He looked very young, Cathy thought. Probably barely into his twenties, with a pale, sandy moustache on his top lip to make him look older. But he seemed to know his subject. He reached into his leather jerkin, pulled out an object and casually tossed it on the desk. It took a moment to register. Then she gripped the chair arms, hearing the gasps around the room. Robins laughed.

'There you are. That's a stick of dynamite. Don't worry, it's completely harmless right now. But you can see what it looks like. They vary; this is what we use.' He turned to Faulkner. 'You said the man they were stolen from uses them for demolition.'

'That's right.' His voice was a croak, eyes fixed on the explosive.

'Theirs will be a little bigger. That weighs around half a pound. You need a detonator to set it off. A fuse. There are different types, but they all work the same way. They create a small explosion that triggers this bigger one. I know it doesn't look like much, but a stick of dynamite can do a hell of a lot of damage if it's placed properly.'

'What about eight of them?' George asked. 'What could they do?'

Robins stared at him, and his voice became very serious. 'In the right hands, possibly more than you want to imagine.'

He continued, becoming technical as he talked about the science, but Cathy had stopped listening. She'd heard enough. All she could do was stare at the explosive on the desk. After the soldier left, they stayed quiet for a moment, wrapped in their own fears.

'What kind of engineer is Minuit?' Terry asked. He lit a match and tried to make his pipe draw. A burning shred of tobacco fell on his suit jacket and he batted it off. 'Would he know how to use this stuff properly?'

'According to what he told us,' Dan replied, 'his background is heavy machines. But,' he added, 'he said he worked in a mine in Saarland when he was younger, helping to install some lifts. Mines use explosives. He very likely learned there.'

'You lot might be gung-ho about all this town hall idea,' Hartley said. 'I'm not so sure. You might as well say he's going to blow up Leeds bridge or somewhere in the railway station.' He glared at her. 'It's all guesswork.'

For once, she was pleased to hear his doubts. They needed to challenge everything.

'I don't know about the town hall, but I'm willing to believe he'll go after something in town,' Faulkner said a quarter of an hour later, when they'd finished talking. 'Why would he stay here otherwise?' He nodded at Hartley. 'Your ideas are good, too. We'll get the army to inspect the bridge and go through the station. I'd rather take precautions.'

'Minuit couldn't clamber all over the bridge even if he wanted,' George said quietly. 'Not after Cathy broke his wrist.'

She smiled to herself. It had been worth the bang on the head for that.

'That still leaves a few options.' Faulkner thought for a moment. 'If he wants to try to for the town hall dome, we can do something to stop that.'

'What?' Cathy asked.

'Have the council install a tall metal gate on the stairs. One with a good lock. If we ask for a rush job, they should be able to do that in the next day or so.'

'He's not a fool. He'll go for something military or industrial,' Hartley said. He placed a cigarette in his mouth and struck a match. 'Pound to a penny.'

'Maybe he will, but the army's covering those,' Faulkner reminded him. 'His chances would be slim. But I'll make sure the Forge and the factory stay on high alert.'

'I have to go and meet someone,' Dan said. In the doorway, he turned. 'We need to take precautions. That's sensible. But don't forget the most important part. We have to find Minuit. Find him and kill him.'

'Can you stay a minute?' Faulkner asked her as the squad left.

'What is it?'

He played with the packet of cigarettes, started to open it, then pushed it away.

'How sure do you feel about the town hall?'

'Sure?' Cathy wasn't sure how to answer. 'I don't know. All I can say is I saw it and I knew in my gut.'

'Intuition.'

'Something like that.'

'Bob has a point about the bridge or the railway station.'

'He does. There might be other places, too. But George was right; Minuit isn't in any fit state to be climbing around the girders and we're as certain as we can be that he doesn't have any help. Besides, he'd have to do it at night; someone would spot him otherwise.' She saw him nod. 'Think about it: if anything happened to either of those places, it could be explained away as an accident. There can't be any other explanation if he blows the top off the town hall.'

He closed his mouth and nodded slowly. 'I have to tell you, I hope you're wrong.'

'So do I.'

He held up Derek's report. 'Now, what about Jackie Connor? DS Johnson seems determined to nail him for this execution, whether he did it or not.'

'Jackie's as alone in the world as Minuit,' she said. 'Everyone he trusts has vanished without trace. He has nowhere left to run, and now this. You can bet he's heard what Johnson is doing from one of his police sources.'

'I don't doubt that.'

'Do you think the timing seems a little curious?' she asked.

'What do you mean?'

'Bob brings the petrol tanker back, still full. Then Frankie Weir's body turns up, bound and shot in the head. Connor's supposed to have done that while everything's falling apart.'

'You don't buy it?' Faulkner asked.

'No more than you do. It's like I said earlier: who gave Bob the tip about the petrol tanker? It was still full, wasn't it?'

'Yes.'

'I'm honestly not asking because I don't like the man. I just wonder if there's something else going on.'

He shrugged. 'We got lucky. I'll take that. Maybe there was a falling out among thieves. Someone could be trying to set Connor up with this Weir murder. I don't know and I don't care.

Let Johnson do his worst. If he can catch Connor, then we step in and spirit him away to stand trial for treason. Orders from the top.'

That wouldn't make SIB any friends in local CID.

'Murder or treason,' she said. 'He'd hang either way.'

He nodded. 'But this would be *our* result. Those are my orders. Along with a very curt reminder that we need to find Minuit and do it sharpish.'

Too many thoughts were spinning round her head as she knocked on Annie's door. The talking inside grew louder as someone pulled the blackout curtain aside. Pam, the older sister. Married to a gas fitter who'd joined the navy the day after war was declared. She'd moved home again after he was posted to sea, and was still working one of the big sewing machines at Burton's.

'Come on through, we're all in the kitchen. I've not seen you in ages.' Her face looked fuller, cheeks big and round, and one hand rested on her belly.

'How far along now?' Cathy asked.

Pam beamed with pride. 'Four months. Jack's last leave. Going to be grand to have a bairn around. Me mother can't wait. Come on. Oh.' She turned quickly. 'While I remember, I have some material that would suit you down to the ground. A pal at work gave it me, more than enough for a skirt. It's still in my locker at the factory.'

'Thank you.' Pam had always been generous, and the best seamstress of the lot of them.

The room was warm, damp with steam, a pot of water simmering on the range; it was good for Mrs Carter's lungs. She was a large woman, wrapped in a pinafore, a turban covering her hair. Her husband was a foreman at Hope Foundry, round-faced, with shirt sleeves rolled up to show thick forearms covered in scars from the hot metal.

'Sit yourself down, luv.' Mrs Carter felt the teapot. 'It's still hot if you fancy a cup, or our Annie has that bottle of mother's ruin she thinks I don't know about.'

'Give over.' Annie grinned. 'I know you've had a sniff or two from it while I've been away.' She turned to Cathy with a hangdog expression. 'Do you mind if it's a night in? They packed so much stuff in my brain today that I think it's going to burst. I don't even have the energy to change out of my uniform, and I have to report back to base first thing in the morning.'

'If she's too tired to chase fellas, you know it must be bad.' Pam laughed, taking a cigarette from the packet.

'That's fine. It's been a long day for me, too.' Too long. She was happy just to sit here. Cathy pulled off her headsquare.

Annie stared in horror. 'What have you been doing to your hair? You look like somebody dragged you backwards through a hedge.'

'I . . .' she began. Then: 'We've been busy. I thought these liberty cuts were supposed to last.'

'You still have to look after them a bit. Get yourself over here in the light. I'll pop upstairs for my stuff. I can't let you go walking round like that, I'll never be able to hold my head up. I hope Edna from the salon hasn't seen it.'

'No.'

Two hours, a couple of glasses of gin and tonic. Hair repaired; it looked better than ever, she thought as she examined it in the mirror. Plenty of gossip and laughter and putting the world to rights. A perfect way to chase away work for a while.

'What was your course about today?' Cathy asked as they stood in the hall, the first chance to talk on their own.

Annie tried to sound offhand, but she could hear the pride in her voice. 'Some new stuff the boffins have developed. Still hush-hush. They're going to train a few of us up on it. It means a week away down south.'

'Down south? That's posh. You're doing all right for yourself, aren't you? First the promotion and now this. You're really going places.'

'We'll see. I still reckon they picked me by mistake.'

'There was a plane went down last week . . .'

Annie nodded. 'One of ours. A training flight. We could see it was in trouble from the control tower, just shouted at Ronnie and Ted to bail out. Nothing left to salvage on the crate, but they're both fine. We can replace planes, but we can't afford to lose pilots.'

'At least they're safe. And you're going to be Auntie Annie.' The name made her laugh.

'Oh God, stop it.' She rolled her eyes. 'It makes me sound like an old maid. Me mam and dad will spoil the nipper rotten, and I won't get a wink of sleep on leave with all the feeding and crying.'

The sirens began, calling into the night. A glance up at the sky. Still some clouds, but not enough to deter a raid.

'I'd better make sure Da gets into the Anderson,' Cathy said. 'The hair looks a treat, it really does. Even better than last time. I can't thank you enough.'

A hug. 'You've got something big going on, too, don't you?'

'Is it that obvious?'

'How long have we known each other? You're all on edge. Tell me about it next time. Let me know when you need more stockings, too. Joe's good, gets them regularly.' She stepped back and gave the hair a final inspection. A palm to smooth the side. 'At least I won't be ashamed to be seen with you now.'

TWENTY-ONE

By the time she pushed the metal door aside her parents were in the shelter, wrapped up warm, already deep into a game of pontoon under the hurricane lamps.

'Where's Dan?' He'd come home with her on the tram.

'He had to go out again. How long ago was it, Henry?'

'An hour or so. Said he had to meet someone.'

Her mother frowned. Always the worrier. 'Do you think he's all right, Catherine?'

'I'm sure he's fine, Ma. He knows how to look after himself. There are shelters everywhere.'

Somewhere off in the distance she could hear the anti-aircraft guns firing and the thud as bombs hit. Nowhere close, and Cathy wondered if Leeds might escape again. Then the sound of the aircraft drew close and she knew. Steady, inescapable. They were here.

Her mother sat with her head back, as if she might be able to gaze all the way to the sky. Her father huddled in on himself, fingers tight around an enamel mug of cold tea. His eyes were clouded, caught in the memories of comrades and trenches.

Explosions rattled and thudded through the ground. Hunslet. Holbeck. Staying south of the river, thank God. Each second seemed to stretch into an hour. She held her breath, a trickle of cold sweat down her spine, praying the bombs wouldn't come any closer. Then . . . just as she exhaled, she heard the planes turn away. The drone became a hum and faded into the silence of the night.

The fire crews and rescue teams would be busy. Bobbies desperately trying to bring some sort of order.

Close to midnight when the all-clear finally sounded.

Her sleep was plagued by dreams of shadows and destruction.

'The council have promised a gate to shut off the clock and the dome. Someone up top must have put a rocket up them,' Faulkner chuckled and raised his eyebrows 'They *claim* it'll be done by dinnertime tomorrow.'

'Who's going to have keys, boss?' Terry asked.

'Whoever's in charge of maintenance at the town hall, the police, and a third one for us. Uniformed patrols to go in every day.'

Impressive on paper, but could it keep Minuit out? More important, was it really the target? Yesterday she'd felt certain enough to argue for it. Now the doubts were tip-toeing around the edges of her mind again.

'What's going on with Johnson and Connor?' she asked Smithy.

'You were right, there was nothing to see at Weetwood Lane. I think he wanted to show me he's on top of things.'

'Is he?' George Andrews asked.

'No. Johnson still believes he can track down Moore and Graham, too. I was tempted to tell him what had happened to them.' He shrugged and turned to Faulkner. 'All their narks are saying Connor's done a vanishing act.'

'It won't be for long. Something's going to break soon.'

Wasn't it?

Dan arrived not long after nine, wearing a clean shirt, washed and shaved, hair neatly combed.

'We have something,' he announced. She could hear the relief in his voice.

'Something concrete or a rumour?' Hartley asked.

'Definite. Minuit is still in Leeds.'

Nothing more than confirmation of what they knew. Janet Benson hadn't been seeing a ghost on the Headrow.

'Where?' Faulkner asked.

'We don't know. But his wrist is broken, and he's been scrambling round for days trying to track down Connor. No luck.'

'If *he* doesn't know where Jackie is . . .' Cathy said.

'Exactly. Your pal's on the run and he's left Minuit on his tod.' Dan waited as that sank in. 'One more thing. Minuit is now calling himself William Jackson. Known as Bill.'

She felt the excitement buzz around the room.

'Anything more?'

Dan shook his head. 'That's it for now.'

'He's bound to be staying somewhere in town,' Faulkner said. 'No more boltholes that we know that he can use. I know we've done this before, but we need to go round the hotels and guest houses again.'

'Lodging houses, too, boss?'

'Not yet,' he answered after a moment's thought. 'He still has money, remember, and he's passing himself off as respectable. He'll need somewhere he can scrub up properly. Work in pairs. Bob, you and Terry. George, you're with me. Cathy and Dan.' On the way out, he caught her arm and spoke quietly. 'Back here by one. We're going to the town hall.'

'You had a useful night,' she said to Dan as they strode up towards the small hotels along New Briggate that catered for performers from the Grand Theatre and the City Varieties.

'A long one. I must have made it home not long after you left for work.' He laughed. 'Just had time for a brush up, cup of tea and Ma's inquisition.'

They should use her to interrogate spies. 'That name . . .'

'It's definite.'

Cathy climbed the grand steps of the town hall. Up to the top floor of offices. Mr Rathbone, the chief maintenance engineer, unlocked a wooden door and disappeared through it. She looked at Faulkner. He shrugged. They followed.

The morning had felt like a waste of shoe leather. No hint of Minuit, Jackson, whatever name he was using, at any of the hotels she and Dan tried. She'd left him on the telephone to his bosses as she and Faulkner set out.

'This is the best spot to put up a door,' Rathbone said as he slapped a palm against the wall. 'Everything's very solid, we're not too high up. Easier for transporting the materials and tools. The Lord alone knows why you want it, though.'

'We had a tip,' Faulkner told him. 'Better not to take chances.'

'I daresay,' the man answered doubtfully. 'It'd be a rum devil who wanted to hurt this place, though. Even the Jerries haven't managed to hit it yet.'

Don't tempt fate, she thought.

'How soon will the door be installed?' Cathy asked.

'The way it's looking right now, miss, they'll have it in place tomorrow. They came in to measure it all up first thing. I'm sure you can see the problem, though. Can't bring it up here in one piece. Not enough room, you see. They'll be drilling and fitting to beat the band.'

He was a pleasant man, somewhere close to sixty, she guessed, with an easy, genial smile. Carefully trimmed eyebrows, no hair sprouting from his nostrils or ears. Someone who took pride in his appearance. White hair, a high gloss on his shoes, a watch chain in his waistcoat.

'Could we go further up?' Cathy asked.

'Course we can, miss.' Another climb, then he took a key from the ring he was carrying and unlocked a door. 'Step out and take a look if you like.' He grinned. 'Best view in Leeds.'

He was right, Cathy thought. She stood on the ledge outside the clock faces, holding on to the stone parapet that extended round the tower. Gusts of cold wind buffeted them, but she didn't care. This was better than standing on the roof of the Avro factory or Matthias Robinson's. Even with a hazy sky, she felt she could see for miles. It all stretched out before her. Across the river and off into the distance. On another side, the Civic Hall, then the university at the top of the hill. To the west, a view up the Aire valley towards Kirkstall. She knew she wasn't seeing the whole city, but it still seemed to go on forever. Smoke and soot and dirt. The tiny people and cars on the Headrow. It was wonderful. It was breathtaking.

'I never get tired of it,' Rathbone said. She'd been transfixed; she hadn't even realized he was standing beside her. 'Magnificent, isn't it?'

'Yes.' It seemed too small a word for everything she was feeling. Her home city, all laid out like this. How much would still be standing once the Luftwaffe really began hitting them? This would be something to carry in her memory.

'Come on,' the man said. 'I'll show you the dome. That's why you're here, after all.'

It was solid, no doubt about that. The Victorian builders had done a good job. Minuit would need a ladder of some sort to reach the very top with the explosives. Probably more difficult than he'd first imagined, especially with his wrist. Still, if he could manage it, eight sticks of dynamite had the power to turn the dome into rubble in an instant and let the sky pour in. She breathed in and out. There was no doubt in her mind now. Minuit wanted this place.

On the way back down, Rathbone gave them the history of the building. But Cathy wasn't listening. In her mind, she was seeing the view again. She would be for the rest of the day. Standing out there had been a rare privilege.

'Did you go out and take a look?' she asked Faulkner as they walked up the Headrow.

'Never had a head for heights. Do you still think he'll try and blow it up?'

'I'm certain he'll do his damnedest.' She turned and looked back. 'That place is part of Leeds, part of who we are. If he succeeds, he'll hurt us all. It's not something that could be fixed overnight, and you couldn't explain it away. We'd be living with it for a long time. A constant reminder.'

He sighed. 'Maybe so. But we can't afford to ignore all the other places.'

'No. I agree' She believed, she *knew*, but she saw Faulkner's face. He was right; they couldn't bank on this.

'If the council does get that gate in tomorrow, it'll help. But you saw that dome. With a broken wrist he'd have a hell of a job putting explosives in place. He might have taken a gander at it and decided to go after something easier. We don't know. That's the problem. He could have reverted to his original targets.'

'Then . . . we'd better hope we find him before he can do anything.' She frowned.

'We're right back where we began.' His voice was bleak. 'The only help is that Connor's problems and what you did to him are buying us time to catch him.'

'We haven't managed it yet.'

'Remember what your brother said: we can't afford to fail.'

'I know. I can hear the clock ticking. You can bet Dan does, too. Loud and clear.'

Cathy tuned the radio to the Forces Network after the news. Ambrose and his Orchestra, pleasant music in the background. A good way to wind down from the day.

She'd just pinned up the hem of a skirt she'd been working

on for months, ready to start sewing, when her mother said, 'The coalman was here today. He thinks coal will be on the ration by the end of the year.'

Very likely. If this war dragged on long enough, about the only thing they wouldn't need stamps for would be air. As her fingers moved, her mind returned to the clock tower, looking out over the city. A surprise, something to cherish for the rest of her life. If only she'd had a camera . . . but a few Kodak snaps would never capture it the same way.

'Do you know when our Daniel's coming home?'

'No, Ma.' He'd been gone when she returned to the office with Faulkner. No sign of him before she left for the day. Maybe he'd show up in the morning with a solid lead for the squad, something to put them firmly on the trail of Minuit, or Jackson, or whoever he was today. Maybe.

'That job keeps him busy, doesn't it?' her father asked in his whispering voice.

What could she tell him? Not the truth. 'He's quite important these days. If he carries on like this, he'll end up as one of the real brass.'

'A proper muckety-muck, eh? Who'd have thought that? He doesn't look happy, though.' He gave her a knowing look.

'Dan's under a lot of pressure, Da. Same as the rest of us.'

Her father nodded slowly. 'I'm sure it'll all work out.'

A smile and he picked up his paper again, peering through his spectacles at the pages. On the radio, Ambrose was leading the band through 'It's Time to Say Goodnight' as he wrapped up the broadcast. Cathy pushed a thimble on to her fingertip and continued sewing, and her mother tipped her head back and closed her eyes.

'We have an invitation,' Faulker told her as she entered the office and removed her headsquare.

'What do you mean?'

'Four o'clock at the town hall. The gate up to the tower. The council's showing it off and giving out the keys.' He grinned. 'It was your idea, so you can go and represent SIB.'

Cathy laughed. 'Sounds like a cracker. Champagne and canapés, too? Wouldn't miss it for the world.'

The others filed in. Everyone except Dan.

'Any sign of him this morning? He never came home.'

Faulkner shook his head as he glanced at his watch.

'You'd better get yourself off to Johnson's briefing,' he told Smithy. 'I'd like chapter and verse about what's going on there. If he has a lead on Connor.'

'On my way, boss.' He downed the rest of his tea and limped off, leaning on the walking stick.

'The rest of us . . . it's more of the same, unless Dan turns up with something good in the next two minutes. Hotels and guest houses again.' Cathy heard the protests; it was the last thing she wanted to do. 'Proper police work,' Faulkner told them. 'You haven't forgotten how to do that, have you?'

She was paired with George Andrews, going up around the university. Plenty of grand houses made over into guest houses or offices. Enough walking to take them through the morning.

She'd given up expecting anything until Mrs Speight on St John's Road spent a long time studying the photo of Minuit.

'I'm fairly sure it's him. William Jackson, you said.'

'That's right.' Her heart was fluttering. She glanced at George. He was staring intently at the woman.

'The one who's a guest here is called Wilson. His hair's a bit longer than it looks here, and he's growing a moustache. He must have a bad wrist. It's heavily bandaged. No pot on it, though.'

Cathy took a quick breath and glanced at George. 'The left one?'

'Yes.'

He'd arrived on Saturday, she told them. It was Wednesday now.

'That sounds like him,' Cathy said. Not a doubt in her mind.

'He said he's doing some research at the university,' the woman continued. 'Engineering. Very polite. Full board, breakfast and evening meal.'

'Which room is he in, Mrs Speight?'

'Number four. First floor back, looks over the garden. Shares a WC and bathroom.' A quick smile. 'They all do.'

'Could we have a look inside his room?' Cathy smiled. 'It's very important.'

'I don't know,' she answered warily. 'He's been no trouble at all. Paid in advance for a full week.' She straightened her back. 'What's he supposed to have done?'

'It's what he might do,' George said. 'Remember, there's a war on.'

The silence seemed to stretch out forever. The woman studied the photograph again, and Cathy's police warrant card next to it on the counter, before she made up her mind and reached for a bunch of keys.

TWENTY-TWO

'Sod all,' George said in disgust.

He was right. The room was tidy, bed made, blackouts drawn back to let in the daylight. But not a scrap to identify the man who was staying there. A single shirt in the wardrobe, tie, underwear and socks tucked into a drawer. A spare bandage for the wrist. A bottle of aspirin. Copies of yesterday's *Daily Sketch* and the *Manchester Guardian* on a table.

Minuit didn't have anything hidden here. Not under the bed or the mattress, taped behind the dressing table or the wardrobe. No false bottom in his suitcase. Everything completely ordinary and innocent.

As she searched, her heart leapt into her throat with every creak and noise in the building. The man was armed; at this stage he'd probably have little hesitation in shooting to escape.

'Time to give up?' Cathy asked after they'd gone over every inch of the room and left it looking the way it had when they entered.

'Might as well,' he sighed.

She returned the key to Mrs Speight. 'Please don't tell him we were here, or that anyone had been asking about him. It's important.'

The woman squinted, undecided for a moment before she nodded. 'Aye, all right, lovey. I'll do me best.'

Cathy called the office from the phone box on the corner.

'Stay right there,' Faulkner ordered. 'Your brother's here, we'll be over in a few minutes. Keep watch.'

'What if he comes back?'

'Wait for us. Whatever you do, make sure he doesn't leave.'

They made a pair, strolling along the block arm in arm, stopping to look at the shoots poking through the soil, enjoying the displays of daffodils in the gardens as the Humber glided to a stop beside them.

'Has he returned?' Faulkner asked.

'No,' Andrews replied. 'The woman who owns the place says he's shown up around six the last two nights, not gone out again.'

'Nothing useful in his room,' Cathy picked up the thread. 'The landlady said there'd been nothing in the waste basket.'

Dan leaned forward from the back seat. 'Was he carrying a briefcase?'

'Yes.'

'He's not a fool. He's going to be suspicious of everything, and he'll make sure he's always ready to run.' He opened the door and stepped out. Bob Hartley followed.

'Minuit knows Dan,' she said.

'I can give a positive identification.' He raised the collar of his overcoat and pulled down the brim of his hat.

'He's evidently growing a moustache, but we know it's him.'

Cathy stared at him. 'What are you going to do?'

'Kill him,' he said simply.

'What?' She was open-mouthed with disbelief. 'Right here in the middle of the street?'

'Somewhere quiet.' His voice remained calm. 'We have people who make the body disappear and clean up.'

'That's . . .' Cathy struggled to find the word.

'That's war.'

The metal gate in the town hall tower was sturdy; the workmen had done a fast, solid job. A uniformed inspector from the police took his key, signing the book with a grand flourish. Cathy wrote her name in a rounded hand and Rathbone the maintenance engineer put his initials on the paper.

'Happy?' he asked.

'That should keep anyone out,' she said. It was impressive; Minuit would need to be able to pick locks to get past it. She started back down the steps, then turned.

'When was it last checked up there?'

Rathbone thought, running a hand over his hair.

'There should have been a patrol late yesterday, but I wasn't here, so I can't say for certain.'

'Today?'

He shook his head. 'No need. The workmen arrived first thing. Why?'

'Would you mind if I took a look?'

An indulgent smile. 'Go ahead if you want. But I doubt it's changed since you saw it.' He took out a torch and flicked it on. 'The battery's good. Just leave it at the desk downstairs.'

It felt strange to be all alone up here. She could make out the faint echo of people below, but as she climbed the steps it was eerie, too full of shadows.

Standing by the gate she'd felt a sudden grip of fear. What if the spy had crept in during the night and hidden his explosives in the dome? A quick look, just to satisfy herself. Otherwise it would stop her sleeping. Probably stupid, but . . .

She'd locked the gate behind her; nobody would have a chance to take her by surprise. She paused every few steps, playing the torch beam all around, eyes searching for anything at all.

By the clock, she looked longingly at the door to the ledge, wishing she could go out for one more look at Leeds. A small sigh and she moved on.

The air was still and cold. The torch gave the only light. The corners were filled with cobwebs and rat droppings. But nothing left by man.

She went as high as she could. The dome was empty. She examined every crevice the light could pick out, but no dynamite. So much for her imagination. Stupid, anyway. If he'd brought it up here, he'd have tried to set it off. No sense in waiting. The inspection had set her mind at ease.

At the desk, she handed the torch to the watchman. Standing on the front steps of the town hall, brushing off a cobweb and patting the head of the stone lion for luck, she breathed deep. The air felt fresh and welcome after the stuffiness of the tower. Very soon it would be dark. She could already make out the faint light from the slitted headlamps of the cars passing along the Headrow. Time to go back to the office to drop off the key, then home. Her legs ached from the day's walking.

She saw the man approaching, crossing Calverley Street towards Victoria Square, looking as if he was on his way to the town hall. As his left hand swung, she caught a glimpse of a bandage on the wrist. He wore an overcoat, hat on his head, just like thousands of others, the shade of a brown moustache on his upper lip, and in his right hand he was carrying a briefcase. He glanced up, noticed her and veered away. So smoothly done that it almost looked natural.

Almost.

It was Minuit.

Cathy tied on her headscarf and she hurried down the steps. At least it would offer some kind of disguise.

He was moving away from her in long, quick strides. Already he'd nearly reached Great George Street.

This was him, the man who'd knocked her out. The one who'd battered Daisy Barker. With his broken wrist, a loaded pistol in his pocket and eight sticks of dynamite somewhere. It was sheer luck that she'd come out at the wrong moment for him.

'SIB.' Faulkner's voice, weary and disheartened. A thin, crackling connection. She had to shout to make herself heard.

'I've just seen Minuit.'

'What? Where?'

She told him how it had happened. 'I think he's probably heading back to the hotel.'

'Dan and George can catch him there.' He was trying to keep the eagerness out of his voice. 'You did right not to follow.'

'Thank you.' The sensible thing, she thought. Even if she'd caught him up what could she have done to a man with a gun? She had her police whistle, but it would have taken too long for a bobby to arrive.

A pause on the other end of the line, just a fraction of a second. 'Are you absolutely positive it was him?'

'Yes.' Somehow, he'd recognized her and turned away. Nobody else. It was Minuit. 'Look, there's nothing hidden in the tower. I just checked it myself.'

'Christ,' he said as he took her meaning.

'He might have stashed it somewhere else. Exactly.'

She felt as if she could hear him thinking.

'I'm going to call the police and the bomb disposal people and tell them we've had an anonymous tip there might be explosives somewhere inside the town hall. They can roust out the maintenance staff, too. You wait there and team up with their officers in charge. No mention of spies or any of that.'

'Of course. Just make sure you get him.'

'We will. I'll send Smithy over to help, too. You know what to do.'

She did: wait. She'd grown used to that. Cathy knew she wouldn't be going home for a few hours yet.

She stood in the growing darkness with Detective Sergeant Gilchrist and Sergeant Benjamin, a cocky Welshman with a lilt to his voice, in charge of the bomb disposal squad that was combing the town hall room by room.

'If there's anything in there, my men will find it,' he said with a grin. 'Better than a pack of bloodhounds, they are.'

'We need to search everywhere,' Cathy told him.

'Don't you worry.' Another grin.

There had been plenty of curious looks when the police first went through the building, calmly telling everyone to leave. No panic, though. It was a little after five, nothing more than a slightly early finish to a Wednesday afternoon.

It had taken twenty minutes from the time she called Faulkner for the police to arrive, another five for the soldiers. Not long after, Smithy appeared.

'Everything in hand?'

'As much as it can be,' she told him. 'We just stand around and let them get on with it. Just think, you could still be at home, enjoying all the comforts.'

He laughed, pushing the glasses up his nose. 'Chance would be a fine thing. My wife made a fuss, but she's very big on duty. She's on the board at our church. As soon as the doctor gave the nod, she was on at me to come back.' A sigh. 'I don't mind, really. I'm happy to do my bit. I just wish I didn't have to see Johnson.'

'Overbearing?'

He snorted. 'Like having a steam roller go over you again and again. That squad of his takes every word he says as gospel, and half of it's complete rubbish.' A small, mild shrug. 'Not our business, anyway.'

'Is he close to catching Connor?'

'He keeps saying he is, but I don't believe a word.'

A corporal came through the front door of the town hall and spoke softly to his sergeant.

'Right. Carry on.'

'They've cleared most of the rooms up to that gate,' Benjamin said. 'Just the basement and the great hall to go now.'

The worst parts. The government had opened one of the British restaurants in the basement. Plenty of places to hide dynamite down there. The hall . . .

'The organ,' she said. The men turned to look at her. 'There's a big organ at the back of the hall. All those pipes.'

'We'll take care of it, don't you worry,' Benjamin told her.

Another half-hour of standing in the cold, darkness rising around them. Making small talk, aware of the men working inside. Constantly watching for Faulkner to turn up with news about Minuit. But he never came. Finally the soldiers marched out, the bobbies behind them.

'Found four sticks, sir,' the corporal said to the sergeant.

'Only four?' Cathy asked. A shudder of fear ran through her. 'Eight were stolen.'

'Only four in there, miss,' the corporal leading the squad said. 'I'd stake my life on it. Two hidden away in a toilet at the back of the restaurant, the others behind the organ.'

'What about fuses?' Cathy asked, trying to remember the jargon. 'Detonators?'

'Nothing, miss. If you want my guess, he was taking it in bit by bit, looking for places to keep it out of sight.'

That made sense. What had Minuit intended to do in the town hall today? What had he been carrying in the briefcase?

Benjamin's voice interrupted her thoughts. 'Are you positive there are eight missing?'

'Yes,' she replied, glancing over her shoulder at the building.

'Take the men back in there, Corporal. Tear the place apart until you're sure there's nothing else in there.'

'Very good, sir,' the man answered. 'You said you'd looked beyond the gate, miss?'

'This afternoon.'

'If you have the key, we'll take another dekko.' He gave her a kindly smile. 'It can't hurt. We are the professionals.'

'Yes,' she agreed. 'Yes, of course.' Eyes trained to search. In case she'd missed something. They needed to find those remaining sticks.

She stood, feeling cold and starting to shiver. Nothing to do with the temperature. Fear.

'I'm going to ring the office,' she said. Maybe they'd caught Minuit and the danger was over. God, she hoped they had. She was so tense she thought she'd shatter at the slightest touch.

The telephone box stood on the other side of the Headrow. But when she dialled, the number just rang and rang.

'Well?' Smithy asked.

'Nobody there.' She tried to smile, but it was a weak, sad effort.

Another hour and a half. Deep into the night now. Hardly any traffic, very few people walking around. Plenty of clouds to deter the bombers. At least that was something.

Finally the corporal appeared again, the others behind him. Solemnly, he returned the key to Cathy.

He saluted his sergeant. 'Not a dickie bird, sir. There isn't an inch we haven't examined now.'

Benjamin looked at her and the police sergeant. 'My men are good,' he said. 'I'd back them to the hilt. If they say there's nothing more, I believe them. No detonators either, Corporal?'

'No, sir.'

'Without those, the dynamite's useless.' He drew himself up. 'We'll take what we've found back to the barracks.'

'Thank you.'

'Glad to help. It's something different, a bit of excitement. Maybe talk about it over a drink sometime?'

She smiled and nodded vaguely. The soldiers marched off to their lorry. The police had already vanished.

'You get that a lot?' Smithy asked.

'What? The flirting? Oh, he probably tries it on with every woman he meets.' She'd paid it no mind. Too many other things to fill her thoughts.

'At least you were right about the town hall.'

'Just not right enough.' There were still four sticks of dynamite and the fuses missing. Minuit must have been keeping a second target in mind. And still no word about him. No Faulkner driving up in the Humber. She had a sinking feeling in the pit of her stomach. Somehow, the spy had escaped again.

* * *

Quarter past ten by the time the tram began to rattle and shake its way up York Road. The office had been empty when she returned. She'd scribbled a brief report for Faulkner. As she finished, a wave of exhaustion crashed over her.

She knew bad dreams lay ahead, but she needed to sleep. She was drained, no use to man nor beast without a few hours of rest.

The house was quiet, her parents already in bed. The door to Dan's room stood open, but there was no sign of him.

She'd barely closed her eyes when the questions began: What if the engineers had missed something? How could they be completely sure? They were only human. Where was the rest of the dynamite? Where was Minuit?

TWENTY-THREE

The men looked as if they'd been awake all night, too. Unshaven, bags under their eyes, suits creased and rumpled and the worse for wear, they arrived from the canteen with mugs of tea. All except Terry Davis, keeping watch on the hotel in St John's Road.

Cathy sprang up, searching their faces. Desperate to know. 'Did you get him?'

Dan shook his head. 'He never came back to his hotel. We spent the night looking everywhere we could think of.'

'He's gone to ground somewhere,' Faulkner added. 'Maybe seeing you worried him. Would you swear it was Minuit you saw?'

One of the questions that had broken her sleep. 'No doubt. Right down to the bandaged wrist. And he was heading towards the town hall.'

She explained what the bomb disposal men had found, watching as their expressions harden it horror as they listened. George Andrews lit a fresh cigarette from the nub of the last.

'Still four sticks missing,' he muttered.

'Along with the detonators,' Smithy added. 'I was there; those men were thorough. It means he can still go after another target.' He looked around apologetically. 'I need to get to Johnson's morning briefing on Connor. Not that there'll be anything to learn.' He gathered up his walking stick and left.

'Minuit could be going back to the Forge or the Avro place,' Hartley said, but Faulkner shook his head.

'It's too late. They're both too well protected now. We've cut him off from the town hall. Just in time, it seems. But he's no fool, he'll have some backups.' He turned and looked at Dan. 'Do your people have a list of other possible targets?'

'The government has prepared lists of military targets for every town in the country. I saw the one for Leeds before I came up here. The other main ones are the Royal Ordnance plant in

Crossgates. Barnbow. They fill shells, and there's another in Thorp Arch near Wetherby that does much the same thing. Fairbairn Lawson on Wellington Street. They produce guns and armour.'

Faulkner was writing the names. 'Is that the lot?'

'The Olympia works on Roundhay Road. That's the Blackburn aircraft plant,' Dan replied. 'But we considered them all to be lesser targets than Kirkstall and Yeadon.'

'Lists don't mean a thing,' Cathy told him. 'You didn't have the town hall, but he was going after it.'

He dipped his head in acknowledgement.

'We need to see these places,' Faulkner said. 'George, you and Bob take Fairbairn Lawson. Make sure their security is up to snuff.'

'We can probably forget Thorp Arch,' Cathy said. 'It's too far out. He'd need a car or have to haul his stuff on the bus.'

'We'll leave that one for now. Barnbow and Olympia.' Faulkner glanced at her. 'You and me.'

'After last night, I need to spend some time on the phone to my office,' Dan said. He looked subdued. Minuit had outfoxed him again.

'Which one do you fancy first?' Faulkner asked as Cathy turned the key in the Humber's ignition.

'Olympia works,' she said. No reason beyond some familiarity; for years she'd passed it when she'd taken the tram to Roundhay Park. As she sat down to drive, the screwdriver they kept between the seat and the back pushed into her hip. They didn't need it now the car was working properly. She jammed it further into the gap. That was more comfortable.

The air had a faint haze. Better than last November, when the fogs had been bad. Policemen in white coats and gauntlets on point duty, flaring gas fires beside them so they could be seen. Half of Leeds with bronchitic coughs. At least it would be spring soon, whatever that brought.

Blackburn Aviation had a sprawling site, she thought as they pulled into the car park. Bigger than she remembered but nowhere near the size of Avro or the Forge. It couldn't be. There wasn't the same kind of space in the city, hemmed in on one side by the main road, and a steep, wooded hill rising sharply behind the works.

Just a couple of hundred yards down the street was the Astoria ballroom, the old Palais de Danse where she'd spent her share of Saturday nights. Then Harehills, with its densely packed streets of through terraces and back-to-backs. Any explosion here could cause devastation.

The assistant director of the works was named James Pascoe, a man with a damp handshake and a constant blink, who gave them the tour.

'We mostly build Sharks and Baffins and Ripons here,' he explained. 'Not as glamorous as bombers, I know, but all vital for the war effort.'

'What other security do you have besides the gate and the fence all around?' Faulkner asked when they'd finished.

'Nothing.' He blinked. 'We haven't needed more than that.'

'You do. Much more. We've had a tip that someone might attempt some sabotage, and this place would be ripe for it.'

She watched as Pascoe's face turned pale. 'You mean a fifth columnist?'

'Something like that. Ring Carlton barracks this morning and ask them to send out a unit.' He paused for a second. 'Better than anything bad happening, isn't it, sir?'

'Yes. God, yes. Thank you.'

'What do you think?' he asked as they headed for Crossgates.

'I'd say it's a miracle someone hasn't already strolled in and destroyed the place. Half the supplies must walk away from there every week. It's like a colander.'

'If Minuit was going after that, he'd have already done it and been on his way without any problem. At least the army should sort them out. What about this other place?'

'Barnbow? They made shells in the last war. There was a big explosion, killed thirty-five women. It happened not long after I was born. Quite a scandal, they kept it secret for years.'

'National security?' he asked.

'Yes.' Cathy turned off the road and pulled up by the barrier where a pair of soldiers with rifles kept watch.

Faulkner smiled and held up his identification. 'Sergeants Adam Faulkner and Cathy Marsden, Special Investigation Branch. We'd like to see the head of security, please.'

'Nothing to worry about there,' Cathy said as she drove down York Road and back into Leeds. The place had been a cacophony of banging metal and voices, with the radio playing in the background. Like Blackburn Aviation, most of the workers were women.

'They've done an impressive job of keeping it safe,' he agreed. 'But that leaves a big question, doesn't it?'

'What he's going to do with the rest of the explosives.'

'Yes.' He nodded towards the city that lay hazy in the smoke of factory chimneys at the bottom of the hill. 'You're the one who knows Leeds. I need you to think of something.'

'We're doing it again,' she complained. 'We're flailing around. Trying to second-guess him.'

His eyes flickered towards her. 'It worked with the town hall.'

They'd been lucky there. Inspired. She'd taken a guess and come up with the single piece of truth among the cesspit of lies that surrounded Minuit. Then there was Connor, with his treachery. Selling his country out to the Germans for the right price. Greed and not a scrap of honour in his soul.

It was enough to make her wonder if there was anything in the world that wasn't for sale.

'Is the army checking the bridges?' she asked as they walked along Commercial Street after parking the car.

'They said they would.'

'We should ask them. Have them look at all of them,' she added. 'Mind you, Minuit won't be climbing around himself . . .'

'No,' Faulkner said with satisfaction.

A thought came to her. 'What if he's managed to find Connor again?'

Dan was sleeping, arms making a pillow for his head on the desk. He stirred as they entered, blinking, trying to stifle a yawn, and gazing around uncertainly.

'Has anybody else been back?' Faulkner asked.

'Not yet.' Her brother's voice was thick, not quite awake. He looked curiously young as sat up and pushed the hair off his forehead. The boy she remembered from all those years ago.

'Why don't you go and relieve Terry watching the hotel?' Faulkner said to her. 'No need to give it more than a couple of hours. I doubt Minuit will be back.'

No, Cathy thought as she walked across town. He was too wary for that. He'd rather walk around with just the clothes on his back than be caught. Things could be replaced. Easy to do with the money he had.

And he might still have four sticks of dynamite stashed somewhere. Enough to create plenty of damage and destruction.

She had time to think as she stood on St John's Road. Terry had been glad to see her, hunched in his overcoat and looking miserable after so many hours.

'First thing, I'm going to find a café and get myself warm,' he said as he rubbed his hands together in anticipation. 'I'll stay there until I can feel the heat all the way to my bones.' He pointed into the distance. 'You'd better keep away from that corner down there. The wind rattles past. I thought it was going to take my skin off.'

'No sign of him?'

'Not a whisper. I know we have to do it, but the whole thing here is a waste of time.'

By the middle of the afternoon Minuit hadn't returned, and Cathy felt as if she'd worn a groove on the pavement after walking up and down so much. At least the weather was a little warmer, another tease of spring with the clouds still low and thick.

The office was full, thick with the smells of tobacco, Brylcreem, and stale sweat. Everybody there but Dan.

They were no further along than they'd been at the start of the day.

'Fairbairn Lawson was a waste of time,' Bob Hartley said. 'The place is tight as a drum. As loud as hell inside. What are we going to do? Start checking every bloody building in Leeds?'

'We're going to do whatever has to be done,' Faulkner told him, then turned to Derek Smith. 'How are things moving with CID and Connor?'

'If you listen to Johnson, they're on the verge of arresting him.'

'Are they?'

Smithy shook his head. 'Not a chance. It's all smoke. His squad's loyal, but even they admit it's all talk. They say it very quietly, of course. They don't have much.'

'Not much, or nothing?' Cathy asked.

'Nothing.'

Faulkner looked at her for a moment, then said, 'I want you all to try and imagine this. The worst of all possible worlds. Connor out there, back together with Minuit. It's probably not that way, but it's possible.' He waited just long enough for the idea to sink into their heads. 'We all need to rest. Go and think about it and we'll have a bright, early start tomorrow.'

As she was leaving, he called her back.

'No more inspiration on targets?'

'Not yet.'

'Keep working on it. We need all the help we can get. He has to know his time's running out.'

'That was very tasty, Ma,' Cathy said as she pushed the empty bowl away. Mutton stew, ready when she walked through the door. The two letters sitting on the stairs would have to wait. One from Annie, with her big, looped handwriting. But it was the other that she was desperate to read. From Tom.

'It was, and all,' her father agreed. For once he'd eaten everything in front of him.

'The butcher let me have a lovely piece of scrag end,' she said. 'Mind you, I'd been queueing three-quarters of an hour to see what he had. The greengrocer on the parade had just had some forced rhubarb delivered, so I've done us rhubarb bread pudding from one of the Ministry pamphlets for afters.' Worry flickered in her eyes. 'Do you know when our Daniel's going to be home?'

'No idea, Ma. I haven't seen him.'

'It doesn't matter, Edith,' her father said. 'They're both caught up in something important. Right, luv?'

'Yes, Da.'

She was patient, washing and drying the pots and putting them all away before carrying through the tea tray, then rushing upstairs to her bedroom, snuggling under the covers and opening the envelope. He must have been able to send it when the troop ship stopped at Gibraltar. Her eyes picked it out on the map she'd pinned to the wall. An impossibly small speck.

> Dear Cathy,
> I've been feeling all at sea for a few days, but it hasn't been bad. Evidently this was the hardest part, or so I've been told. I hope it's true. At least we're warmer now, down to shirtsleeves and getting a bit brown. Mostly it's been boring, not much to do besides sit around and play cards. Plenty have been groaning and going green, and that's with it apparently moderately calm.
> Didn't see any of the other side on the way here, and we were all relieved at that. We've been given our orders, and quite a way to go yet. This is a very short break, a chance to stretch our legs where the ground doesn't move under you, and to get this letter on its way.
> I've written to my mum and dad, too, and a postcard to the old garage in Leeds. Not much point in your replying to me until we're settled. I don't know how it would find me. Pity, I'd love to hear from you. I miss you a lot. Nothing like a real separation to make you realize how you feel, is there, and this looks set to be a long one.
> Lots of love,
> Tom

She smiled, bringing the paper to her face, hoping she might be able to draw in the scent of him. But there was nothing. He was safe, that was the important part. By now he was probably in a barracks somewhere, sweating in the desert heat.

He missed her. God knew she wished he was here. They'd go out to the Majestic or the Scala again and dance the evening away. Pick up where they'd left off before he put on a uniform. Some day . . . how many women in Britain were sitting and thinking the same thing? Wives, girlfriends, all wishing this would end and their men would come home safe.

Annie's letter was barely more than a note.

Dear Cathy,
Remember I told you about the course? Got my orders this morning, all my warrants for travel and everything. No point in saying where, the censor will just cut it anyway. Honestly, I'm a bit scared. I'm a hairdresser, not one of these with a brain for this important stuff. I told you I keep telling them they've made a mistake, confused me with someone else, and I'll end up feeling like a complete fool and bawled out by the CO when I get back.

Cross your fingers for me. When I have my bit of leave we'll go out and make a proper night of it. Oh, pop round our house when you can. Pam said she'd brought home that material for you.

Love,
Annie

Another smile. Annie always seemed to arrive at full speed. She closed her eyes for a moment, hearing the song drifting up from the radio downstairs. 'Annie Doesn't Live Here Any More'. She chuckled. Good timing.

TWENTY-FOUR

He must have crept into the house while she was asleep with no siren to disturb her. Dan appeared at the breakfast table looking sleek, washed and shaved, hair neat. But his eyes were still sunken, the flesh stretched tight across his face. He avoided her gaze, making small talk with his parents before going to fetch his briefcase.

He'd already reached the end of the path by the time she'd buttoned up her coat and grabbed her little case with the flask and sandwiches for firewatching. With that, her handbag and gas mask case, she was laden like a pack horse.

'Hang about,' she called, and Dan turned, a flash of annoyance crossing his face.

'Get a move on, then,' he said. 'You had a busy day yesterday,' he said as she hurried to keep pace.

'We're all busy. What about you? Did you dredge up anything worthwhile?'

He gave a bitter shake of the head. 'I spent most of the day with my agent. We went around every single one of his contacts. Our friend's vanished off the face of the earth.'

'You know he hasn't,' she said. 'He's still right here.'

Dan stayed silent for a while as they walked to the tram stop. He looked tormented; something was tearing him apart inside.

'My people are running out of patience.'

'What? The XX bosses? Out of patience with you?'

He nodded.

'How do you mean? You're still here.'

'They'd have probably replaced me already, except half our people are out with flu. As soon as enough of them recover, they'll be sending someone else.'

Now she understood why he'd been short with her. No need to say the word; it would be ringing loud and clear in his head. Failure. The golden boy tarnished. He'd pay the price for it, a career that would tumble into oblivion.

How much had it taken for him to admit that to her, of all people? She wasn't sure how to respond. No point in sympathy; he'd never accept it.

'What if we find him before that?'

'Then everything will be forgiven and forgotten.' A sad, hopeless smile. 'Not much chance, though, is there?'

'You can't say that. Things keep happening.'

'Not the right ones. Every time we've come close, he's been too quick for us.'

Nothing more until they reached the office, the first ones there.

'Are you going to tell the others?' she asked.

'Faulkner knows. That's enough.' He stared at her. 'I'd appreciate it if you didn't say a word, either. Especially to Mum and Dad.'

'Mouth shut,' she promised. 'And maybe . . .'

'No,' he told her. 'Don't.'

He'd never failed at anything in his life. He'd kept climbing higher and higher, and now the abyss had opened up, right in front of him.

Smithy had gone to Superintendent Johnson's morning briefing.

'Someone gave me a tip yesterday evening,' Bob Hartley said. He swallowed the last of his tea. Cathy glanced at Faulkner, but his eyes showed nothing. 'I was in the Duncan and got talking. A lead to someone who might know where to find Jackie Connor. Don't know if it'll come to anything.'

'Take Terry with you,' Faulkner said. They shrugged into their overcoats, tapped down their hats and left the office.

'I had a thought,' she said.

'Places Minuit might try to destroy?' He lit a cigarette and blew a plume of smoke up to the ceiling.

'There's the market, everybody knows about it, and it's looked grand ever since it went up. But I don't think he could do it.'

'Still possible.' Faulkner began to write. 'Anything else?'

'The Corn Exchange. Then there are the churches: The Parish Church, St John's, Holy Trinity. Four sticks of dynamite could easily bring down the spire, and it would fall on to Boar Lane. You know how much traffic goes along there. Pedestrians, too.'

'I'll contact the engineers. They can search those places today.'

'Then something else occurred to me,' she continued. 'What if Connor had kept a stick or two for himself?' For a few seconds the room was silent. 'Would you put it past him?'

'No,' he replied slowly. 'I wouldn't.'

'If you're right, we don't know how much Minuit and Connor each have,' George said. He raised his eyes and gazed at her. 'Or what they might do with them.'

'There's one more thing,' Cathy said. She had their complete attention. Time to air the ideas that had arrived when she lay awake during the small hours. 'They found the explosive at the town hall, but no detonators. Why wouldn't he hide them there, too? About the only thing I can come up with is that Connor hadn't given them to him before his world collapsed.'

'I'm not so sure about that,' Faulkner said.

'I'm not, either, but it would help explain why Minuit hasn't done anything. I had all sorts of strange theories firing through my head. Maybe Jackie thought he had the Germans over a barrel and they'd pay him more.'

George let out a low whistle. 'Holding the Jerries to ransom. That would be a bloody dangerous game.'

'Guesswork,' Faulkner said. 'We can ask him when we find him.' He paused. 'But we're no closer to that. Fingers crossed that Bob comes up trumps again, or Johnson gets some kind of break. I had headquarters blistering my ear again this morning. We need Connor, we need Minuit, and we need them yesterday.'

Cathy walked. She showed the spy's photograph to people. All she got in return was a shake of the head, a quick no, and her sense of frustration building.

She didn't want her brother to fail. The pain, the fear on his face when he told her . . . she couldn't ease it. Words wouldn't help. The only way was to find Minuit and do it quickly.

But there was nothing.

The café was tucked in the middle of the dilapidated block of New Briggate between the chest clinic and the dispensary, just down from the Wrens, a hundred yards from the little park on North Street where an anti-aircraft gun sat, pointing at the clouds.

The place was always busy; hardly a surprise when there was never a shortage of meat in their food. Every scrap of it black market. But it was a place where coppers and councillors never had to pay for their meals; who was going to do anything to close it down?

The shepherd's pie warmed her after a morning outside, rich enough with lamb to leave her feeling full and lazy. She'd been aware of someone cautiously eyeing her, the boy who moved around, clearing the plates and wiping the tables. No more than fourteen or fifteen, on his first job after leaving school.

She scraped up the last of the mashed potato and put down her knife and fork. He was there in a few seconds.

'All done?'

His hands were very clean, the skin puckered; he must wash all the pots, too. Spots across his face, fiery red blotches. Poor lad; she remembered those years.

'Yes, thank you.'

'You're Sergeant Marsden, in't you?'

Cathy studied him again. She was sure she'd never come across him when she was in uniform. How did he know she was a copper?

'That's right,' she replied warily.

He grinned. 'No charge for the force.' He nodded towards the man standing over the stove. 'Mr Turnbull's policy.'

'Thank you,' she repeated. It seemed the least she could say.

The boy glanced around and lowered his voice. 'You remember Polly?'

Polly? There had been so many names since she began with the police. Ten or fifteen Pollys at least.

'Polly Barlow,' he prompted. 'From the club.'

In a snap, Cathy placed her. One of the young women taken into custody from the Glory Club. Held overnight because she didn't have her identification card. Taken home, with Cathy and George threatening the father who'd raped her.

'I do.'

'She's our Jessie's best mate. My sister,' he explained. 'We live next door but one. Everybody's grateful for what you done there.'

'I'm glad it helped.'

'The old sod won't dare show his face on the street for a long time. Not if he wants to keep his teeth.'

It was all in the open now; sooner or later someone would give Polly's father a taste of his own medicine.

Still, Cathy raised her eyebrows. 'I think it's safer if nobody mentions anything like that.'

He nodded, suddenly looking older than his years. Frowning, as if he was about to say something, then thoughtful.

'Why don't you pop back for your dinner tomorrow? Chicken pie. It's proper chicken.'

A curious invitation. 'I'll try.'

'You should,' he told her. 'You really should.'

Nothing in the afternoon, the day ending with Dan looking glum and alone in the office. As she left, Cathy put a hand on his shoulder. He shrugged it off, never glancing at her.

Brenda had already reported for firewatching duty. But last week's desperation had vanished. She looked to be bursting with news.

'You must have heard from him.'

She nodded. 'The letter arrived last Saturday.' Her eyes were gleaming with joy. 'Bobby's on his way home.'

Cathy put on the helmet, set out the stirrup pump and buckets. Everything in order, ready, but she doubted they'd be needed; the cloud cover was too thick. Not even fully dark yet, and not as cold as last week. Maybe spring was on the horizon.

'What happened?' she asked once they'd settled back inside the building.

'It was hard to piece it together because of the censor, but he was in an accident and his leg was badly broken. They're sending him back to England for more treatment. Rehabilitation, they said.'

Relief seemed to radiate from her.

'Is he going to stay with you?'

'I don't know yet. But he'll be over here, won't he? Close, not thousands of miles away. And he's not dying.'

Cathy squeezed her hand. No sense in telling her the injury must be bad if he needed rehabilitation in England. Bobby's war was probably over. 'I'm really pleased for you.'

A quiet shift, exactly what she'd expected. Her parents were in bed, lights off, when she climbed the stairs. Dan's room was empty.

She'd made no mention of the young man in the café. Growing as bad as Bob Hartley, she thought, keeping quiet about her sources. But what was there to tell? Nothing more than a strange invitation to have some chicken pie.

It teased her mind all through a fruitless Saturday morning. What did she have to lose? At the very worst, she'd have a free meal.

Cathy had just begun to eat when she looked up and saw a young woman standing by the table, looking down at her.

'Do you mind if I sit here?'

'Help yourself.'

She took off her headsquare and shook out her hair, pale and curly. Nobody Cathy recognized, in her late teens, maybe nudging into her twenties.

A grateful nod when the boy brought her a cup of tea. She spooned in some of the sugar substitute and made a face as she drank.

'This stuff tastes awful, doesn't it?' She smiled. 'I should do without. Just habit.' A pause. 'You're Sergeant Marsden.'

'Yes.' The whole world seemed to know her name.

'My name's Jessie.' Her eyes flickered towards the counter. 'My brother said you'd been in. Polly Barlow's my best friend.'

'How is she?'

'Better now. Found herself a decent second job, usherette at the Gaiety cinema down on Roundhay Road. Her dad's never going to lay a hand on her again. The whole street saw you drive up. Me and Robbie were watching from the window.' She grinned. 'Better than going to the pictures.'

'I'm pleased things are better for her.' She wondered where this was heading.

Jessie glanced around to check nobody was listening.

'I've got a boyfriend.' A frown. 'Sort of, anyway. His name's Ciaran. He's not the steady kind. Works for all sorts of people.'

'Anyone in particular?'

'A few things for Jackie Connor.' She let the name dangle long enough to light a cigarette and blow out smoke. 'You're with the Special Investigation Branch, aren't you?'

Interesting. Very few would know that, or what it meant. 'I am. We're looking for him. He's disappeared.'

The young woman nodded. 'Jackie can be hard to find when he wants. Ciaran's been taking him things. He has an old banger of a car, delivers stuff, you know. I went with him on Thursday night. Out in the middle of nowhere.'

Cathy felt a twitch of her pulse, tightness in her chest.

'Where?'

Jessie simply smiled.

'Why are you telling me?'

'You were good to Pol. She was so grateful when she came round to see me, burst into tears. Do you have a friend like that? Someone you'd do anything for?'

She thought of Annie. 'Yes.'

'Then you know what it's like. Me dad left just after Robbie was born. Tiny little thing when he came out. Said a shrimp like that couldn't be his.' She stubbed out the cigarette with short, angry strokes. 'Me and Polly, we were born the same year. Always lived in the same street. Same school, everything. She told me what was going on, but I didn't have a dad who could go round there. You're the first one who really helped.'

She finished speaking, drained the cup, making a face, and pushed a folded piece of paper across the table.

Before Cathy could say anything, Jessie had gone.

She rushed through the rest of the meal, the paper feeling like it was burning a hole in her pocket. Back in the office, she opened it. An address, neatly written in a girlish hand.

Nobody else around, no idea where they'd all gone. Nothing to do but wait. Sometimes luck showed up when you least expected it.

It was close to four o'clock when a despondent Faulkner arrived with Smithy and George Andrews. She'd spent two hours watching the hands on the clock crawl round.

'Connor,' she said. It was enough.

'You know where he is?'

She held up the scrap of paper. 'This is where he was the night before last.'

He studied the address and looked at the map. 'How did you find out?'

'Someone who wanted to repay a good deed George and I did for a young woman,' she replied. Understanding dawned on Andrews' face. 'Completely out of the blue.'

'Reliable?'

She'd weighed that during the afternoon, examining the exchanges she'd had with Jessie and her brother. The woman seemed honest, sincere, wanting to pay a debt. So earnest. If she was that good an actress, she'd be in films, not living in Harehills. Then again, Minuit had conned Dan and an experienced interrogator. In the end, it came down to a guess. Placing a lot of trust in someone she'd never met before. That and her gut feeling.

'I think she's kosher.'

'It's very convenient, isn't it?' Faulkner said. 'We're looking, getting nowhere, and this comes up.'

'I know,' she agreed. 'I've thought about that.' She gave a weak smile. 'I'm not a big believer in luck, but . . .'

'How did she know we're looking for Connor?' She saw the doubt on his face, but he was right to be sceptical.

'Come on, boss, it's hardly a secret,' Smithy told him. 'Us, Johnson, probably half of bloody Leeds is hunting him.'

'She knew I was SIB.'

That was enough to keep them quiet for a few seconds.

'You're the one who talked to her,' Faulkner said eventually. 'Do we go with it?'

Cathy felt the crackle of tension in the air. 'We have to, don't we? It's a chance to find him.'

'It could be a set-up.'

'That's possible,' Cathy replied. Who knew what might be waiting for them?

'We'll never know if we don't look,' George said. Silently, she thanked him.

'This address,' Faulkner said slowly, playing with the piece of paper. 'Do you know it?'

She shook her head. 'About the only thing I can tell you is it's out near Eccup reservoir. Probably a farmhouse, something like that.'

'Anyone with him?'

'No idea.'

'There's no chance of finding out who owns it today. We'd

better pray that this woman told you the truth.' Faulkner pursed his lips then exhaled slowly. 'It'll be pitch dark by the time we can get everyone together and find the place. I'm not going to risk going in at night when we haven't even seen it. As soon as it's light tomorrow. With a little luck, he'll still be asleep. Everyone in dark clothes.' A smile. No suits for once. 'George, you had that bit of commando training, didn't you?'

'If you can call it that. Just a two-week course before they decided I'd be better in the military police.'

'You still have more idea than the rest of us: you're in charge.'

'What about me?' Derek Smith asked. 'The leg . . .'

'You get to stay warm in the car and coordinate everything.' He looked at Cathy. 'I'll pick you and your brother up at half past five. Be ready.'

Things were moving fast. They were close; she could feel it. See it in the way everyone looked. 'We will.'

'I'll tell the others when they show up.'

TWENTY-FIVE

Cathy waited in the half-light, hidden by a tree. The house stood twenty yards away, a farm with some smaller buildings around a small yard. The blackout curtains were closed, no sign of life inside.

George had done a very quick recce after they arrived. Nothing to indicate whether Connor was really here.

'No farm equipment at all, but there's a car in the barn.' His grin was wicked. 'I disconnected two of the sparking plugs. Nobody will be escaping that way.'

They'd had to tramp over some rough ground. Fields that had become overgrown. Nobody was working this land. She was glad of the trousers, the shoes she'd worn on the beat and her dark police greatcoat to cover everything. Warm and practical, even if it wasn't as glamorous as the material she'd collected from Pam the evening before, the rich, dark blue velvet with tiny white stars.

'Three yards. Ample for a skirt. As soon as I saw it, I thought it would suit you down to the ground. You'll look a right bobby dazzler.'

'It's gorgeous.' It really was. Wonderfully soft, a perfect colour. But . . . 'Why doesn't she want it?'

Pam hesitated, pulling on her cigarette. 'She was given quite a bit and she's used it for a few things. I think it might have vanished from somewhere. You know what I mean.'

Passing stolen goods to a copper . . . it was funny. Everyone had a little fiddle and this was too lovely to refuse. No one would ever know.

She listened to the day coming awake all around her. The crows and the magpies. All the others would be waiting for the signal. There was no cover close to the farmhouse. If someone inside decided to start firing . . . better not to think about that.

She could see Dan, wearing his coat and hat and a dark jumper, one of four figures crouching against the side of the house. He'd been quiet at home last night and silent in the car as they drove around out here to be sure they were in the right place.

This had to be it. The only one around.

Had Jessie told her the truth? They'd find out soon.

Hartley's tip had come to nothing. Another dead end. This was the only thing they had.

The plan was ramshackle. Go in through the windows in case Connor had booby-trapped the doors. After that, room by room until they found him.

If he was there. The words none of them spoke.

A soft whistle, hardly any louder than a bird call, and the men began to move. She heard the sharp sound of breaking glass and saw them climbing in.

Cathy held her breath, expecting gunfire. But the silence returned.

Faulkner had ordered her to stay back, to be ready in case someone tried to run. Her mouth was dry. She watched as the light grew.

'He's been there,' George said. He gulped down smoke, taking deep drags on his cigarette as he paced around the Humber. All the tension was starting to drain from him. 'He must have left last night. Yesterday morning's newspaper on the table, plates in the sink. No layer of dust anywhere. The lights and the water still work.'

'Anything to show Minuit had been with him?' Cathy asked.

'Couldn't tell,' Terry told her.

'No surprises waiting?'

'Nothing,' Faulkner said. He stood with his hands in his pockets, kicking at the dirt in front of his feet. 'Someone must have tipped him off.'

Had Jessie set them up? She found that hard to believe. Yet if it wasn't her, the only people who knew about the raid were the members of the squad.

And it couldn't have been any of them. Could it?

She looked around at the dark, scowling faces. Impossible. Not even Bob Hartley would do that.

'Anything useful inside?'

'We picked up everything we saw,' Terry told her. 'Not much. No spare clothes in the drawer or the wardrobe.'

'Come on,' Faulkner said wearily. 'We might as well go to the office.'

'I'm looking for Jessie.'

The woman looked her up and down. 'Wrong house, luv. Four doors along.'

Cathy knocked and waited. Eyes would be watching. Some would remember her. Nothing to be done about that. She was here to find out if the girl had tricked her.

It was her brother who answered, the one who worked in the café. Robbie.

His face was bruised and cut. He held himself carefully, as if every part of his body hurt. She eased past him and closed the door.

'What happened?'

The voice from the top of the stairs made her turn.

'Someone saw me talking to you yesterday. They thought Robbie might know what it was about. They beat it out of him. Made me watch.' Jessie sounded calm, holding in the anger that burned behind her eyes. 'It's Sunday. Me mam's gone to church.'

Cathy turned back to the boy. 'Who did it?'

'Ciaran Burns.' Jessie spat the words. 'Jackie's helper. My boyfriend. Was.'

'Where do I find him?'

'Marsh Lane tenements. Number four. He lives with his parents and two sisters.'

Cathy put her hands on the boy's shoulders. 'I'm sorry,' she said.

'What about Ciaran?' Jessie asked. 'Is he going to be sorry, too?'

'Has he had his call-up papers?'

'He laughed about ignoring them. Thought it made him a hard man.'

A deserter and a criminal. That could make him SIB business.

'Then he's going to wish he'd never been born.'

They stood on Duke Street, close to the blocks of flats that extended up Marsh Lane. Right by the start of the Bank, the area where so many Irish had settled and their descendants still lived. The block was solidly built, the brickwork blackened by years of smoke. Large posters on the gable end advertised Swan Vesta matches and Bisto gravy, as if the country was still at peace and life was normal.

But the wreckage from the goods station nearby gave the lie to that. Bomb damage scattered far and wide. Piles of rubble. Metal twisted and thrown into grotesque sculptures. A few days since the last raid, but the smell of destruction and charred wood still hung low in the air. The stark reminders of war. A miracle the block hadn't been hit.

'You know what to do,' Faulkner said.

Cathy nodded. She'd knock on the door of number four, big Terry Davis right behind her. Show the warrant card and ask for Ciaran. Dan and George would be waiting in case he tried to slip off down the back stairs. The boss and Bob Hartley at the front.

'He can lead us to Connor and Connor can give us Minuit.' They felt like the first words Dan had spoken all morning. 'Let me question him.' Some ghost lurked behind his gaze. 'We need this wrapped up.'

This was his final chance. Ciaran Burns could be his lifeline. She thought about those bruises and cuts on Jessie's brother. The work of a bully.

Cathy felt Mrs Burns's fists hammering against her back as Terry dragged Ciaran from the flat and down the stairs. Blows from something harder, and the woman screamed and cursed until they were safely away from the block.

The young man was bundled between the members of the squad, suddenly looking very young and frightened. Cathy saw a rusted Morris parked down the street. Burns wouldn't be driving his old banger again for a few years.

'Deserter, are you?' Hartley asked, his face inches from Ciaran.

A dull, confused nod as an answer.

Dan grabbed the young man's shoulder, made him turn.

'Where's Jackie Connor?'

Cathy felt Ciaran looking at her, beseeching. She thought of Robbie's face and turned away.

'He'll kill me.'

'No, he won't.' Her brother's voice was menacing, as dark as night. 'Trust me on that one. Not when we're done with him. And you're going to tell us where to find him.'

They had him. He'd tell Dan everything. It wouldn't take long. Threats would be enough; the young man was petrified, his bravado all gone. She didn't want to be there to watch.

'I'll walk back to the office.'

'Are you sure?' Faulkner's eyes flickered towards the tenements. 'Will you be safe?'

She nodded towards the flats. 'They're done.'

'As soon as we know . . .'

'I'll be ready.'

She walked, happy to feel pavement under her feet after an early morning in the countryside. Streets, roads, they felt familiar. Comforting. Where she belonged.

It wasn't too far, up Kirkgate, past people going to the morning service at the Parish Church, then along the empty street. She had time to think.

Connor had beaten them again. He'd kept one step ahead. But that wasn't going to last. Cathy glanced at her watch. Half past nine. They'd be questioning Ciaran Burns for a little while yet. Ample time to have something to eat and drink in the canteen at work.

She'd only been back in the office for five minutes when the others filed in. Barely time to make herself look presentable.

'Did he tell you?'

'Yes,' Faulkner said. 'A quarter of an hour and he was happy to give us everything. Not much of a hard man after all.'

She glanced at Dan. He wore a shadowy, secret smile.

'What did you do with him?' She'd promised Jessie that Ciaran would pay for giving her brother a beating.

'Gave him to the military police at Carlton barracks. He's going to have a few months of hard labour in the glasshouse before he learns to be a soldier. After that, we drove past the address he gave us. He's supposed to take Jackie some whisky this afternoon.'

'Very handy,' Cathy said. 'Where is it?'

She stood outside Marshall's mill, squinting at the upstairs windows of one of the terraced houses on the other side of the road. Ready to shout a warning if Connor appeared with a gun when the squad knocked on the door of number six. Sunday morning, the only day of rest, and hardly a soul around. Someone along the street was playing Glenn Miller's 'Moonlight Serenade' on a gramophone. She hummed along as she stood, waiting and ready.

Dan and Terry Davis strolled around the corner, pausing for a second to stare at the Temple Mill, with its front looking as if it had come from ancient Egypt. A comment, a nod, and they moved on.

Stopping in front of the house. Terry stood to the side as Dan knocked on the door. Cathy held her breath, eyes on the windows upstairs, ready to yell at the slightest movement.

This was it. The certainty raged through her. Another minute and they'd finally have Jackie Connor.

A question from inside, then Dan gave the password Ciaran Burns had told him. She saw the door crack open before Dan forced it wide, Terry barging in right behind him, a gun in his hand.

She gave a long, low whistle, the signal for the rest of the squad, then hurried down the street and into the house.

Cathy noticed the pinafore draped over the back of a chair by the table and the copy of *Woman's Own* poking out from the magazine rack. Someone had let Connor use their house.

The man was kneeling on the floor, wrists cuffed behind his back. He was in his shirtsleeves; it was warm in the room with a good fire burning in the hearth. A stony, defiant stare on his face.

'Nobody upstairs,' Hartley called, then she heard his feet clatter back down.

'We're not going to do anything with him here,' Dan said. 'We'll take him to the safe house. No close neighbours to hear him there.'

No threat; just a matter of fact statement. Connor's face was stone.

She studied him. He didn't seem nervous, although he had to know what would happen in the end: a hangman's noose.

She felt let down. Months of pursuit had ended as easily as this. No fight in him, no resistance. He hadn't even been carrying a weapon. No chance to run this time.

She'd built him up in her mind for so long that he'd almost become a myth, something too big to be real. Someone with the devil's luck to preserve him; she'd seen that when she chased him through the Leylands and into the market.

In the end he'd been as ordinary as everyone else. Brought down in a single moment.

Connor had been the hard man. The boss who had his fingers in everything across Leeds. A deserter, a man who betrayed his country for a few pounds.

Now he had nothing. His men were gone, his empire had turned to sand, and he didn't know how it had happened.

Through the open door, she heard the Humber draw up outside, engine purring. Dan and Terry bustled Connor into the back seat.

'Coming?' Faulkner asked.

Cathy shook her head. The questioning was going to be brutal. Dan needed information, and he had to have it quickly. They'd do well enough without her.

'I'll poke around and see if I can discover who lives here. It might be useful for later. He persuaded someone to let him use the house.'

'Your brother will crack him.'

She had no doubt about that. Too much depended on it. It was the only way he might catch Minuit and avoid going back to London in disgrace.

'Make sure you're around later. As soon as we know . . .'

'Of course.'

The house was a back-to-back; Connor couldn't have slipped out another way, even if he'd wanted. Now to find out who lived here. Letters and bills were stacked behind the clock on the mantelpiece. The same as every house she knew. Habit; her parents did it.

John and Victoria Dobson. She knew his name. A small-time crook who had done jobs for a few gangs. Too old for conscription. If Connor was relying on people like him and Ciaran Burns, he was scraping the barrel.

Up the stairs. One larger room, the old mattress on the double bed sagging in the middle. The other was smaller. She could smell him in here. The hair oil, the sweat. Cigarette butts in an ashtray with *A Souvenir of Scarborough* in faded paint around the rim.

A leather valise sat on the floor. Locked. Downstairs she found a knife and forced the catch; Connor wasn't going to complain.

Cathy pulled out a shirt, a pair of socks rolled into a ball. Underwear. Beneath them, a notebook and some papers held together with string. She smiled. Something to keep her busy in the office while the others were asking their questions.

TWENTY-SIX

The telephone ripped through her concentration. She'd gone through the notebook, jotting down information, then moved on to the papers. With this, they should be able to wind up every single one of Connor's dealings.

'Special Investigation Branch, Sergeant Marsden.'

'It's Faulkner. What are you doing?'

She started to tell him, but he interrupted.

'Sounds like nothing that can't wait. I need you to come up here.'

A wave of panic caught at her throat. 'Why? What's happened?'

'You'll understand when you get here.'

'Dan—'

'He needs you here more than anybody. The house is on Clarendon Road. Called . . . what is it? Wild Dene. It's on the gateposts.'

'Now?' she asked, but the line was dead.

A grey afternoon. Not raining, but dampness in the air as she hurried along the street. A long road, with the old graveyard up at the top on one side, and Woodhouse Moor on the other.

The houses were solid, detached, a way to show off the owners' wealth. But the war had reached them, too. The carefully tended front gardens had become a tangle. No staff to deal with them. With petrol so tightly rationed, the cars were probably on blocks in the garages.

She'd been walking a good five minutes before she reached Wild Dene. The name was etched sharply into the stone. Another long drive, the house imposing. When she'd been a beat copper she'd sometimes had to call at places like this. They always made her feel small. But that was the intention.

Cathy rapped on the door. It was opened by woman she'd never seen before. Middle-aged, with a hard, suspicious mouth and penetrating eyes. Her hair was drawn back in a bun.

'Sergeant Marsden?' She inspected the warrant card and pointed down the hall. 'Second door on the right.'

It had been a grand room once. Sparsely furnished now. Bare, scarred floorboards. A cheap table and chairs, an old cloth-covered settee in front of the fireplace. At least that was in good order, keeping the room warm.

Most of the squad was there: Smithy leaning on his stick, George, Terry, Faulkner. Easy enough to guess what Bob Hartley and her brother were doing. Cathy shrugged off her coat and untied her headsquare.

She looked at their faces. 'Why do you need me here so urgently? Has something happened?'

'It's Connor,' Faulkner said. Her heart lurched. Had Dan killed him? 'He wants to talk to you.'

'Me?' It sounded like a joke, but they all looked deadly serious. 'Why me? He doesn't even know who I am.'

'He does, name and rank. He was impressed by the way you chased him that day. That you didn't give up.'

She'd never been likely to do that when it was their best chance of catching him. But in the end she'd failed.

'They've been working on him,' George told her. 'Getting damn all in return.'

'He says he'll tell you everything. But only you.'

She was dazed. Why would Jackie Connor want to talk to her? She didn't believe his reason, not for one second. But they needed answers to stop Minuit. *Dan* needed them. Time was running out.

'Where is he?'

'In the cellar. You'll want your coat, it's chilly down there.'

A steep flight of wooden steps led down from the kitchen into a well-lit, open area. Things were stored, covered by sheets turning black with mould at the edges. Ahead, a closed door. Every muscle was taut, every nerve jangling. If someone touched her now, she'd scream.

Cathy knocked.

Dan pulled it open. He was sweating, eyes wild, a man barely holding on to control. Not the person she knew. He took hold of her arms and pushed her back from the door. She heard it close behind him.

'I don't know why he wants you, but he insists on it.' He spoke quickly. 'We dragged a few things out of him but he says he'll only tell the rest to you.' He paused, drawing in a breath. 'He claims he knows where we can find Minuit. I don't care about anything else. Just get that from him. You understand?'

There was desperation on his face. Her brother hated having to rely on her. He needed her to do something he hadn't managed himself.

'Yes.' She didn't hesitate. 'How badly have you hurt him?'

'Enough.' He turned away, not looking at her. 'He's not in any fit state to attack you.'

'Good. You'd better get Bob out of there.'

'I need to know everything he says. Every word.'

'You will.'

She didn't want this responsibility. She hated it. Catching Minuit rested on her shoulders. One more thing that came with this job.

Hartley emerged, glaring daggers at her. 'Go on, see if you have any luck.'

Her chest was tight. Cathy felt she could hardly breathe. She stepped inside and closed the door.

The room was larger than she'd expected, about twelve feet by twelve. A flagstone floor, bricks for the back wall. Lit by a single bulb.

Jackie Connor was sitting on a hard-backed chair, looking straight at her. Just a man, no master criminal. In pain from the beating he'd received. Unable to outrun her now. Someone who knew his time was ebbing away. After all she'd ever imagined about him, there was nothing to scare her at all.

'Sergeant Marsden.'

His voice was thick, lips swollen. Nostrils crusted with drying blood, cuts across his cheeks.

'They gave you a pasting.'

He tried to shrug and winced at the pain. 'Not the first I've had. Comes with what I do. I knew the odds when I started.' He gave a small cough, turned his head and spat. 'Your brother's good. Nowt like that other one. He just likes to hurt.'

Nothing fancy about his accent. Pure Leeds, even broader than hers. Money hadn't changed that. Curious, she asked: 'Where did you grow up?'

'The Bank,' he said, surprised at the question. 'What about you?'

'Quarry Hill.' A stone's throw from him. Like it or not, they had beginnings in common. Things they both naturally understood.

He chuckled. 'That brother of yours, too? He's tried to hide it behind his airs and graces.'

'Why did you want me here?'

'To remind them I have a price.' His eyes shone. 'That I still have a little power.'

'And I'm your price?'

'That's it. You're a good runner, too.' The way he said it make it seem like enough. 'I thought you were going to catch me.'

'I didn't, though, didn't I?' She could admit it to him. Who was he ever going to tell?

'It were you who found that place in Woodhouse, weren't it? Dottie told you?'

'Yes.' It was safe to say. He'd never be able to hurt her now.

'And you must have put two and two together to come up with Ciaran Burns.'

'Does it matter?'

'Happen not. I like to know what happened, though.'

Enough talk. Maybe he really wanted to know. Or perhaps he was stringing her along to give the spy time to escape. She shivered in the cold of the cellar.

'Minuit,' she said.

'It were all carefully arranged. The right person to fool everyone. He's clever. Very dangerous. The bugger even scared me a few times.'

'Where is he?'

Connor continued as if he hadn't heard her. 'The money were too good to refuse. It was a game to play. The club, buying into the demolition company and stealing them explosives.'

'But no detonators.'

'Oh, I got 'em.' He had a sly gleam in his eyes. 'Held 'em back. Told the Jerries they'd have to fork out more. Minuit threatened to kill me. I laughed in his face. Told him if I was dead, he'd never have them. They paid up in the end.'

Greed. As simple as that.

'They only found four sticks of dynamite at the town hall.'

Connor tried to shrug; it seemed too painful. 'Ask him. I passed over all eight. As soon as he saw the Forge and that factory were too well guarded, he needed somewhere else. He was the one who came up with the town hall.'

That answered one thing. Now the big question. 'Where is he?'

He smiled, showing gaps where two of his teeth had been.

'Is it worth my life?'

'I'm not the one who can make that kind of promise.'

'I know.' Another grin. 'But tell me anyway. Lie to me.'

Could she do it? He was a deserter, a criminal. He'd hurt people, probably had a few killed. Worst of all, he'd betrayed his country. Did he deserve anything? Dan's face flickered through her mind. The information would save him. Was it worth a lie to do that?

Or was it simply a game, one final joke? Another show of power to let him pit sister against brother.

She ran her tongue over her lips to moisten them, feeling him watching, intent on every small movement she made.

TWENTY-SEVEN

'No.'

He laughed, an ugly sight with his damaged mouth. Over very quickly as his face creased in pain and he pressed down on his ribs; broken, at a guess.

'I had a bet with meself,' he said once he'd caught his breath. 'Said you'd turn me down. Glad I can be right sometimes.'

'Now what?' Cathy asked. She didn't know what he was going to do, couldn't predict it from the expression he wore.

'You were honest, so you win the prize. I'm going to tell you where Jan Minuit is going to be until nine o'clock tomorrow morning.'

'He's adamant that Minuit won't be moving before tomorrow morning,' Cathy said. 'Connor's supposed to go and hand over the detonators. He's still got them hidden.' The others listened in silence. Eyes full of hope and anticipation. It could all be over soon. 'The spy was leaving messages all over. Jackie finally contacted him. He's promised to bring the detonators, and more money to help him escape. The plan is to show up at the place where Minuit's been hiding before nine tomorrow morning. Everything open and in the daylight. Minuit will hold on until he realizes Jackie won't be coming.'

'It gives us a few hours to plan,' Dan said.

'Go in and take him as soon as it's dark.' Bob Hartley paced around the room. 'He won't be expecting us.'

'No.' Faulkner's voice was sharp. 'We're going to go in properly prepared. Where is he, Cathy?'

'An empty workshop in one of those streets between Whitehall Road and the river. Just out from the city centre.'

'Do you think Connor told you the truth?' George asked.

'Yes.' The man seemed to have tired of everything, ready for it to be over. She glanced at her brother. 'Why don't we keep him handy, just in case?'

Dan nodded.

'We need a careful look at this place, and then we'd better keep watch in case he tries to slip out during the night,' Faulkner said. 'We have good maps in the office.'

It was dark outside as the Humber came to life and nosed through the streets towards Briggate. Every one of them silent, locked in their own thoughts.

She wanted her own revenge on the spy. For the knock to the head, still an occasional twinge to remind her now. And for what he did to Daisy Barker. She hadn't forgotten that.

A dank, drizzly Sunday evening. A quick look at the area, keeping out of sight of the workshop where Minuit was hiding. Not a soul around in the back streets that spidered down between Whitehall Road to the water. The roads were broken, neglected cobbles, the flagstones damp. A touch of fog and she could have been walking into a horror film.

With these clouds, they'd have no raid tonight. How long before the next one? Or the big one?

A few more hours and this should be finished. Her brother would escape the axe. He'd been quiet since she climbed the steps from the cellar. Listening. Thinking. Knowing how much depended on everything falling just right.

Connor . . . like she told them, he knew he'd been defeated. He'd stopped wriggling and accepted what was going to happen. No complaints or last-minute pleas for mercy. In a grudging way, she had to admire him for that. As she said goodbye, he'd given her a final, broken smile.

'See?' he said. 'You didn't fail.'

Maybe. Maybe not. The jury was still out on that.

The air in the office felt brittle.

George and Bob Hartley were keeping watch on the workshop. At midnight, Dan and Terry would replace them. Four o'clock, she and Faulkner would take over. With his stick and his bad leg, Smithy would escape standing in the cold.

Cathy took the Georgette Heyer novel from her bag. It could fill the dead hours and carry her away from all this. Ten minutes and she put it away; the words couldn't weave their magic tonight.

Her mind couldn't settle to anything. Even thinking about the pattern for a skirt from the material Pam had given her didn't help.

Connor still seemed willing to talk after he'd given her Minuit's address. Why not? She'd never see him again. She had a few more questions to ask.

'Where have you hidden the fuses?'

A small shake of his head. 'Not saying. It doesn't matter. Minuit will never have them.'

'Frankie Weir. Was that you?'

His chuckle became a cough. When it subsided, he said, 'Dozy beggar. He had it coming.'

Cathy stiffened as he reached into his pocket, but he only brought out a packet of Gold Flake. His fingers were trembling from the effort of striking a match.

'Why? What had he done?'

'He threatened to tell your lot where to find me unless I gave him some brass.' His eyes flashed. 'Couldn't be having that, could I? Not someone like him trying to put the squeeze on me. I arranged to meet him. You know what he did? He bragged to me about letting one of your mob know where to find the petrol tanker. Deserved what he got just for that.' Well, well, she thought. Now she knew who Hartley's informant had been. Past tense. 'One shot and that was it. Nothing to it.'

'Johnson thinks you did it, but he doesn't have any evidence.'

Connor grinned. 'He couldn't find his arse with both hands and a map.' He stopped suddenly, a blush rising in his cheeks. 'Excuse my French.'

Terry sat silent, gazing at nothing as he puffed on his pipe. For a moment, Cathy wished she smoked. It might help. But with their father's ruined lungs, she and Dan had never picked up the habit. Probably the only kids on Quarry Hill who hadn't.

Was this how soldiers felt before combat? Willing the time away while they also prayed for the hands on the clock to stay still?

Smithy pulled a deck of cards from the desk and began to play patience. At quarter to twelve, Terry knocked the tobacco from his pipe into the ashtray. He and Dan stood, wrapped themselves in their overcoats and hats, and disappeared without a word. She watched them go, heard the soft click of the door closing and the faint sound as they moved towards the stairs.

Half an hour and Cathy raised her head, hearing a low mutter of voices. George and Bob, coming in and trying to shake the chill from their clothes.

'Any sign?' she asked. Words. Something, anything to break the oppressive silence.

'Not a peep,' George Andrews replied. 'Impossible to tell if he's in there or Connor's been playing us for fools.'

Hartley stared at her. 'Maybe he thought you'd be more gullible than the rest of us.'

'Enough.' A single, sharp word from Faulkner and the silence returned.

She must have dozed. It had been a long day. Cathy was exhausted. She felt as if she'd barely paused since the early start at Eccup. The scrape of a chair woke her, bleary-eyed, unsure where she was for a moment, the first stirring of a headache where Minuit had hit her. Her mouth felt like a sewer. Cathy reached for her mug, swilled the tea dregs around and swallowed them. Not much better.

Half past three. She stretched out her back in the chair. She remembered looking at the clock a little before two. Her head felt clearer. She glanced at Faulkner. He was awake and alert. Of course. Always on top of every single thing; she wasn't sure how he managed it.

Twenty-five to four.

Twenty to. Another look at Faulkner. He raised his eyebrows and she nodded. She buttoned up her police greatcoat. For a second, she considered taking the gas mask case. No. Too cumbersome, and the Jerries wouldn't be coming tonight. A deep breath. She was ready.

The night air had a clammy edge; she felt dampness against her face. As she walked, a melody sprang from nowhere, keeping pace with her footsteps. 'I'm Getting Sentimental Over You'. The first song she and Tom had ever danced to, the night they'd met at the Majestic. A flood of thoughts arrived: had he reached North Africa yet? She had no idea how long the sea journey would take. Would the ship be safer in the Mediterranean? Where would he be in the desert?

She felt the fears start to crowd around her mind.

'You're miles away,' Faulkner said quietly.

'Sorry.' She managed an apologetic smile.

'For what it's worth, I believe Minuit's in there. But if we try to force our way in, it's going to end up like something out of a Western film. He doesn't have anything to lose. I'm not going to take that kind of risk with people I command.'

'What, then? Wait for him to come out?' she asked.

'It's going to be very tricky, however we do it. That seems the least dangerous way.'

'Nine o'clock,' Cathy said. 'Whitehall Road will be busy. What does Dan say?'

'We haven't talked about it.'

'It's his operation.'

'And my squad.'

'He told me they're going to send someone to replace him.'

'He told me. He's going to be hoping against hope that Minuit's in there. I don't want you torn between family and squad.'

'I don't know if I can be anything else,' she answered. But . . .'

'We're here.'

Dan was waiting, hidden from the workshop by the next building.

'I'm going to stay,' he said.

'Go back to the office. Take a break for a few hours,' Faulkner told him. 'You'll be dead on your feet.'

He held up his hand, rattling a tiny bottle. 'I'm fine. Our agent gave me these.'

Dexedrine. She'd heard about them from some of the troops who'd returned from Dunkirk. Little pills to keep them awake and sharp. And alive. In his place, maybe she'd be swallowing something, too.

'Then keep quiet and stay still,' Faulkner ordered. 'Watch the back of the building – there's a way out.'

'All we bloody need,' he muttered once her brother had gone.

Cathy stood on her own, deep in the shadows, keeping watch on the front of the workshop with its big double doors. No sign of movement, but Minuit was too professional to give himself away. Nothing would happen until close to nine. And then what?

Far in the back of her mind the song began to play again. 'I'm Getting Sentimental Over You'.

These were the worst hours: nothing happening, but they still had to keep alert and ready. She'd never done any surveillance when she was in uniform. Nothing more than walking a beat and supervising women police constables.

She shifted her weight from foot to foot, trying to keep the numbness out of her legs and the cold from the rest of her. It was worse than firewatching, and still a few hours to go. A plain clothes officer had once told her that his job was hours of boredom leading up to a minute of action. Tonight she truly understood the boredom. It deadened the brain.

A solitary vehicle passed on Whitehall Road, the thin slit of headlights picking out the black and white markings on the kerb. The only sound to disturb the night. It faded to nothing.

Another quarter of an hour and she heard the thin snap of a twig. Cathy melted deeper into the shadows, holding her breath.

'It's me.' Faulkner's voice, a whisper that barely carried a few feet. 'Anything?'

'No.'

'I've just spoken to Dan. He's as on edge as anyone can get without exploding.'

'Can't you send him back to the office?' she hissed.

Maybe he shook his head; his body was lost in the night. 'I don't have any power over him.'

'Is he a liability?'

'When we go for Minuit, keep an eye on him.'

'I'll try.'

'Good. Why don't you walk around for a few minutes? I'll watch here.'

The offer was welcome. Her footsteps echoed along the empty streets. Leeds was quiet, the clouds hanging thick over the city. As she walked, she kept glancing over her shoulder. Nobody at all. Cathy checked her watch. Almost half past five; she'd only been out here for an hour and a half. Ten minutes and she was back, ready to carry on. As Faulkner faded off into the blackness, she felt refreshed.

* * *

What was Minuit doing in there? Trying to sleep? Pacing around, anxious, checking his gun, thinking through all the possibilities. The chess player, planning four or five moves ahead.

She felt the lightening of the sky before she saw it. A few objects began to take on vague form. Cathy moved to a place where she couldn't be spotted but could still see the front of the building.

Then the day seemed to arrive in a rush. Blink, and black turned into grey. Blink again and it was close to full light.

Soon.

Her nerves were ready to scream. She knew they'd calm as soon as things started to happen, once she was moving.

This was where it was going to end. Finally.

Traffic was beginning to move along the road. The metal rhythm of tram wheels, the hiss of tyres. Monday. A new week for most. Another day for her.

The rest of the squad would arrive soon. The Humber would be parked somewhere close, ready to make the spy disappear. The men would be positioned all around the workshop to stop Minuit making an early escape.

She kept her eyes on the doors, willing something to happen. Still only seven o'clock in the morning. Two hours. How was she going to last that long?

'The boss sent me to relieve you.' The voice made her jump. Just Terry Davis, moving silently for a big man. 'Half an hour for something to eat and a hot drink. There's a café a hundred yards down the road.' He grinned. 'Don't worry, we'll keep the fun until you get back.'

Grateful, she hurried away, blending with a mass of people alighting from the early bus. Half of them looked up, checking the skies. They'd become a nation of watchers, connoisseurs of clouds. But their lives depended on it.

Powdered scrambled eggs, fried bread, a rasher of something that could have been bacon. But it was hot and filling, washed down with tea so weak it was barely brown. Cathy smiled as she remembered her mother's damning judgement: wet and warm. Still, it hit the spot and it was a chance to sit down for a few minutes. By the time she returned to stand near the workshop, she felt sharp.

* * *

'We're changing the plan.' Faulkner was whispering; she felt the warmth of his breath tickling against her ear as she looked at the doors.

'What are we going to do?'

'By quarter to nine Minuit's probably going to start feeling very nervous, wondering whether Connor's really going to turn up. Bob and Terry are going to try and pry the back door open. George will be waiting with them.'

'What about you and Dan?'

He nodded towards the workshop. 'Either side of the front door. I'm banking on Minuit trying to escape that way.'

'Don't you think he'll suspect a trap? He's no fool.'

'I'm sure he will. But we'll be forcing his hand. He might panic a bit and gamble that he stands a better chance out here than trapped inside.'

She turned her head to stare at him. His plan was so threadbare it had holes.

'Do you really believe this has any chance of working?'

'I think we'll take him by surprise. That'll give us the advantage. Smithy's going to be parked nearby in the car'

'Where do you want me?'

'With me and Dan. We don't have anyone else. Smithy's not agile enough for this yet.'

'Why not try to go in the front door, too?' Cathy suggested. 'Make him feel pressured on both sides.' He seemed hesitant. 'It's going to be dangerous, however we do it. This way it'll be contained inside. No danger to anyone passing.'

'We can't afford to fail.'

'I know that.' She turned back to gaze at the building and thought of her brother. 'Believe me, I know.'

TWENTY-EIGHT

Cathy stood to one side of the doors, protected by the stone wall. Dan was on the other side, his face tight and ugly with concentration. Faulkner crouched by the lock, selecting the right pick from the kit in his hand.

She hardly dared to breathe. It was so close now.

Faulkner's hands moved. Then he stood, nodded to Dan and let out a piercing whistle. In a few moments they could hear sounds from the back of the building. Faulkner pulled down on the handle and pushed hard, his whole body behind it. The door swung wide and they ran in.

Just for a second, Cathy held back. Her heart was hammering in her chest. She ducked, as if she expected gunfire, but there was only silence. A mix of bright daylight and deep shadows made her blink as she entered.

It was a bleak, abandoned space that smelled of the oil and ancient sweat that had seeped into the stones. Dead leaves and mouse droppings littered the floor, cobwebs hung in the corners, dirt everywhere. A partition in the back corner marked out the office. Five work benches littered with dried wood shavings. A fireplace still full of dead ashes. A pile of boards that someone had forgotten still stood upright in the corner with three stinking, dead rats in front, maggots crawling over the decomposing bodies. She moved away from the stench.

No Minuit. Nothing to show he'd ever been here.

Connor had lied.

A scream of metal and a crack of wood as the lock on the back door gave. Terry and Bob Hartley rushed in, guns in their hands. Faulkner pointed to the small office.

The lock gave as soon as Terry kicked it. He stepped away as it swung back, then ran in.

She held her breath.

No voices from inside. Nobody there.

Cathy glanced at her brother. His head was bowed, shoulders slumped. Defeated.

She felt empty, sick. Guilty. She was the one who'd fallen for Connor's lie. Stupid. He'd beaten her again. Maybe Hartley was right. She had no place doing a job like this.

Minuit was still roaming around Leeds with four sticks of dynamite. Here to destroy.

Cathy breathed in sharply as something cold touched the back of her neck. Her body straightened. She started to turn, but a man's voice, no louder than a breath, whispered behind her ear, 'Keep still.'

She did exactly as she was told, and gazed straight ahead. Her legs began to tremble, and she tried to swallow, but her throat was suddenly too tight.

'Gentlemen.' He spoke quietly, but the word boomed like a cannon in the room. Every head turned.

Bob Hartley had his gun raised, killing in his eyes.

'Put it down,' the man ordered. She felt them turn one to one another and saw the angry glare before Hartley's arm fell to his side. 'Much better. You missed the obvious place. I was behind those boards. People see what they choose.' A pause. 'All you noticed were dead rodents.'

'What now?' Faulkner asked.

'Now Sergeant Marsden and I will go out to that car you have parked around the corner. Your man Smith will get out and I'll tell her where to drive. Obviously, if anyone tries to stop us, I will shoot her. She won't survive, believe me.'

He spoke so calmly that she knew he meant every word. Her heart was ready to explode. She looked at the others, feeling helpless. Truly terrified.

She heard Faulkner's voice cut through the silence. 'You didn't succeed. Everything's still standing.'

'But I did, Sergeant. I'm walking out of here alive, that's success.' A long pause. 'Did anyone tell you I was employed by your government to test this XX system. No? No word from your superiors on that, Mr Marsden?'

A final lie. But it was enough to sow a few brief moments of confusion and doubt. She saw horror spread across Dan's face until he realized. It kept them still as Minuit began to move her.

His left hand held her arm as he made Cathy into his shield. Together, they backed out of the workshop.

'I know you value this lady, so you won't follow.'

They kept moving.

'No screaming,' he warned her.

She nodded. Her mind was numb. All she could do was move her feet, praying she didn't stumble or fall.

'I know where the car is parked. There's a room upstairs with a good view. That's why I picked this place.' They walked normally, nobody paying attention to them, the gun in his right hand prodding her back. Another few steps, and he guided her down a side street, towards the car waiting on the other side of the road. 'Do you like the coast, Miss Marsden?' He sounded amused, almost jaunty, making idle conversation. 'Not quite the season for the beach, but no matter. Bracing sea air, isn't that what they used to say in the railway adverts?'

Cathy struggled to find her voice. She pushed back the tears. 'Is that where we're going?'

'My rendezvous. A boat to pick me up. Everything arranged before I arrived.'

'They gave you plenty of time.' Something to keep him talking, to distract him as she tried to think of a way to save herself.

Her breathing was light, fluttering. She refused to let him see her terror.

'They allowed me time for any problems.'

'And also in case you failed?' she said.

She felt the gun barrel rise and fall against her back. A shrug.

'There are other agents. It only needs one. This proved it can be done.'

'And the rest of the dynamite?'

'I've left it somewhere safe for the next man. Or it might be a woman.'

The Humber was only ten yards away. If she got in, it would all be over. They'd have failed. Whatever she did, it had to be soon. Before the final chance slipped away.

He must have read her thoughts: 'Remember, Sergeant, a bullet moves faster than you ever can. You'd make a very satisfying target.'

'You could have killed me up on the Moor.' She'd wondered about that ever since it happened.

'More fool me. You broke my wrist. That's given me a lot of problems. Now, you'd better hope that you stay alive.' He pushed the gun barrel against her spine.

He wanted her compliant. Too frightened to resist. He was succeeding. Cathy tried to steady the thoughts flying through her brain.

Minuit was good at this. Every step of the way, he'd kept ahead of them.

If she drove to the coast, the spy would never let her return. Someone would find her body on the sand with a bullet in her brain.

A shiver rippled through her body.

She stopped by the passenger side of the Humber.

'Bend down, tap on the window,' he told her. 'Let him see your face.'

Smithy smiled. Only for a moment. Then he recognized Minuit and spotted the gun.

'Leave the keys in there and place your gun on the back seat. Very good. Slide out this side. Make it calm and quiet.'

Minuit drew her back as Smithy obeyed.

'Very good. Now walk away.'

Smithy limped off, leaning on his stick, looking back after every step. The spy let the distance reel out. The door of the Humber hung wide.

'Get in,' he ordered.

Cathy obeyed, sliding across to the steering wheel, feeling impotent and defeated. Something bumped her back. The screwdriver. Her eyes flickered towards Minuit. He wasn't looking. She pulled it from the seat, gripping it tight.

The spy bent his body, head out of sight for just a second as he lowered himself into the car. He had the gun in his right hand, down on the seat to steady himself.

Another moment and he'd be in control again. It would be over. He struggled to close the heavy door, head turned away.

One chance.

Cathy brought the screwdriver down on the back of his hand. She put every desperate ounce of strength behind it. His skin tore. She pulled it out, then down again. He screamed. She was going to make him pay. For this. For what he'd done to her on Woodhouse Moor. For the beating he'd give Daisy Barker. She pushed harder, forcing the screwdriver all the way through his hand and pinning it to the leather. Cathy gave a grim smile as she saw blood start to flow over the seat.

The spy tried to hit her with his left hand, but she pushed it away. She pried the gun from his fingers and brought it down hard on his broken wrist. He bent forward, head on his knees, sobbing like a child as he tried to staunch the blood.

Cathy sat back, shaking and panting as she tried to aim the gun. For a second she ached to pull the trigger, to kill him right here.

The desire kept rising. It would only take a little pressure and he'd be gone.

She waited until it passed.

She'd beaten him. She'd ripped off the mask that Minuit had worn since he came ashore in England.

He yelled, eyes bitter with fury, and swore at her in Dutch. His way of dealing with the pain. The humiliation of being beaten by a woman. She looked around, willing the others to hurry up. But for the first time in weeks, even waiting felt satisfying.

She could breathe. She was alive, not sure if she was going to laugh or cry.

The car doors were wrenched open. Faulkner reached in and touched her shoulder.

'Are you all right?'

She knew what she wanted to say, but she couldn't make herself form the words, as if there was a barrier between her brain and her tongue. Instead, she held out Minuit's gun for Faulkner to take.

Cathy turned her head. Dan was standing over Minuit. No sense of triumph on his face. Nothing more than relief.

Hands helped her out of the Humber. She stood, frightened for a second that she'd stumble and fall. A few people gathered to look. Like a good, practised copper, Smithy moved them along. So ordinary it made her smile.

'Do you think you can make it back to the office if I help you?' Faulkner's voice.

'I . . . maybe.' She didn't know. Any kind of distance felt too long.

'Come on.' He smiled and took her arm. 'We'll go to that café down the road. Get a cup of tea in you.'

'Yes.' It sounded like the best thing in the world.

Cathy drank two cups, sweetened with some real sugar the waitress brought from the back. Faulkner didn't try to coax her into talking, didn't say a word. She wasn't ready to speak yet, she just wanted to sit and hear everyday noises. She knew she was in shock. The clatter of pots and murmured conversation around them kept her steady. Slowly, inch by inch, the world began to align itself. She felt as if she'd come back from somewhere far away.

'Any better?' he asked finally and she nodded.

'I can probably get to the office now.'

'After that it's home for you.'

'But—' It was Monday morning. She couldn't go home.

'An order,' he told her, but he had a kind smile in his eyes.

Cathy sat at her desk, reliving what had happened. So much, things that had piled one on top of the other, Ciaran Burns, Connor, Minuit . . . they arrived in a rush that pulled her along, all the way to the workshop. She jerked as she remembered the feel of the gun barrel at her neck.

Sooner or later, Minuit would have shot her.

A simple little movement, the twitch of a finger.

The end of everything she'd known. All she'd loved.

Cathy felt herself begin to tremble again. Gently at first. Then the shakes came. She let them.

Rivers of tears rolled over her cheeks. She couldn't have stopped them if she'd tried.

She had no idea how long it lasted. But finally it subsided to small shudders.

The feeling . . . that would never leave. She'd come close enough for death to stare into her eyes.

Cathy wiped at her face. With horror she saw dried blood all over her right hand. She grabbed her bag and dashed to the toilet to wash and scrub her skin until every trace was gone.

Cathy studied her face in the mirror. Very pale, the shadows deep and dark under her eyes. No surprise; she felt even worse. The liberty cut looked beyond repair. For a second she felt sure the tears would come again.

No. She couldn't give him that. Once was all he'd earned.

Cathy splashed cold water over skin and tugged a brush through her hair. Not much improvement, but it would have to do for now. She felt drained. The operation with Minuit had been secret from beginning to end. The only people she could talk to about this were her brother and the men in the squad. The other choice was to keep it all inside. She knew which it would be.

'I've borrowed that Austin,' Faulkner said. 'I'll run you home.'

'Where are the others?'

'Going over the workshop. Maybe Minuit left something there.'

She made herself think, to focus on *something*. 'They won't find anything. He was too clever for that.'

'Very likely,' he agreed with a sigh. 'Still, we have to look.'

'Dan?'

'He's with . . . he'll be asking plenty of questions. Savouring it all,' he added.

'After that?' She knew, but she still wanted to hear it.

'Minuit will disappear and none of this will ever have happened.'

'He said he'd hidden the rest of the dynamite for the next spy.'

'Your brother will find out where it is.'

Maybe Dan would drag out the information. Or maybe not.

Cathy looked down at her lap. A tiny fleck of blood at the edge of a fingernail. She scraped at it. The spy would be gone and none of this would have happened? How did you rewrite history?

She exhaled. 'Would you mind if I took the tram? Don't worry, I'll be fine.'

'Sure?'

'Yes.' She needed the time alone. To try and feel normal again.

It didn't seem right to step on to Brander Road in the daylight. As if she was skiving.

Rest, Faulkner had told her. But she was scared of the things she'd see when she closed her eyes.

As she'd walked down Kirkgate a hand had touched her arm.
'Miss?'

Cathy had drawn back, nervous, distrusting, suddenly terrified. A woman was facing her, a face she'd seen somewhere before. Late twenties, dark hair, with an uncertain expression. Harmless. But Cathy was in a daze, not fit to talk to a stranger. Not now. What could the woman want?

'I'm sorry . . .'

'The other week, down on Boar Lane. You pulled my Emily out of the way of that tram.'

The picture clicked into place.

'Is she all right?' It was the only thing she could think to say.

'She's fine.' A smile. 'She has her bear. I think that means more to her than anything. I don't know how to thank you.'

Cathy shook her head.

'I was there, that's all.' She'd forgotten it had ever happened. Her mind was too full for this. 'I'm very sorry, I have to dash.'

Simple, ordinary tasks to try and help her make sense of the day. Then she heard the click of the front door and put the pinking shears down on top of the blue material. The sound of footsteps going upstairs. Cutting out the skirt could wait.

Her parents were looking at each other, the usual worried frown on her mother's face.

'I'll go and see him,' she said. 'He's probably jiggered.'

'Ask him if he wants something to eat,' Mrs Marsden said. 'I've kept a plate warm for him in the oven.'

Dan was sitting on the bed, suitcase open in the middle of the floor. It felt like the room of a guest, not a family member.

'When do you go back?'

'Tomorrow afternoon. I need to tie up a couple of things first. I phoned the office. They're pleased as punch, of course. Full of congratulations. Crisis averted.'

'You're back in their good books again.'

'For now.' He looked up at her. 'What you did there . . .'

'What about it?' Cathy said. She could hear the anger lurking. 'He was going to kill me. I was trying to stay alive, that's all.'

'It took a lot of courage.'

She gave him a watery smile. 'No, Dan. It took a lot of fear.'

She paused, aware of what she'd said. 'Did you pry anything else from him?'

'No. He already knew what was going to happen. No reason for him to say a word.'

So the dynamite was still out there somewhere.

'Is it all done?' She wanted to know, to put a full stop on that story.

A nod as he looked away, the word unspoken.

Things seemed a little easier the next morning. As long as she didn't have time to sink into her thoughts, Cathy could cope. Dan was carrying his suitcase as they walked up to the tram stop. All the uncertainty had vanished from his face.

'Glad to be going back to London?' Cathy asked.

He gazed around at the houses. 'Yes. I don't feel I belong here.'

He never had; Dan had always seemed out of place in Leeds, as if it had never truly been his home.

'Back to the grindstone?'

'Interviews tomorrow with the top bods of XX about what happened up here. Questions about why it took so long.' He frowned. 'That might be a tiny black mark. But since we uncovered a traitor, too, maybe not. After that, business as usual.'

The success of catching Minuit had swept away all the traces of self-doubt she'd seen in her brother. Now he was facing the world with confidence again. He'd already rid himself of the tiny bits of Leeds that had crept back into his speech. Shedding another skin.

She couldn't do that. It would be a long time before her life felt normal again. If it ever did. She was only beginning to understand that Minuit had turned her inside out. He'd hurt her. Wounded her inside. She had no regrets about what she'd done to him. It had been the only way to survive. No sorrow at his death. He'd have killed her without thought. But he'd left her with questions she didn't know if she'd ever be able to answer.

'Did you talk to . . . Elizabeth, was it?' Cathy asked.

'Only for a minute. I told her it was all done. She said it was probably best if we didn't talk again until the inquiry gave its verdict. After that she's being posted away from London.'

He tried, but he wasn't good at disguising the hurt.

'I'm sorry.'

'Doesn't matter.' He tried a weak smile. 'We have a war to win.'

She'd never love her brother, but maybe she'd begun to understand him.

In the office, she watched Bob Hartley cleaning out his desk. A few days' leave with his family in Carlisle, then report to SIB in Glasgow a week on Monday.

'I bet you'll be glad to see the back of me,' he said.

Cathy paused, hand on the doorknob.

'Why lie? I'm overjoyed.'

'You did well yesterday.' He seemed to force the words out, as if he begrudged every one.

'Thank you. I wish you the best.'

EPILOGUE

Leeds, Friday 14 March 1941

The sirens began at quarter to nine. Cathy checked the equipment. Sand in all the buckets, plenty of water in the tank of the stirrup pump. A perfect night for the Luftwaffe. Hints of sun during the day, a little more warmth in the air. Still clear, plenty of stars up there. Far off to the east, she saw searchlights start to rake the sky. A few seconds later she made out the deep, ugly drone of the aircraft, relentless and terrifying as the noise grew and grew until it filled her head.

She saw the coloured tracer from the ack-ack guns, the puffs of smoke as the shells exploded around the bombers.

They were a darker shape against the blackness. She stood, mesmerized; impossible to shift her gaze.

The bombs began to fall. Incendiaries. Down along the river first, fires flaring brighter than day. Guides for the wave of planes that would follow.

Louder, louder, until they were right overhead. She couldn't hear herself think. Bombs kept dropping. One landed on the roof, bouncing just yards away.

Cathy screamed. A quick breath and the training kicked in. They only had seconds before the fire began. She grabbed the incendiary with the scoop and plunged it into the bucket of sand. Brenda was there, pouring on more sand to smother it. The pair of them worked the stirrup pump, soaking the bucket with water until they were certain it was no danger.

All across Leeds, blazes burned.

They stood, grinning like fools. Cathy felt her heart racing, coughing from the pall of smoke over the town. Leeds was turning to flame.

Suddenly she was aware that the bombers had gone, their engines fading as they headed home.

Brenda began to laugh. Cathy joined her, letting it come until her stomach muscles cramped and her face was red. Relief at this. At the whole damned week. Letting it out. They'd done it, they'd stopped an incendiary. One fire halted before it could begin. Their own small victory over the Germans. That had to be worth something.

As she walked down Kirkgate after her shift, the stench of burning was everywhere. Smoke clung to her clothes and skin. From the tram she could see the fires down along the river, crews reflected in the light as they tried to extinguish the blazes.

Her euphoria began to fade as she walked down Brander Road. They'd had the incendiaries, but she knew that was only the first part. This was going to be the big raid they'd all expected for months.

It began a few minutes after midnight. They cowered in the Anderson shelter, the three of them clutching each other as the bombers flew so low they seem to be skimming the rooftops. Her mother was whimpering, holding tight to her father's arms.

Wave after wave of explosions. One after another until her nerves were flayed to shreds and she wondered if the world would end.

Finally, after she'd given up hope, it stopped. They stayed in the shelter for a long time, afraid of what they'd see outside, that the smallest things might bring the Jerries back.

They emerged cautiously as the all-clear sounded, not sure what they'd find. No damage she could see. In the house, nothing had rattled off the tables or shelves.

Cathy stood in front of the mirror, blackouts drawn back on a grey Saturday morning. She buttoned her uniform jacket, drawing a hand over the sergeant's stripes on the sleeve and rubbing the police badge of her cap. It all felt wrong. This wasn't her, not any longer.

But for one day . . . it was the only thing to do.

Outside the Special Investigation Branch office, she paused for a second, standing taller. Cathy grasped the doorknob and turned it.

Faulkner was at his desk.

'I have to,' she told him. 'Just for a few hours. To help.'

Very slowly, he nodded. 'Report back here on Monday morning. Good luck.'

'Marsden. I'm very glad to see you. I can use everybody today.' Inspector Harding looked harried, eyes red, notes all over her desk.

'I had to, ma'am.'

'We have problems everywhere, but Armley and Holbeck seem to have been hit hardest. That and the city centre.' She took a breath, exhaled and her voice calmed. 'I want you to take charge of the constables. Barker knows Armley, put her and someone else up there; Civil Defence will have the details of where they're needed. Send a couple more to Holbeck, around Marshall Street. You and one other in town, Park Row, by the railway station and the market.'

'Yes, ma'am.'

'Heavy rescue's going to be busy, there's plenty of bomb damage. Make sure people have the gen on where they can go for help. The National Assistance and places like that. The constables should know, but—'

'I'll go through it with them.'

Harding gave a strained, tired smile. 'I suppose this is a very limited engagement?'

'I'm afraid so, ma'am.'

'Doesn't matter, I'll take what I can get. By the way—' Cathy looked questioningly as the inspector began to smile '—that hair isn't regulation. But I think we can turn a blind eye for once.'

'I don't care if you are a bobby.' The air raid warden stood at the top of Park Row, arms akimbo, facing her down. 'You're not coming anywhere closer unless you put on that helmet you're carrying. Dangerous down there. Orders, see?'

Cathy placed it over her hair and tightened the strap under her chin. WPC Betty Rains did the same. Reluctantly, the man moved aside.

They'd seen some damage: two of the water tanks in the middle of the Headrow turned to ruined metal and the scorched, shattered ground of an incendiary fire that made her remember the night before. Windows smashed up and down the road and the glitter of glass all over; shop assistants were trying to sweep it all up.